Crossing at
Sweet Grass

Crossing at
Sweet Grass

Laurie G. Robertson

CROSSING AT SWEET GRASS

iUniverse books may be ordered through booksellers or by contacting:

iUniverse
1663 Liberty Drive
Bloomington, IN 47403
www.iuniverse.com
1-800-Authors (1-800-288-4677)

ISBN: 978-1-4917-9779-2 (sc)
ISBN: 978-1-4917-9778-5 (hc)
ISBN: 978-1-4917-9777-8 (e)

Library of Congress Control Number: 2016908919

Print information available on the last page.

iUniverse rev. date: 08/10/2016

To all people who love an adventure back in time and to those who supported me, especially Debby. Thank you.

The Eagle Feather

An eagle feather
flutters in the wind.
It has traveled far,
soaring across the prairie,
gliding over mighty rivers.
Now on a tree branch
it dangles before me.

Clasping it,
I brush it across my cheek
and wonder what secrets
are locked inside.
I too have secrets.
Adventure had beckoned me
to escape dull farm life.
Fate has taken me to a wild land.

It is all survival now.
How can I know the
promises this feather holds?
Wind picks up;
the feather escapes and whirls away.
I follow it home.

Contents

Preface

This story came to me in a series of dreams, adventures, and research. A friend and I traveled through the Dakotas, Nebraska, Wyoming, and parts of the Oregon Trail to research and experience these beautiful lands and people. I hope you enjoy this historical romantic adventure of Kallie's travels on the Oregon Trail and into the wild Black Hills. Thank you, Deb, for helping with editing and providing wisdom and encouragement.

Major Character Listing

Kallie's Family

Brothers: Michael and Caleb
Parents: Patrick and Ona
Neighbors: Millicent and Steward Luther
Husband: Armand
Sister-in-law: Elizabeth
Brother-in-law: Jacob

Brave Eagle's Family

Mother: Pretty Shield
Father: Chief Flaming Arrow
Brother: Speckled Eagle
Girlfriend: Dawn Star
Dawn Star's aunt: Walks Far

Friends: Bear, Running Brook
Weasel Tail, Meadow Grass
Flying Crow, Short Bull
War Chief: Black Hand
Shaman: Lost Buffalo; wife, Yellow Willow

Chapter 1: *The Capture*
Ahiyuslonan: To Come Dragging Along

Kallie could no longer struggle against the rapid rhythm of the horse's pounding hooves. She desperately tried to calm herself by thinking escape might be possible. Since her captor hadn't killed her along with the menfolk, maybe the savage would free her when he was done with her. The attack had happened so suddenly. In one brief moment, their solitary wagon had been attacked, her husband and brother-in-law had been massacred, and she and her husband's sister had been left unprotected. The warrior had swooped her up, shouted an exultant war cry, and draped her across his horse.

Racing across the prairie, the horse moved far ahead of the other warriors. As Kallie lay sideways on the horse's back, her body ached. Blood drained to her head as she clung desperately to the horse's mane. If she lost consciousness, she would plummet to the ground. The sweat from the horse lathered in her face. Inside she screamed with terror, but her throat was too dry and swollen to cry out.

She had seen her captor's face for only a brief moment, and his steady gaze had unnerved her. Kallie's lean and muscular body had shaken uncontrollably when he had grabbed her from behind and lifted her onto his horse.

The summer sun was at its zenith. The brutal afternoon heat robbed the air of any moisture. Mud from the rains had turned into dusty clouds. The horse's gait slowed, and the rest of the war party caught up. Soon battle cries quieted, and the horses needed to be watered. The group stopped at a rocky ravine where lush green willows and

1

cottonwoods provided a sanctuary from the sun. Leaves fluttered in the wind, creating a rustling sound in the gentle breeze. A river was close by.

Even though the ravine was shady, it provided no comfort for Kallie. She figured the savages would soon split the bounty held in the cumbersome wagon they had dragged behind. The wagon held the only earthly possessions of her life. Soon everything she had left would be gone. Her thoughts were disrupted by her sister-in-law's screams. Elizabeth pleaded with the two braves as they callously pulled her into the bushes.

Kallie stood in silence. Her long wavy hair had unraveled from its braid. All her strength had left her, and she was terrified. Her face held no expression except for the defiance in her eyes. Her cotton blouse, trimmed with lace, was torn, and her blue skirt and shawl were ripped and muddy. Her captor moved toward her, holding a large knife. Kallie stepped back. Her hands were still bound in front of her. The tight knots had cut into her wrists, rubbing them raw. Looking into his eyes and then again at the knife, Kallie moved to avoid touching him. His fast, direct manner quickly overpowered her. Grabbing her hands, he sliced through the rawhide knots that shackled her.

In a desperate attempt, Kallie screamed and darted past him. She ran like a frightened doe flushed from its hiding place. Kallie stumbled over tree stumps, and branches whipped her body. She gasped for air. The savage had stood there for a moment but then chased after her. She struggled toward the river, jumping over rocks at the shore.

When the savage grabbed her sleeve to turn her around, she lashed out with ferocity. Thrashing, Kallie dug her fingernails deep into his face. Blood ran down his cheek; her claw marks extended from his eye to his mouth. Reacting, her captor struck her face with the full force of his fist. The other men watched from afar. Kallie felt herself crumple to the ground and slip into darkness.

As she regained consciousness, Kallie was confused. The side of her face throbbed, and her eye felt swollen. She looked down to see her hands had been tied again. Her composure turned to terror as her captor tugged the ropes to lift her up. The savage touched her clothing with suspicion and pulled at it. She noticed how his sunbaked hand contrasted with the whiteness of her top. While the others looked on, the man cornered her. He moved in so close his breath prickled her neck. Without warning, she raised her knee and hit him in the groin with a sharp jab. Dropping to his knees, he doubled over. She was surprised by her strength and agility but feared she would now be killed. While submitting may have been the best thing to do, she had, once again, let her temper control the outcome. The kick had been an automatic response. Now she had to run before it was too late. Instead of ropes, this time it would be the knife. With her captor incapacitated, this was her final chance to escape.

Even though her hands were still tied, Kallie ran to the riverbank and crossed the river, balancing on the big flat-topped rocks. She reached the opposite shore and ran toward cover. Rushing into the brush, beating the saplings down as they whipped her, Kallie plunged ahead into the unknown. Fear gripped her. She ran until she had to catch her breath. Needing to assess the situation, she stopped to listen. The pounding of her heart and labored breathing were the only sounds she could hear. Sensing something was lurking close by, she looked up and met the yellow eyes of a young mountain lion. Helpless with her tied hands, she had no defense.

Kallie backtracked until she could hear the rumbling of the river again. She realized something had frightened the young cat. It no longer followed her. Smelling lavender, Kallie moved toward the plants and bent down to hide. It was there that she discovered a small cave hidden in the rock outcroppings where the river widened into a shallow expanse. Part of the water's flow was dammed with sticks and rocks, creating a deep pond of clear water surrounded by willows and huge boulders. The beaver pond was sunny and a peaceful refuge in the midst of her misery. Kallie crawled through the small opening into the dark cave. The lavender smell comforted her as its sweet fragrance enveloped her surroundings. Still bound by the burning rope, she could not free her hands. The more she moved them, the tighter the knots became.

From the cave opening, she observed a beaver gathering sticks to repair its huge mounded home. In this gentle oasis, painted turtles relaxed on logs, absorbing the sun, and fish nibbled at water insects.

Dragonflies landed on the lily pads for only seconds before the leopard frogs jumped at them. The lily flowers were in season, and their pink petals accentuated the landscape. The air was moist and refreshing. Her observations were interrupted by sounds of splashing. Kallie peered out. It was her captor. He seemed to no longer be hunting her. The Indian warrior casually swam naked and then stepped out of the pond. He possessed a hard, sinuous, muscular build. His wet skin glistened in the bright sunshine, and his long black hair dripped down his back. After he dried off, he put on his breechcloth and bent over to slip on his moccasins. He slowly gazed around as if he could sense her presence. Patiently observing, primal in his stance, he turned in her direction. Searching the ground for tracks, he darted into the woods, following her original path. Kallie watched apprehensively until she could no longer see or hear him.

In her hiding place, Kallie closed her eyes and allowed the scent of the lavender to comfort her. She decided to stay hidden even though her tracks might betray her. As her apprehension grew, her breathing became deeper. The sounds of the river rushed louder, while flashbacks of the raid filled her mind. The images haunted her until she heard a rustling in the bushes. As she cautiously peeked out, two fierce dark eyes stared coldly back at her.

Startled, Kallie immediately dropped her gaze and, with quiet resignation, slowly crawled out of her hiding place with her head bent down in submission. The savage grabbed her arm and lifted her up with a swift, powerful jerk. She fell backward, but his strong arms held her waist in a tight grasp. Placing her against his body, he forced her up against a boulder, which was scorching hot from the midday sun. The other braves jeered and laughed in the distance. This painful indignity angered and humiliated her.

Her captor's breathing slowed, and he loosened the knot and then retied her hands tightly behind her back. He then took the rope, cinched it around her throat, and forced her to sit on the ground. He left her there and yelled something to one of his companions. After the man's companion acknowledged him, her captor stormed toward the woods.

Left in the dirt, Kallie heard the voices of the other men. She did not recognize the strange dialect or know what kind of Indians had captured her. The savages passed by, all ignoring her with the exception of one who looked different from the rest.

Nonchalantly, he tugged on the rope that bound her, brought her head close to his, and spoke in English. "I'll loosen these, but you have to stay close. If you try to escape again, I'll wet the rope so it dries around your neck extra tight. I will let my other two friends retrieve you, and I will be slow to find you. They will not be kind." He took off her bonds, pointed toward the river, and said, "Wait down there." Then he left to catch up with the other braves.

As she stumbled down the river path, Kallie heard the soft cries of Elizabeth, her sister-in-law, who also had endured a terrible ordeal. When their eyes met, Kallie felt pity for her even though she had never trusted her much. Elizabeth had been such a strong woman but now was reduced to fragility after losing her dear husband and brother.

Kallie had not been so lucky in love; her husband, Armand, had become crazy when drunk, which was often. Remembering the crack of his whip and his whiskey breath filled her with hatred. She felt nothing but coldhearted relief that he was now dead and could no longer hurt her. Cautiously, she moved closer to Elizabeth, who was crouched down on the riverbank, staring ahead with swollen, tearful eyes.

In a hushed tone Kallie said, "Elizabeth, they seem done with us, and the one who cut my ropes pointed to the water. Do you think we could wash off this dirt and destruction?"

Elizabeth continued to stare into the distance and said nothing. Kallie cupped her hands and drew a long, cool drink of river water, relieving her thirst. Then she ventured up the trail to investigate. The heat of the day had intensified, turning the muddy river trail into dust. She peered through the bushes. The laughing braves were gambling. The horses quietly grazed, swatting the buzzing flies with their tails. The covered wagon was left untouched in the baking sun.

Kallie ran back to the riverbank and spoke in a soothing voice. "Elizabeth, the savages seem distracted. It's a good time to bathe if we want to be left unmolested."

Elizabeth retorted, "We'll never wash this filth off us." But still, Elizabeth peeled off her dirty dress and entered the river wearing only her ripped undergarments. Kallie completely disrobed and waded into the deepest part of the river. Even under these circumstances, the water felt glorious to her. This was her first refreshing moment since long before the raid. Kallie swam across the river to the other shore and then back again, letting her body flow with the current. The sensations from cool water ran through her, and she closed her mind to the future. The women rinsed the dirt from their clothes the best they could before laying them out to dry.

Kallie stood on the bank and let the sun dry the wetness of her nude body. She tipped her head to wring out her hair. When she heard a rustle in the bushes, she grabbed her clothes to cover herself. Turning her head, she met the eyes of her captor. Kallie froze in place, but the man lowered his eyes, turned away, and moved along the path.

Kallie had no idea what her captor or the other men were doing. She sat on the riverbank, positioned as far away from them as possible, as if this would make her safer. She pretended that maybe they would forget about her and Elizabeth and leave them alone. Kallie's wet hair dripped and helped soothe the painful whip marks on her back. The sores had been slow in healing and throbbed. As Elizabeth stared off, Kallie crouched down and twisted her wedding ring off her finger. She tossed it into the river and watched the silver band sink to the muddy bottom. Rubbing her ring finger, she thought back to Armand, now dead on a swollen riverbank. Initially, his charm had enticed her so. He had rescued her from a destitute farm life after her parents had died from fever, and she had happily left with him. Whiskey quickly dashed her hopes about their exciting new life together. Armand had turned so mean that, instead of helping him during the raid, she had run toward the woods to escape him.

Leaving Elizabeth, Kallie picked a handful of comfrey leaves growing nearby. She placed the leaves upon a boulder and took a rock and crushed them into green pulp. Adding just a drizzle of water, she formed a paste and clumped it on a big elm leaf and placed it over her swollen eye.

Carefully, Kallie brought another poultice to Elizabeth and softly said, "Elizabeth, place some of this on your cuts to speed the healing. You'd best get ready now—finish up with your dressing."

Elizabeth, coming out of her stupor, reacted with angry eyes. She snarled, "You are acting like my brother Armand's death is a relief. Oh, my poor, dear husband, Jacob, is dead also. You ran away while the rest of us were fighting. Kallie, you just ran away. I shall never forgive you!"

Kallie said nothing in return because it was true. Pondering her new situation, she shivered while reflecting on recent events. She could not stop thinking about Armand's stiff body and his lifeless blue eyes staring blankly at her. Yet she felt justified discarding her wedding ring. She was entering into the unknown with a strange warrior who now controlled her life. She wondered if her fate was to die.

The intense heat of the afternoon passed, and the silence was broken by distant laughter from the men. Ravenous from hunger, the women began foraging for food. Although they found a few berries and roots to eat, they weren't satisfied. As both of the women drifted farther away from the men, Elizabeth said, "This may be our only chance to escape." She broke into a frantic run and stormed ahead, disappearing around the river bend. Kallie resisted because she remembered the one warrior's dire warnings about running away. Kallie heard Elizabeth scream and ran to investigate. Elizabeth had been stopped in her tracks. The same warrior who had threatened her was on horseback and thwarted Elizabeth's escape attempt. Both women were fearful. The warrior took out his knife and moved it across his tongue, and he stared until they both lowered their heads.

Speaking in a combination of French and English, the savage introduced himself as Bear. He was an impressive man whose facial expression was not as severe as those of the others. He was friendly but indifferent to their plight. Instead of hurting them, he got off his horse and motioned for them to follow behind him.

Kallie noticed Bear walked differently from the other men, and his clothes were more colorful. Red war paint started at the top of his face and met stripes of yellow extending from his eyes to his jawline. White shell earrings decorated his earlobes. Besides the fringed, black-striped buckskin leggings that caressed his thighs, he wore only a dark breechcloth. A necklace made out of strips of long white shells ran parallel across his muscular chest. Three eagle feathers flared from the back of his long black shiny hair. On his shoulder was a beaded case filled with arrows.

His magnificent horse followed him. The horse's black mane was braided and tipped with a large dangling feather. Huge red circles were painted around the horse's eyes, and his forehead displayed a beautifully beaded medallion with geometric designs of blue, white, and red. When they arrived back to where the wagon was, Bear motioned the women to sit. He pointed. "That is Flying Crow, and the other is named Weasel Tail."

Kallie did as she was told and sat down. Her heart ached when she saw Flying Crow and Weasel Tail ransacking the dilapidated wagon. She and Armand had once been so proud that it had been made of seasoned wood and reinforced with iron. The wagon top was doubled thick canvas waterproofed with linseed oil. All of her precious belongings were scattered on the ground. Even her medicine pouch—which contained laudanum, quinine, hartshorn for snakebite, citric acid for scurvy, and valuable opium—was tossed. Kallie carefully felt the hem of her dress, relieved that her vial of love potion was safely hidden. Her neighbor Millicent had given her the vial of brownish-looking substance as a going-away gift. Millicent had warned her to hide it wisely, for the potion was powerful and could be used as a weapon.

The brave named Flying Crow held Armand's fiddle. Laughing at the sounds, he tugged the strings roughly. Bear gathered all the whiskey flasks, and Armand's pistol and knives, along with a few cups, utensils, and soap. Their belongings were carelessly stuffed into buckskin pouches. Elizabeth perked up when she saw Bear pull out her beloved Bible. She desperately reached out for it, but Bear ignored her and turned away. Curiously looking at the thick book, he ripped out a couple of pages. Inspecting the paper, he stuffed it into his pack, ignoring Elizabeth's scowl.

The massive brave named Weasel Tail picked up Elizabeth's silver hairbrush. Both women instinctively looked at each other, carefully observing where he packed the precious item. The rest of the belongings were left scattered in the wind. Kallie's throat tightened in anger and despair at the sight of it. Her possessions, left discarded in the bushes, represented the last of her world. The muscular men loaded her horse, Clara, with the stolen items. Clara reacted nervously to the men's strange scent. She whinnied to Kallie for rescue, but Flying Crow sternly jerked the horse back in his direction. Glaring, he made it obvious that Kallie's treasured horse was no longer her property. Disheartened, she bit her lower lip and looked down to avoid making the situation worse.

Elizabeth looked panicked when Weasel Tail lifted her onto Clara. He tied Elizabeth's hands tightly behind her back so she could not escape. Bear's horse was packed with bounty. Motioning Kallie to come closer, he bound her hands with twisted rope made out of buffalo hair. It extended several feet behind his horse and would force Kallie to walk at any pace he set. Leaping upon his horse in a swift, graceful motion, Bear made a clicking sound to start his horse moving.

The war party continued along the river, heading north. The brave who had captured Kallie had disappeared. The others never looked back at her as they advanced forward, so she left the most obvious trail she could. She hoped that if a rescue party came after them, they could follow her trail. Tired and hungry, she could barely keep up with the pace of the horse. The muscles in Kallie's legs tightened with stiffness, and her feet blistered. She had lost her bonnet, so her skin was sunburned. Flies buzzed around her. She prayed for strength, but the torture continued until early evening. The extended rope became taut by her resistance, and the horse began to drag her. She struggled to stay alive.

Chapter 2: *Reflections of Rage*

Iyoyakeca: Be Distressed

Brave Eagle rode as if his life depended on it. He had told his best friend, Bear, to watch over his captive and keep her safe from the other two. Bear had nodded his head and waited for more explanation, but Brave Eagle had given none. He had leaped on his horse, Wind Racer, and galloped toward open country, leaving everyone behind, including his captive. He would meet up with the group later.

Exhilaration from the raid still surged in Brave Eagle's blood. Earlier in the day, he had led the war party with great determination, for he loved the glory of blood and battle. He had made coup, representing his bravery. He had felt alive again, and adrenaline had surged through his veins. Feeling powerful and invincible, he and his friends had ridden with the wind.

He was proud of the red dot on his coup feather that indicated his killing deed in the raid. Although he was already known throughout the land for his horse-catching and trading abilities, many tales about this summer sojourn would fill the winter nights. The captive would bring him prosperity and prestige when he traded her at the great Sun Ceremony. There, numerous tribes gathered together for trade and worship. His hostage would bring a high price.

His lip tasted of blood, and uneasiness overcame him. He thought back to his unexpected struggle with his captive. Weasel Tail and Flying Crow had laughed loudly at him after witnessing it. Humiliation had quickly turned to anger as his friends' glances, once full of admiration, had changed to mockery. He felt the heat of embarrassment even now as he thought about it. He pressed into his horse's flanks to drive him faster.

He rode hard until he came to a pond, a place to water his horse. Brave Eagle stared into the water's green depth, ashamed that his anger had once again controlled him. It seemed to always control him. The action against the white woman opened the wound locked deep inside him. His knuckles whitened as he attempted to crush a stone within his clenched fist. Giving up, he sent the stone sailing across the waters until it sank, leaving nothing but concentric circles rippling away from the splash. Refusing to grieve his wife's untimely death, he had been holding an angry grudge against life. He cursed the earth itself, and his heart had turned to stone. Now, as he was caught within his own torment, his emotions rushed out in a rage.

His heart ripped open and unleashed his grief. Sitting with his head down, Brave Eagle wept. He endured the pain of his fears until he was completely drained of emotion. Shaking, he stood up and looked at the sky. For the first time since her death, he wished his wife, Two Moons, peace in the spirit land. The breeze picked up, and he smiled, sensing Two Moons had heard him. He thought to himself that it might be time to live again. Wind Racer briefly touched his nose to the side of Brave Eagle's face. His horse turned his ears straight up and moved his head up and down, making Brave Eagle smile.

Brave Eagle thought about the day's events. Before riding off, he had peered through thick willows. The other woman captive hugged the shore and cried sorrowfully while his captive climbed out of the water. She had mesmerized him, for he had never seen a naked white woman before. He thought about her agile body, curvy buttocks, and the graceful way she had moved. He had watched as she wrung out the water dripping from her wavy hair. As she tipped her head to the side, wounds had become noticeable. They were angry red whip marks that snaked down her back. Noting their severity, he had wondered to himself if the woman was like a horse that did not respect urging or whipping. His cheek still throbbed from the four long scratches carved by her nails. With such a fighting spirit she would bring a good price, though he would have to keep her wounds hidden from prospective bidders.

The expression on his white captive's face lingered in his memory. He remembered the instant their eyes had met. Her eyes had reminded him of the green river stones he used to polish as a boy. Her skin was smooth and white. Her hair was wild and curly. Following the curves of her feminine body, he had wondered about her age. She looked all of twenty years. She was a strange, alluring creature, an object of curiosity. Something stirred in him, and he felt unsure of his intentions. He decided it was time to leave. He rode hard but felt strangely relieved. After some time, the war party appeared on the horizon. He galloped toward them. The group stopped advancing. Soon he heard the other men cry out with joyful whoops, acknowledging his impending arrival.

When Brave Eagle reached his companions, he looked down at his captive. She looked away from him, but he sensed both her anger and fragility. He cut the rope that bound her hands, gripped the young woman's waist, and placed her on the horse with the other woman. Just as he suspected, she was too exhausted to struggle.

The group started to move again, and the horses kicked up dust. Brave Eagle and Bear rode alongside the women. Bear said, "At the next festival there will be great stories over the campfire of our brave deeds and coup. The two captives are young and will make valuable trades this year." Bear flexed his arm muscle and went on, "The raid was done without any repercussion from the white enemies. The summer rains have obscured any signs of struggle. It is such a good omen."

Brave Eagle nodded. "The horse racing will be good. I look forward to competing against men from other tribes and strange horses. It is always an exciting challenge."

Bear said, "Your equestrian skills are widely respected. I am proud to wager on you."

Brave Eagle laughed. "You always wager on me, but when I win a race, you give away all your winnings. If you keep that up, you'll never get the horses you need to marry. And besides, such strange behavior causes women's tongues to wag."

Bear's expression darkened, and he changed the subject. "Brave Eagle, what will your trading price be for your white captive? Do you need me to be your negotiator? You know I can get the best prices."

Brave Eagle ignored the question, instead asking, "Have you noticed the color of her hair? It is a chestnut brown with hues of red that show in the sunlight. It is the same color as my first horse."

Bear said, "That yearling was your pride and joy, your most treasured possession at the time. That was when I first met you, during the Sun Festival."

Then Brave Eagle confided, "I do not know what I will do with her. She will not look at me. Her behavior both angers and excites me. The captive is a strange breed."

Bear asked, "My friend, if she was a captured wild mustang coming in from the prairie, what would you do with her?"

Brave Eagle answered quickly, "If I broke her hard and fast, I would have an obedient horse but one with no trust. She would be skittish all her days. However, if I left my scented blanket close by, eventually the mare's curiosity would overcome her initial fear of my smell. When she investigated and discovered the blanket did her no harm, she would eventually come to accept me. Taming her would take longer, but the mare and I would share a mutual trust."

Bear agreed. "Yes, but let me know if you want a negotiator. I could get a good price for her, and besides, I thought you were going to marry Dawn Star."

Brave Eagle did not answer. The other two men had stopped and were discussing something. Flying Crow abruptly interrupted, "I want that captive off my horse. It is too much weight."

Bear left the group of men and told the captive, "Flying Crow wants you off his horse. You will ride with Brave Eagle."

The other woman cried out. Bear looked irritated and pulled out his knife. When he flashed it at her, the woman quieted immediately.

Placating Flying Crow, Brave Eagle tugged his captive off the captured horse. The woman's long chestnut hair slid down to her waist. The lace surrounding her collar had been torn off, revealing a hint of her cleavage, and the sweat upon her chest glistened. Slow and deliberate, her breathing accentuated her breasts as the soft breeze rippled her tattered blouse. A thick crust of dried mud had formed around the hem of her skirt. The woman trembled, but he grabbed her waist and lifted her onto Wind Racer. Then he jumped on behind her.

Soon his captive surrendered to the rhythm of the ride. She leaned back and pressed into his chest. He could not escape her presence as their bodies meshed. His every breath touched the side of her face. She was strangely arousing to him. The swaying of his horse gently rocked her, and she seemed calmer. He wondered about who this woman was and why she was in such a defenseless situation.

His captive seemed to relax as sounds of sparrows and bobolinks echoed across the land. Evening clouds streamed along the sky, and the setting sun cast colors of yellows, pinks, and purples. As they moved closer to the river, clumps of cotton grass blew in the wind. Her curly hair gently brushed by him with each surge of Wind Racer's motion. The curve of her breasts rubbed against his arms, and he felt an overwhelming desire. He and the woman swayed with the horse's rocking motion and moved as one. The others followed closely behind until finally darkness settled in. It was time to set camp.

Chapter 3: *Encounter with Weasel Tail*

Kiciza: To Quarrel with One

The horses finally stopped. Kallie watched each man scout in a different direction for a proper campsite. Her captor pointed to an area along a river bluff, and the others nodded in agreement. As they rode toward the bank, her captor pulled out a shiny hunting knife and wrapped his arms around her. In one swift motion, he sliced through the ropes and released her from bondage. Blood rushed back into her hands, giving them a tingling sensation. Her captor slid off his horse. His powerful arms clasped her waist. As she slid into his hold, their eyes met, and a charge of excited feelings raced through her body. She was surprised but couldn't seem to help it.

Each man helped set up the simple camp. Weasel Tail collected wood. Flying Crow took a fire drill stick from his beaded pouch and rapidly twisted the stick until a spark was produced. He ignited kindling by blowing on the twigs until the sparks became a small fire. Then he made tea water by dropping heated rocks into a skin water bag. Her captor seemed to be scanning the area, maybe for a possible ambush.

Bear gave her and Elizabeth a small piece of pemmican and said, "Sit here until Brave Eagle gives the okay to move." Famished, Kallie and Elizabeth devoured every morsel of the buffalo meat mixed with fat and berries and did what they were told.

Fatigued, Kallie slumped over onto the ground while the others sat around the glowing fire. She watched Bear give Elizabeth another piece of pemmican, for which she uttered words of gratitude, and then she promptly devoured it. He threw a piece on Kallie's lap and walked away.

While the others were distracted, Elizabeth snatched Kallie's pemmican. Frantically, Elizabeth bit into the meat until someone clutched her wrist and pulled it away. Looking sharply at her with disgust, Brave Eagle placed the pemmican back in Kallie's pocket. He pushed Elizabeth toward Flying Crow, who was looking at her.

Brave Eagle motioned to Kallie to lie down on a buffalo robe. She obliged. Tired, she lay rigidly waiting for him. Pondering her fate, she gazed up at the immensity of the heavens shrouded with stars sparkling like diamonds. She spotted her favorite constellation, Orion, the great hunter of the sky. Drifting in and out of sleep, Kallie heard Flying Crow, who had used Elizabeth, come back to the fire and talk with the other men.

Kallie fell into an unsettled dream state. Yellow eyes of a young cougar stalked her. As she looked at them, they turned into her dead husband Armand's cold, brutal eyes. His agitated look pierced her like a sword. Blood dripped from his wound as he mournfully called out her name. Startled, she woke from the nightmare and sensed it was a premonition of more danger ahead. Distant wolves howled under the light of the crescent moon, causing her to shiver. The nightmare had unnerved her.

She was surprised to find Brave Eagle next to her and listened apprehensively to his slow, rhythmic breathing. He slept with his back turned to her. She could not escape from her confused feelings. Anger welled up inside her when she thought of his rough treatment toward her. Never would she forgive him. Even so, she was strangely aroused as they rested together in the darkness. Somehow, it was comforting. Their mutual attraction might be her only chance of survival. Regardless of his behavior or her mixed emotions, she needed him. Her other possible ally might be Bear, who, although indifferent, knew English.

From her bed, she watched Bear wrapped in his blanket, crouched by the small fire. Bear let out a frustrated sigh and poked the last of the glowing coals. She thought it odd he would seem restless and wondered why he was up so late. When Weasel Tail came to relieve him, she knew it must be watch duty. As Bear stood up, he looked right at her. She could not read his expression, but he seemed sad. Bear turned away, crawled onto his sleeping mat, and fell asleep.

Kallie awoke to the bobolink's morning song but was startled by Bear, who stood over them. He looked at Brave Eagle's embrace of her and reached to shake his friend. Brave Eagle opened his eyes, let her go, jumped up, and started packing.

She heard Bear wake Elizabeth. He spoke in English. "We are going hunting. If you try to escape, we will track you down. Then you will be tied to a tree and left to starve. Do not leave this place. Enemies could be anywhere."

Bear further explained, "We are several campfires away from our village, and our food supply is gone. We have been discussing whether to feed you or not. Weasel Tail thinks there is no time and you are slowing us down. The rest of us are in favor of replenishing our food supplies. We are going hunting."

Kallie noticed the braves had finished preparations. Bear continued, "If you try to escape, we can easily track you." Flying Crow, who stood by Bear, took out his knife and put it to Elizabeth's throat, making a sawing motion. Terrified, she nodded her head that she understood.

Elizabeth pleaded with Bear, "Help us, please. Surely you must find it in your heart to help us back to civilization."

Bear said, "You are to stay. Weasel Tail will hunt you down and kill you. Do you understand?"

Elizabeth again nodded yes. As soon as the dust clouds had settled, she leaped up and said, "Kallie, get up! The savages have left. This is our chance to escape!"

Kallie asked, "Elizabeth, what are you talking about?"

Elizabeth impatiently blurted, "They went hunting. They'll be gone for the day. This is our chance to escape. It may be our only chance."

Incredulous, Kallie asked, "Where would we go if we escaped? I heard wolves close by last night. Do you really think we would get far? We haven't eaten a decent meal in days. That man called Bear told you he would kill us if we tried to escape. Can you not comprehend that?"

Veins in Elizabeth's neck popped out as she shouted, "Kallie! You want to stay with these brutal savages. Have you no shame? Why, if my brother Armand were alive, he'd whip you again. You stole his money, and now you're disgracing his memory."

Kallie glared. "I'd horsewhip you if I had the chance. I'm glad for all your suffering. I'm trying to survive, and that is all. Elizabeth Ann Perkins, you're acting all high and mighty. How far do you think we would get? They would track us down like varmint dogs. Remember what will happen if we try to escape. Remember the knife across your throat? Didn't you hear the threats of what they would do after they found us?" She fumed while she watched Elizabeth storm off toward the river, thrashing through the alders.

Elizabeth yelled, "Kallie, the Lord helps those who help themselves. Hurry, now is the time to run!"

Kallie ignored Elizabeth's commands. She realized the last of the coals were going out. Quickly gathering up a small amount of starter shavings, she ignited the coals until they glowed with a bright orange and then buried them under rocks. She walked to the river and splashed cold river water on her face to calm herself.

Kallie knew her sister-in-law was stubborn. She remembered back to the first time she had seen Elizabeth and her husband, Jacob. It was when a large revival called the Second Great Awakening came to town and had attracted folks from all over. Their wagon was a prairie schooner with huge white sails. Its sideboards held painted, colorful scenes from the garden of Eden. The backboard had the words "Repent before the Lord" painted on it. A huge wooden cross hung on the back of the driver's seat. Jacob's blue eyes were piercing, and his tight lips formed an unnatural snarl. This made him look untrustworthy. He had shouted his lecture about sin, hellfire, and lepers. After his intense sermon, Elizabeth had informed the townspeople about new Christian activity in Oregon. The crowd hushed as she spoke of leading the crusade of salvation and about starting a mission school. She then asked for charity and said anything that could be spared would be greatly appreciated in the eyes of God. The money collected would be dedicated toward "giving the benighted ones a knowledge of the Savior." As the preacher's wife, Elizabeth had led the faithful in prayer as she aggressively pushed the collection plate around.

Kallie called out, "Elizabeth, where are you? Come back. We need to search for food. Quit your foolishness."

Elizabeth shouted back, "Kallie, over here. These branches are whipping my face. All right, you can have your way. Let's look for food, and then maybe we can think about escaping."

Weakened by hunger, they moved toward a marshy area. The morning sun slowly evaporated dew that had collected on leaves. The mud squished between their toes in the shallow waters. Aquatic insects floated on top of the still water, and Kallie watched the backswimmers, stone flies, and water striders magically skim across a pond. Occasionally they saw fish feeding, but they could think of no way to catch them. Elizabeth saw a garter snake slither by but refused to consider it food and glared at Kallie for even suggesting it.

Disheartened, Kallie sat down as hunger pains stabbed her ribs. Not caring to admit it, she was hurt Brave Eagle had left her to starve. Lost in thought, she aimlessly stared at the vegetation until she spotted a small game trail. Entering the grove of elms, she dug into a pouch sewn inside her skirt and pulled out the slingshot she had carried since her farm days. Kallie gathered stones. Quietly moving along the trail, she found a hiding place. Waiting with forced patience, she sat motionless while the flies buzzed by her. Beads of sweat dripped down her face. The salty drops rolled onto her lip. A flash of brown movement revealed a small hare nibbling on grass. It stopped every few steps, inspecting the area before advancing. Shaking, Kallie held her breath while taking careful aim. She exhaled and unleashed the rock. It whizzed through the air, striking the rabbit's head. Excited, Kallie scooped up the stunned hare and killed it by twisting its neck.

Thankful for her good fortune, Kallie ran back to camp. She used the coals to stoke the fire and roast the rabbit. Elizabeth's temperament turned sweeter when she noticed the bloody carcass. She mouthed, "I will eat that raw if I have to."

Kallie said, "I'll gather up some lamb's-quarter and chickweed for greens. Elizabeth, don't drift too far, or something will steal our meal. Oh, how I wish the plum berries were ripe." Kallie recalled the reddish-orange berries her mother had prepared into sauces and jams. She imagined tasting succulent berries so sweet the juice dripped down her chin. Remembering the smells almost overwhelmed her. Shifting her thoughts, she surprised herself by thinking about Brave Eagle. She imagined his muscular arms wrapping around her. She closed her eyes and continued to daydream about him.

Kallie and Elizabeth were in better spirits after eating and bathing in the creek. Elizabeth said, "Why, now I feel good enough to escape."

Kallie said, "I hear horses coming." The women quickly hid evidence of their kill and sat close together. Bear and Brave Eagle, Weasel Tail and Flying Crow rode in and dropped their game on the ground.

Bear looked at the women and said, "So you've made a fire, and you found a jackrabbit to eat." He pointed to Elizabeth and said, "Fetch firewood. We will need a fire to dry the meat."

The men hung a pronghorn carcass by its hind legs and quickly skinned it. They butchered the meat by cutting long, thin strips off it and then hung them on a makeshift rack. Kallie figured they were going to dry it for travel meat. Bear allowed her to have a knife, so she cut strips off the carcasses. It was hard work, and she could feel that her back wounds were aggravated and bleeding. She was relieved when Brave Eagle motioned her to sit.

The evening winds calmed under the mask of darkness, and dinner roasted over the fire. The men laughed and smoked tobacco in long, decorated pipes with formidable blades on one side. Kallie's festering wounds began to bleed. She had no choice but to endure them.

Brave Eagle signaled her to follow him to the river. He carried a large leaf containing a sap mixture. Standing behind her, he pulled on her top and helped Kallie take it off. Slowly she removed her blouse and camisole and pushed her braid to the side. Gently, Brave Eagle applied the sap mixture to her wounds, but still she flinched with each touch. She knew by the burning sensation the sap would soothe the festering. Nudging her when he was finished, Brave Eagle turned, leaving her alone. Kallie looked over her shoulder and watched him walk away.

When she arrived back at the fire, Brave Eagle played his flute. Music floated magically through the air, and the notes sounded like the nature surrounding them. His melody was a collection of birdsongs, wind, flowing water, and rustling prairie grass. Amazed at his versatility with his flute, Kallie thought about her childhood. Her father possessed a beautiful voice and played the fiddle at all the social gatherings. During the long winter evenings, he had taught her how to play the pennywhistle so she could accompany him. Now, pulled back to Brave Eagle's music, she was completely mesmerized. She listened, trying to gather subtle clues about this mysterious warrior.

Kallie looked up at the night sky. Venus hung close to the moon. She interpreted this as a sign of hope. Attempting to sleep for the night, she curled up in the robe. When Brave Eagle made his way to bed, he immediately fell asleep. Kallie soon became uncomfortable. She needed to relieve herself but waited until everyone appeared to be sleeping. She got up, careful not to wake anyone, and quietly walked away from camp.

On her way back, Weasel Tail emerged from the shadows. The large, muscular man blocked her way. Kallie froze as she looked into his dark eyes, guessing his intentions. She turned to run, but Weasel Tail grabbed her by the hair and covered her mouth. Biting into his hand, she twisted and struggled, but she was no match for his strength. Weasel Tail subdued her and forced her to the ground. At that moment, Brave Eagle appeared out of the darkness and pulled on her attacker until he released her.

Weasel Tail glared at Brave Eagle. Both of the men's bodies were pumped with tension, and they spoke in harsh tones. It ended when Weasel Tail spat on the ground, uttered a final comment, and made a hurried retreat to camp. Brave Eagle sternly motioned her to follow closely behind him.

Reassured that Brave Eagle had defended her, Kallie reclined and waited for his reaction. There was none. His curious manners, strong brown body, and the security he provided attracted her. Moving in closer, their bodies warmed each other. Slowly, Kallie brushed her hand upon his back. Getting no response from him, she withdrew her hand. His body seemed rigid with anger, and he was breathing hard. She wondered about what had been said between Weasel Tail and Brave Eagle in their heated encounter. Kallie took a deep breath and looked up at the heavens. Maybe an answer would come in her dreams, as it always had before. Locking her fingers together, Kallie prayed she would survive.

Chapter 4: *Silver Hairbrushes*

Kaka: To Comb Hair and Detangle

Camp was still when Kallie awoke. The only sounds she heard were the voices of Brave Eagle and Bear in the distance. When she stood up, she could see them rearranging strips of drying meat on the racks. Shaking off sleepiness, she rolled up the thin buffalo robe. The small fire rocks were hot and ready to use. Careful to avoid Brave Eagle's attention, she took the water skin and walked to the river. Once at the bank, she crouched down, scooped up water with the skin bag, and hung it on a branch. Then she vigorously splashed river water on her sunburned face and washed. Standing back up, she observed the cattails and arrowheads swaying in the breeze. The morning air was already humid and hot.

Before leaving the river, Kallie picked chamomile for tea. She set the yellow flowers on a boulder and pressed a rock against them. The sweet aroma of the crushed flowers reminded her of her growing up on a frontier farm. As a young girl, she had been fascinated with the healing power of plants. Any chance she had, she'd gone in search of a new specimen to transplant into the family's garden. Her mother and father were Irish immigrants who were suspicious of the local flora. She could still hear her father's voice when he had scolded, "If you have time for such foolishness, then you can double up on chores. I have agreed to let you work for the Luther family in exchange for candles and cloth." Her mother had nodded in agreement, glad for the trade.

Life had been so simple when she was a girl. After chores were done, she had ridden her horse, Clara, over to the Luther farm. The Luthers were an elderly couple who had helped settle the valley. The old woman,

Millicent, had a reputation of being strange-minded, but she was kind and gentle to Kallie. It was Millicent who had taught her about the magical healing powers of plants.

Millicent possessed striking blue eyes that seemed to pierce one's thoughts. Her dark dress hid her full body, and where most women would have touches of white clothing, Millicent preferred black. Rolled-up sleeves revealed strong arms, and an apron hung tightly around her ample waist.

By midmorning, Millicent's long gray hair would come tumbling out of its loose bun and give her an untidy look. When visitors came, she did not alter her appearance for them the way Kallie's mother always did. Millicent's rumpled bonnet stayed hung on a hook by the door regardless of how many times Kallie urged her to put it on. Millicent always laughed and said she didn't care what others thought.

Although people sought Millicent's help when a doctor was not available, no one trusted her. Her erratic behavior, strange night walks, and bubbling cauldrons caused rumors to echo throughout the valley. Folks whispered that Millicent was a powerful witch who could cast spells on any unfortunate accuser. Steward Luther remained oblivious to gossip about his wife and stayed busy tending his fields. Mr. Luther was a quiet man who always went to the trading post alone.

Soon Kallie's association with Millicent made people suspicious of her. She was far more vulnerable to people's jeers. Anytime she entered the trading post, people grabbed their children and withdrew from her. During church gatherings, the traveling preacher lectured against the sins of the devil. He would slam his hand on the Holy Bible while shooting accusatory glances Kallie's way. As a result, she had learned to suppress all matters about healing and dreams, never speaking to anyone about them except Millicent.

She had loved working for the Luthers. Tending to their garden and spinning clumps of wool on the huge spinning wheel had been relaxing chores to her. While Kallie spun, Millicent made candles for trade. A large cauldron bubbled, always ready for dipping candles. Rays of sun had shone through the window and lit up glass jars containing strange concoctions of herbal remedies. Like clockwork, Millicent always had a wonderful supper ready for Steward. Remembering the smells of fresh bread and peppered pot roast permeating from Millicent's hearth made Kallie's mouth water. After the main meal of the day, Steward would return to his fields, leaving the women alone to do their chores.

In the late summer, she and Millicent had ventured into the woods to gather wild herbs under the light of a full moon. While they were walking, Kallie would tell Millicent about her dreams. Millicent had explained that every dream told a story, and every strange event represented a deep secret of the soul.

After evening tea, Millicent would crinkle her eyes as she read the tea leaves settled at the bottom of Kallie's cup. Millicent's one lazy eye had stared as she predicted Kallie's future. It was to be an exciting, arduous journey. They had laughed not knowing how soon their lives would change.

By the next spring, after the revival, life never got back to normal. Her brother Caleb had become ill. He shivered from chills, and then the next minute, he burned with fever. Her ma had frantically instructed her to go fetch Millicent. With Millicent's help, Caleb clung to life. The next morning Kallie's mother collapsed with the fever. This time Millicent's medicine did no good, and by nightfall, her mother was gone. Flushed from either drink or fever, her distraught father stumbled to the barn. He did not last through the night. The next morning Millicent told her Caleb would survive, but his recovery would be slow. Kallie's other brother, Michael, and she had the sorrowful task of burying her parents.

Saddened by the memory, Kallie returned to camp with the water. Imitating the men, she used two sticks to pick up hot rocks from the fire. Carefully, she dropped each rock in the vessel filled with water and tea leaves. She could feel Brave Eagle's gaze upon her even though he was by the drying racks, so Kallie swayed in her long skirt and loose blouse to keep his attention. Walking to the fire, he grabbed a bone left from their evening meal and gnawed on it while he waited for tea. As Kallie handed him his cup, she looked into his eyes. When he gazed back into hers, his disposition seemed to lighten. He seemed to have forgotten the fight with Weasel Tail from the night before.

The others slept until the midmorning heat became intolerable. Elizabeth was next to waken and stumble to the river to wash. When she returned, Kallie noticed something was different about her appearance, but she couldn't determine exactly what it was. Elizabeth's long black dress was comely and quite suitable for her missionary zeal, although her long silver crucifix was missing. At times she could be a handsome woman, but Elizabeth usually combed her hair into a tight bun that gave her a sterner look than nature had intended. Sometimes her turquoise-blue eyes sparkled and helped brighten her severe expression. Underneath her dark missionary facade, there was another side to Elizabeth's nature. She wore the most beautiful undergarments Kallie could ever have imagined. Adorned with lace and colored ribbons, her silk bodice competed with that of any brothel mistress east of the Mississippi.

After Elizabeth consumed her fill of tea and food, she looked around. The men, distracted with meat drying and conversation, ignored the women. Unguarded, Elizabeth motioned to Kallie to follow her. The women strolled down the game trail along the river until they reached the bank, where the water rushed by. Kallie enjoyed the quiet morning while picking lamb's-quarter and dandelion leaves. She felt lighter and more relaxed than she had in days. Her thoughts drifted to Brave Eagle until Elizabeth's glare disrupted her thoughts. Suddenly, Kallie realized what was different about Elizabeth.

She exclaimed, "Elizabeth, you've brushed your hair! You got your silver hairbrush back. Oh, how I've longed for it. Let me borrow it."

Elizabeth looked away and said, "Tell me one thing you've ever done for me."

Kallie squinted her eyes before replying, "Elizabeth, I saved you from starving just yesterday, and I'd think that would be enough."

Elizabeth hesitated but then relented. Reaching deep into the pocket of her dress, she revealed her silver hairbrush. She handed it over to Kallie while saying, "All right, here, you can use it. It will feel heavenly."

Kallie struggled with the tangles and knots in her hair until frustration almost made her quit. Finally, she and Elizabeth brushed her hair until it was smooth again. Bending over, she lifted her skirt and ripped a long white strip from her petticoat. She ran the strip of cloth around her long hair to make a back braid. This would help her unruly hair stay in place, at least for the morning. Handing back the treasured item, she looked curiously at Elizabeth and asked, "How did you get him to give it to you?"

Elizabeth smiled proudly and said, "I have my ways."

The women walked by the grazing horses. The animals' tails twitched continually to swat pestering flies. Kallie whistled in a playful manner, and her horse, Clara, quickly came to her. Kallie laughed as she rubbed the horse's nose. Clara had been her faithful companion for many years. The horse was one of the few possessions she had taken when she had left the farm with Armand.

Flying Crow seemed to speak some harsh words. Weasel Tail, wearing Elizabeth's silver crucifix upon his chest, approached the women in anger. Kallie instinctively backed away. Her beloved horse was not hers any longer. Quickly turning, she ran toward the camp, leaving Elizabeth standing alone with Weasel Tail and Flying Crow.

Kallie noticed Brave Eagle had observed the men's behavior but did nothing. She sensed they had acted within their rights. As Kallie approached, Brave Eagle gazed upon the curves of her body. She felt her face flush at his attention, and this confused her.

She knew so little about him. He obviously loved horses. She watched Brave Eagle guide Wind Racer down to the river to wash him. Bear stood by her and Elizabeth and told them a story about the capture of Wind Racer's mother. Kallie understood that he and Brave Eagle had ventured, at great risk, to Comanche territory for trade.

Bear continued, "On the homeward journey, we followed the fresh trail of a mustang herd. We avoided spooking them and ambushed them at a watering hole. A beautiful pregnant mare appeared, and Brave Eagle chased her down."

Bear made a circular motion with his arm and explained, "Brave Eagle lassoed the creature's neck and pulled the rope tightly until its grip slowed the horse. The pregnant mare abruptly stopped and pulled back, allowing Brave Eagle to leap off his horse."

Displaying his bulging arm muscles, Bear demonstrated the strength it had taken to staunchly hold the rope tightly to settle the mare down and hobble the horse's legs. Bear showed how Brave Eagle had pulled the mare's head down to his level and blew his breath into the horse's nostrils.

Bear finished, "Soon after we arrived back at the village, the mare gave birth to a frisky colt." Bear pointed to Wind Racer, who was a beautiful painted chestnut with special long white markings on his face and legs.

"Brave Eagle named him Wind Racer at the moment he saw the colt running and kicking. At only a few days old he ran with a perfect gait as he raced with the wind."

They watched as Brave Eagle lifted the buffalo-hair bridle off Wind Racer's neck and unbraided his mane. He poured the cool river water on the horse and continued to rub him down. Wind Racer raised his head and shook it in response. Brave Eagle smiled, careful to avoid washing the horse's white nose, which was painted with power symbols.

Flying Crow nudged Elizabeth to wash Clara. Elizabeth halfheartedly attempted it but was too frightened of the horse to do a good job. She had always preferred a wagon ride to saddle riding and did not trust horses. When Flying Crow and Weasel Tail moved out of sight, Kallie helped Elizabeth.

Kallie scooped up water with her apron and poured it on Clara. Her horse responded with a neigh. Not daring to show any expression of happiness, Kallie kept her lightness inside. Pretending to be concentrating on the horse, she peered under Clara's neck to watch Brave Eagle. His lean, muscular arms moved with sweeping motions over Wind Racer's body. Brave Eagle wore nothing but a breechcloth, and his back muscles were prominent as he brushed his horse. Fascinated, Kallie watched Brave Eagle's movements and once caught his gaze. She quickly looked away, not knowing how to respond. She continued to peek at him until Elizabeth tugged hard at her sleeve, demanding her help.

Soon it was time to depart. Bear distributed smoke-dried meat, and each man packed his buffalo hide parfleche. As the men grouped together, Kallie noticed they smirked and pointed at her. Brave Eagle reacted with anger at the other men's teasing. Agitated, he lifted her roughly upon his horse. Then he hesitated, turned, and changed his sullen expression into a smile as he shook his head. Laughing with them, he leaped on his horse and waited for Flying Crow to lead the party. Next came Weasel Tail, who proudly wore Elizabeth's silver crucifix. Elizabeth scowled as she followed behind riding Clara. As she passed Kallie, Elizabeth defiantly vowed, "God will save me when the timing is right. I will just have to be patient."

Chapter 5: *The Storm*

Aicamna: To Storm upon and Blow Furiously

Kallie positioned herself for a long ride and took comfort in being close to Brave Eagle, her body feeling his. Her arms looped around him, and her hands rested on his muscular thighs. Together they shared the rhythm of the horse's gait as the terrain changed from rolling hills into rugged, sweeping grassland. The prairie sun was relentless. Heat waves shimmered upward from the dusty earth. The grasses went on forever. There was no shade anywhere.

Approaching a colony of prairie dogs, the horses slowed in order to dodge hidden holes. Prairie dogs poked their heads out of depressions, while others scurried back and forth between holes. Finally, one sentry backflipped a signal of danger, and all the prairie dogs dove for protection. Mice scurried from underneath the horses, and grasshoppers sprang in every direction. Kallie covered her nose at an ill-smelling plant with long narrow leaves and yellow flowers that grew on the sandy soil. Stirring up clouds of dust, the loaded horses moved through the sea of grasses.

Brave Eagle captured her thoughts. Kallie wondered why the other men's clothes displayed colorful beaded designs, but his clothing bore no such beadwork. He wore only silver armbands, buckskin leggings, a breechcloth, and a belt that held his knife. He had packed his arrows and bow, tomahawk pipe, and a hide bag that held his flute. A thin sleeping robe was rolled up with a buckskin shirt that he had worn in the evening chill. Two necklaces dangled from his chest. One had a small, plain pouch attached to it, and the other was a simple arrowhead.

Kallie thought about Brave Eagle's dark eyes, set close together, shining like obsidian when he smiled. His expression reflected the face of a proud, dignified man. His strong jaw, high cheekbones, white teeth, and prominent nose were handsome features. Three feathers were attached to the back of his hair, each positioned differently. As she sat close to him, a feather dangled at her eye level, and she saw it was marked with a red dot. Wind Racer had similar feathers flowing from his braided mane, as if he was decorated to show Brave Eagle's exploits.

They rode steadily throughout the day, and Kallie was amazed at the horses' stamina. It was evening before she sensed the horses were getting tired. She knew they could smell the river by the way they flared their nostrils. When Flying Crow pointed to a grove of willows in the distance, Kallie was elated. Exhausted from riding, she wanted to cry out in pain because of her blistered thighs, aching muscles, and dry throat. Looking back, Kallie empathized with Elizabeth's pained expression. Although Elizabeth looked determined, she was not accustomed to riding long distances. Kallie hoped that both she and Elizabeth could soon dabble their blistered feet in the cool river waters.

At camp, meat was given to the women. Its sweet flavor dissolved in their mouths as they tugged at their jerky strips. The men were in a deep discussion, and their voices rose as they spoke rapidly. Elizabeth ignored them, but Kallie observed their furled eyebrows and looks of consternation. Realizing they were arguing about something, fear ran through her. She bit into her strip and prayed the men would not take action against her and Elizabeth.

Flying Crow broke off a stick and drew a picture of something in the dirt. Kallie edged over to look, but she could not make any sense of it. As the men knelt down and observed Flying Crow's map, their expressions changed. The tone of their voices softened, and their body language became friendlier. All shook their heads in agreement. Something was about to happen.

The group quickly dispersed, and Brave Eagle motioned for Kallie to come. Helping her up on the horse more gently than before, this time he placed her in front of him. They hurried along with the others. Prairie grasses moved slowly in the wind as dusk was setting in. His presence penetrated into her very being. Kallie leaned back so his powerful arms encompassed her and his long black hair hit her shoulders. The proximity of his body became intoxicating as his breath caressed her neck.

As they traveled, she surrendered to him by tilting her head back and leaning on his shoulder. Brave Eagle accepted her in his arms. Lost in her dreams, she felt his body. She could resist no longer. Consumed by desire, she rode close to him toward their destination under the light of the emerging moon.

They set a simple camp late that night. Exhausted from the strenuous ride and the hot day, everyone chewed meat strips quickly and went immediately to bed. Too tired to chew the dried meat, Kallie slyly stashed it in a hidden pouch hemmed in her skirt. Curling up in her blanket, she was asleep in moments. Late into the night she awoke, acutely aware of Brave Eagle's presence. His smells permeated her nostrils as she slowly extended her arm toward him. Kallie placed her trembling hand lightly on his chest. Feeling no rejection, she gently massaged him.

The night sounds were seductive. Following the rhythm of his breathing with her touch, Kallie felt Brave Eagle's hand grip her. As he pulled her close to him, his strong arms overtook her. Kallie did not resist. Shocked by her own intensity of desire, she accepted his touches, turning her mind off to the right and wrong of it. Only the present mattered. Brave Eagle softly stroked her breasts, thighs, and the rest of her body. He rubbed up against her so that when he lifted up her skirt, she was ready for him. His strong, animal, rhythmic pattern brought him in deeper each time, and Kallie found herself responding with each thrust. She completely surrendered to him, wanting more, relaxing until she tightened with an exalted breath that released her. In the night, sounds of the two became one, and heavy breathing turned into soft moans. Kallie noticed Bear, who was on guard duty, look in their direction, place his hands under his chin, and turn away.

Brave Eagle woke, and for the first time since the raid, Kallie thought he looked peaceful. While the morning sun burst through the clouds with colors of red and orange, the men gathered. Just like the night before, Flying Crow seemed to speak emphatically. He pointed to the spiderweb shining in the early sunrays and then to the sky in the direction of the sunrise.

Kallie took a chance and looked into Brave Eagle's eyes, searching for a hint of affection. He ignored her and switched his gaze to Flying Crow instead. Her feelings hurt, she withdrew and stood by Elizabeth.

Elizabeth spoke harshly. "I see you trying to cast a spell on that savage beast. Not for escape but to make him love you! You're disgusting, Kallie. I've never heard the likes of it before! It is trouble. You'd best change your ways, or the Lord will punish you!"

Kallie kept her steady gaze on Brave Eagle and said, "Elizabeth, it is no affair of yours. Besides, I'll survive if he cares for me and maybe you will too. Remember—your husband is dead. Your brother, who was my husband, is dead. Your destiny will be your own doing. You'd best change your temperament; these savages may be your only salvation." The two women stood in angry silence until they noticed a sense of urgency as the men approached them.

Bear grabbed Elizabeth by the arm and said, "Hurry, a storm is coming."

Kallie used Brave Eagle's hands as a step and landed squarely on Wind Racer. His horse shook its head and anticipated Brave Eagle's intentions. They rode hard most of the day, concentrating on making gains in distance and stopping only to water and feed the horses. Kallie did not understand. She saw no clues that storm clouds were brewing. The day's heat was sweltering, just like the days before. There were only thin, sparse clouds on the horizon. Not comprehending the men's concern, she passed it off as one of their many idiosyncrasies.

When the group stopped to rest at the river that snaked through the grasslands, Kallie stood on the riverbank. She watched a soaring red-tailed hawk hunt for prey. Lost in her own thoughts, she barely noticed Brave Eagle brush past her. He jokingly grabbed her, almost throwing her in, but he let her go at the last second. Laughing, she pretended to be shocked. He turned his back on her and moved close to the river's edge when, without warning, Kallie leaped away from a bee. Accidentally, she knocked Brave Eagle into the river. She stood looking at him with both her hands covering her mouth, shocked at what she had done. Surprised, he looked at her with a sly smile. His clothes were wet as he crawled up the bank. There was no time to dry off, and as they rode his moist skin pressed against her. Making way silently and swiftly, Wind Racer kicked up swirls of dust as they traveled on.

At sunset, the weary party arrived at a huge limestone butte along the river. The men appeared visibly relieved that they had reached their destination. Along the butte were several wind-carved caves with openings large enough to provide shelter. An overhang provided protection for the skittish horses. Nervously they grazed, twitching their tails at flies. The men prepared for night in their refuge, and Bear directed the women to collect firewood along the river.

Kallie walked with Elizabeth and said, "What a beautiful evening sky, with the setting sun streaming through such white, fluffy thunderhead clouds."

Elizabeth pointed. "Yes, but look over there." Off on the horizon, an angry black background was spreading throughout the sky. "We'd best hurry to keep out of it."

Kallie said, "You go ahead. I want to walk a bit." She paused to smell the white blossoms of the pale dogwood shrub. The winds steadily increased, and Kallie observed the pink petals from the meadow rose fall to the ground, leaving small fruit on the branch. By the time the green fruit ripened to its deep-red color, she would know her fate. Engrossed in her own thoughts, she approached the river's edge. A push sent her headfirst into the dark green waters. The sudden plunge confused her until she popped to the surface and saw Brave Eagle laughing at her. She acted angry for a split second but then laughed as she climbed up the bank.

Kallie shivered from the winds whipping around them. Brave Eagle motioned he would be back. She slipped away, using vegetation as cover to undress and wring out her clothing. Brave Eagle returned with his buffalo robe and offered it to her. Smiling, she accepted and wrapped it around her wet body. Her soggy clothes fluttered in the bushes nearby.

Crouching down, Kallie shielded herself with the robe. A fragile sunset quickly faded, obscured by thickening clouds. Thunder sounded with a formidable rumble as the approaching storm rolled toward them. Still in the distance, strikes of angry lightning bolts stabbed the earth with a brightness and rapidity she had never seen before. Watching the constant stream of lightning, she was filled with wonder.

Surrounding her in his arms, Brave Eagle moved in from behind and shielded her from the harshest winds. Water from her hair dripped onto him as she laid her head upon his shoulder. His hand brushed against her cheek as they sat watching the approaching storm. Raging winds blasted past them. Brave Eagle placed Kallie on the ground beneath him and took her during the beginning of the storm. Experiencing the feel of his skin touching her silky, nude body, she exhaled deeply. Excited by the sensations as their bodies pressed hard against each other, Kallie was as free as the storm winds.

As lightning intensified, they dressed and scrambled into the large cave with the others. Protected, they were comfortable in their surroundings. Bolts flashed, brightening the cave with each strike as the sound of thunder crashed. The horses became agitated, and Weasel Tail went out to calm them. As he left, a bolt struck so close Kallie felt the hairs on her arm stand up. The air smelled of lightning. The storm's ferocity frightened her. It was as if the world was ending and the heavens had opened up, lashing out torrential rains and hail. The river became swollen, and rising water rushed close to the cave opening, reminding Kallie of the flood she and her wagon party had endured earlier. Elizabeth would not let go of Flying Crow, who reluctantly tried to calm her.

The winds howled, and the small fire danced every time the gusts changed direction. The storm continued for several hours until, finally, the wind began to die down and a soft rain sounded outside. The redness of the cave rock reflected the glow of the fire and had a calming effect. Anxiety lifted, and everyone relaxed and eventually fell asleep to the melodic rhythm of the prairie rain. Brave Eagle gently caressed Kallie and pulled her to him as they lay under the buffalo robe.

Suddenly, the wind shifted violently. The storm returned even more intensely than before. Howling whirls blasted debris everywhere. Sounds of the horses could be heard until their terrified shrieks were obliterated by the loud, ear-splitting sound of a tornado. Kallie closed her eyes and bit her mouth to prevent herself from screaming. Flying Crow held Elizabeth down as she struggled to escape from the cave. The storm endlessly pounded.

Brave Eagle rushed out into the storm after the tornado passed to check on the horses. Kallie followed him and was soon drenched by the driving rains. Her hair was dripping, and she moved her arms to protect herself against the hail. After Brave Eagle retied the ropes and soothed the horses, he and Kallie ducked under a cave overhang. Brave Eagle pressed her hard against the rock wall and kissed her. They could not stop. His lips caressed her neck, and then he bit her. As he took her, Kallie's body trembled and she dug her nails into his back. Their moans and screams were masked under the sounds of thunder and wind. Lightning illuminated their wet, slippery bodies. When they had calmed, they lay for only a moment before the storm drove them back into the cave with the others.

Watching the storm through the cave entrance, Kallie peered over Brave Eagle's body. She saw Bear looking at her, but Brave Eagle pulled her back into his arms and resumed his snoring. The cave fire slowly lost its glow. As the last of the coals were extinguished, lightning still flashed strongly and thunder rumbled in the distance until finally the angry storm dissipated.

Sounds of birds woke Kallie. A red-shafted flicker flew by the cave entrance as she ventured outside. The fierce storm had left a trail of destruction. The river rushed by, its murky waters carrying alders torn from their roots. Huge dirt swaths in the grasslands marked the tornado's path. The air smelled fresh, and sounds of crickets surrounded them. The sun again ruled the prairies.

Carved from the elements, the caves had provided adequate shelter. The walls looked reddish in the morning sunlight, revealing pictures carved into the rock. Fascinated, Kallie moved in closer and discovered etchings of stick men and strange animal designs. Putting her hand over the rock, she followed the carving with one of her fingers. She felt a kinship with the ancient travelers who had sat under the sun carving these pictures. Wondering what secrets were in the designs, she picked up a rose-colored stone and squeezed it in her palm. Rubbing its smooth surface helped ease her worries about the future.

Kallie looked to the horizon and noticed the terrain was changing. She feared that now she would never find her way back to the fort. The dark hills in the distance looked black and forlorn against the prairie expanse. She wondered if that was the group's final destination. When she looked up, Flying Crow had already packed Elizabeth on Clara's back. He stopped to look at Elizabeth, but she, having survived the storm, ignored him.

Bear said, "Flying Crow dreamed that a huge gathering of crows flew in circles above him. They told him there would soon be a summer hunt so big it would feed the whole village. This is a very good omen." Bear smiled. "I love summer hunts. The coats of the buffalo are lighter, so my arrows go deeper. It is much less dangerous to make a kill."

The men lightly conversed until Brave Eagle spoke. She didn't know what was said, but Weasel Tail sneered. Angry looks escalated into an argument. Even Flying Crow joined in, shouting while pointing at her. Brave Eagle then said something that caused the men to stop and stare at him in disbelief. They nervously laughed and seemed stunned. Brave Eagle stood his ground until he too started laughing. The men slapped Brave Eagle on the shoulder while shaking their heads and dispersed to mount their horses.

Bear instructed the women, "Enemies might be close. You are expected to be quiet while we travel. Watch for a sign from Weasel Tail; he is in charge of searching for intruders. You must do as he says, or you will be killed—or even worse, you might be captured. The leader of our enemy, Hawk Claw, makes his captives worthless like a played-out horse." Bear took his hunting knife and ran it across his neck. The women nodded their heads that they understood.

The group cautiously journeyed on a gully trail instead of along the ridge. Traveling this way was arduous because alder branches whipped their legs. When they arrived at a river fork, Brave Eagle stopped his horse while the others turned off and kept going. Kallie, apprehensive about being separated from Elizabeth, searched for some sign of reassurance, but no one even looked back at them. She was alone with Brave Eagle, and her body stiffened with fear as she leaned into his chest. The silhouettes of the others moved toward the horizon and became smaller and smaller. Now they were truly alone.

Chapter 6: *Escape*

Sigluha: Get Out of the Way

They camped in the early afternoon. Brave Eagle spoke little, but that didn't bother Kallie. Years of being isolated on a frontier farm had conditioned her to the quiet. She was comfortable surrounded by the sounds of nature. Searching for edible plants, she found lamb's-quarter greens and some flower blossoms. In addition, Kallie picked white-flowered spring cress and was pleasantly surprised by its tangy flavor. Brave Eagle pulled dried berries and milk vetch pods from his pouch and handed them to her. These items, as he indicated by hand motions, were to be mixed with the other greens. Then he dug out a piece of soap weed root and showed her how to use it as soap. She accepted it because she needed a bath, but she did not feel comfortable disrobing. She decided to save it and continued to search for food.

Wading beside her in a marsh, Brave Eagle dislodged tubers from the muddy bottom. Kallie felt his gaze upon her and was relieved she could hold his attention. She wanted to show him she was knowledgeable about plants, for this would surely add to her worth. This was important because she sensed that the men's comments had stung Brave Eagle's pride. As sunrays warmed their bodies, Brave Eagle seemed to relax. He looked comfortable and was quiet. Kallie figured he was listening for any changes in the magpie's chatter. The red-shafted flicker's song signaled something good, for he smiled when he heard it.

It was dark before Brave Eagle started a small fire to heat rocks for cooking. Kallie mixed herbs with hydrated berries. The riverbank reverberated with night sounds as they ate their meal. When he finished eating, Brave Eagle looked at her. His stare made her feel exotic and beautiful in the fire's glow. Not thinking about life's complexities, she lay down beside him.

The next morning, they again foraged for edible greens. Brave Eagle showed her many plants, motioning with his hands to explain their usage. Gathering his quiver and bow, he signaled Kallie to follow him. She walked softly. He stopped often to smell the air and track carefully. Several sets of tracks led him to a marshy watering hole, where the two of them waited, hidden in the vegetation. Eventually an antelope approached the water, but the cautious buck twitched its ears and ran off. Brave Eagle leaped from his hiding place with bow in hand and chased after it.

In the cottonwoods, sunlight streamed through the trees and, for the first time in days, Kallie was alone. Hesitant about what to do with her freedom, she strolled along the gully picking purple foxgloves. She caught up with Brave Eagle, who was poised with his bow and arrow in absolute concentration. By the time the antelope lifted his head to smell for danger, Brave Eagle's arrow had pierced its neck. The buck ran a few steps and dropped. Brave Eagle knelt down beside it and softly chanted, while moving his arm in all directions. Grunting, he scooped up the animal and carried it on his back to the river for cleaning. With a pleased expression on his face, he signaled Kallie to get his horse. She ran through the brush and, when she came to the bloom of foxgloves, turned toward the river fork. Wind Racer came to her calls and followed her.

At camp, Kallie and Brave Eagle butchered and lay meat strips on a makeshift rack. Portions of meat were kept in a hole dug by the river where it would stay cooler. She started to use the drill stick to start a fire, but Brave Eagle shook his head. There would be no fire during daylight. Instead, they spent time cleaning the area until there were no traces of butchering left.

Walking to the marsh, Kallie waded out to collect cattails. The brown parts of the plant could be pounded into flour that produced edible flatbread. The mud from the pond bottom created gurgling sounds as she pulled out each foot. With her arms full, Kallie finally made it to shore. Brave Eagle took the plants from her arms and placed them on the bank. He placed his hand into hers and walked with her along the river. When they arrived at the deepest part of the river, he stripped off his clothing and dove off the rocks. He motioned for Kallie to join him, but, embarrassed, she shook her head no. Climbing onto the shore, Brave Eagle confronted her. He drew her close to his nude body and slowly tugged on her blouse until she obliged him. She lifted her blouse over her head and released the button on her skirt, causing it to drop. This exposed her cotton petticoat, which barely covered her breasts. Reaching out, he slowly touched the ribbons on her bodice and inspected them. His hands brushed her breasts as he moved his arms down her sides and squeezed her waist. Backing away, he motioned her to take off the petticoat. She slowly did so and stood before him naked, but just for a fleeting moment. Quickly, she jumped into the river, and Brave Eagle dove in after her.

In the clear, cool waters they swam and laughed. Kallie playfully climbed on his back. Brave Eagle dove under the water, and their bodies met in a slippery embrace. Kallie wondered if she could trust Brave Eagle but realized it didn't matter. He was all she had in the world, trust or not.

After their swim, they lay close together on the sunny bank. Kallie listened to Brave Eagle's breathing as his hands explored her body. Embracing him, she allowed sensations to release untamed feelings. Brave Eagle caressed her soft body, cupping his hands over her firm breasts, feeling her erect nipples. His strong, proud body responded to her. Warm feelings enveloped Kallie, and she cried out as Brave Eagle collapsed over her. As their breathing slowed, they held each other, and Kallie listened to the sounds of the river rushing by.

Wind Racer grazed near camp, his tail swatting the biting flies. Under darkness, they finally built a pit fire to cook dinner. They ate large portions of meat and finished the greens and tubers. Brave Eagle threw a bone into the fire and then looked into her eyes. Speaking in his native tongue, he introduced himself as Brave Eagle. Pointing to her, he waited until she replied, "Kallie."

He looked puzzled at the sound of her name and repeated, "Kallie." Smiling, she nodded a yes because it sounded close enough. As the fire smoldered into its last embers, they went to bed, warmed by desire. The night was peaceful and one that Kallie would remember for all her days. She decided to put her worries aside and hoped things were going to turn out all right. One wonderful night would stretch into another until everything seemed normal again.

In the early morning, Brave Eagle went to the river to spear fish. Kallie watched him from a distance. He became like an otter searching for trout. When he found a deep pool, he sat until the fish accepted him as part of the landscape. Slowly, he raised a long stick with a knife tied to it and plunged it into the water. He brought the pole back out by pulling the attached rope. When he lifted the shaft, she saw the attached blade had pierced a flopping fish. Brave Eagle pulled the fish off and poised himself for another catch.

His bronze, lean, muscular body had been shaped and hardened by the elements. His stomach muscles were pronounced, and his manly arms bore bands that accentuated his muscles. She smiled when she noticed he had braided the side of his long hair and tied it off with his three feathers. Maybe, she thought, he had altered his appearance for her.

It had been another pleasant day, and as soon as the cover of darkness came, they started a small fire in a deep pit. Kallie put the fish fillets in the cooking pouch and added the hot cooking stones. While they cooked, she pondered her future. Shaking off her fears, she ate her meal and felt better. Her skin was becoming tan, and she felt refreshed from swimming. Only the uncertainties of her life situation caused her concern.

As a frontier child, she had heard many stories about the savagery of Indians, but Brave Eagle had shown her mostly kindness. Still, she wondered about his intentions. Where was he taking her? Would he use her up and then cast her away in trade? Even worse, would he allow others to torture her until she was dead or disfigured? Soon she would know.

Before dawn, Brave Eagle motioned Kallie to help pack. She noticed a change in Brave Eagle's behavior. He spent more time hiding traces of their camp and continually scanned the area. They would be walking the rest of the way, since much of the meat and skins were placed on the horse. Not all the meat was completely dried, so she knew they were close to their destination. How she dreaded the thought of arriving in his village.

Brave Eagle hunted as they followed the meandering river. With his arrows and bow poised on his shoulder, he moved slowly while looking for animal signs. Kallie quietly followed behind. She held the horse's reins out of nervous habit, because Wind Racer needed no such prodding. Spotting tracks, Brave Eagle motioned Kallie to stop. Tired, she happily complied and rested in the shade. Soon she fell asleep.

Kallie's sleep was disturbed. Frightened, she awoke and wondered how much time had elapsed. An eerie feeling came over her. It was too quiet.

Hiding the horse in the gully trees, she cautiously moved in the direction she had last seen Brave Eagle. As she bent down to search for his tracks, a hand covered her mouth with a mighty grip. Brave Eagle turned her head to show her that it was he. His eyes, intense as a wild animal's, commanded her to be still. Brave Eagle pointed to several Indians in the distance, all searching the ground to track anyone who had recently traveled through. Brave Eagle pointed to the leader and formed a claw with his fist. Kallie remembered Bear's warnings about an enemy named Hawk Claw.

They remained well hidden in the brush, and Brave Eagle's alert eyes never left the sight of the intruders. The braves were painted for battle. The war party paused to listen and smell the air. Hawk Claw seemed to have sensed something. He searched the area carefully.

Kallie knew they had an advantage, since Brave Eagle had spotted the enemy first. If they were found out, she knew the men would fight to the death. There would be no capture, except maybe for her. It would end badly. Brave Eagle prepared his quiver and bow, kept his war club within reach, and gave Kallie a knife from his belt.

Kallie was thankful Brave Eagle had both accuracy and rapidity of shot. Holding three arrows in his hand and two in his mouth, Brave Eagle waited and seemed ready to fire as many arrows as he could. It was either that or become overpowered.

Motionless under cover, Kallie and Brave Eagle hid together, their breathing and fate intertwined. Brave Eagle's eyes were barely visible from the vegetation as the war party passed by. His body stiffened when the leader stopped a hundred feet short of them to watch and listen. Hawk Claw seemed to sense their presence. As the warrior approached, Brave Eagle's hand covered Kallie's eyes. In the confusion, she could hear the enemy coming toward her. Paralyzed with fear, Kallie's chest tightened until she could barely breathe. She relied on inner strength to stay calm and prayed to be spared from a gruesome death. A wolf yelp signal called out. The enemy warrior stepped backward, and Brave Eagle let go of her. She saw the stranger shrug and hurry back to his warriors. The war party continued toward their destination.

Kallie's pounding heart calmed. It had been a stirring adventure in an otherwise quiet day. Sensing the situation to be safer, she laid her head next to Brave Eagle. They watched the enemies weave down the hill like a drawn-out snake. Hawk Claw's party would not discover any fresh trail if they stayed on the east side of the river.

The couple hid in the thicket, ignoring the biting bugs, until Brave Eagle tapped Kallie's shoulder and motioned her to follow. As they emerged from their hiding spot, they ran to a vantage point above the river. Below, Wind Racer was grazing in the bushes, just out of the enemies' view. Kallie knew that rescuing the horse would be a very risky move, but there was no choice. Brave Eagle would never leave Wind Racer behind.

Maneuvering down the hill, Brave Eagle attempted to reach his horse without being detected. Sweat shimmered on his brown skin, and his taut body was tense as he slid down the slope. Brave Eagle had to remain still for long periods of time until he finally made it to Wind Racer.

Kallie remained hidden in a thicket at the vantage point. Peering over the rocky ledge, she watched the war party. They crossed the river precariously close to where Brave Eagle and his horse were hiding. Brave Eagle looked up at her for guidance. She frantically shook her head no to warn him not to come out of hiding. The enemy was too close, and they had stopped to look around.

When the war party moved on, Kallie motioned Brave Eagle to make a run for it. He had only seconds to pass through the open area before reaching the cover of the wooded river terrain. Wind Racer carried a full load but adeptly ran past the clearing and up the hill. Partially hidden from view, Brave Eagle and his horse skirted along the trail, while the war party moved farther down the river. Barely able to endure the suspense, Kallie closed her eyes and prayed. Relief washed over her when Brave Eagle arrived, but it was short-lived. His expression warned her that they were still in danger. They needed to escape quickly down the ravine in case the war party had detected them.

His hand took hers in a strong grip. As they negotiated their way down the arduous descent, Kallie wondered if she was running to her own demise. Lost in her thoughts, she slowed while Brave Eagle pulled her. Miscalculating, he stumbled, bringing Kallie down with him, and they rolled to the bottom. Hot and sweaty, they were now covered with a thick layer of dust. They both laughed. Kallie prayed Brave Eagle cared for her, because each step forward put her closer to his village. For the first time since they had separated from the others, she wondered about Elizabeth's fate.

She could sense Brave Eagle was in a hurry to get home. They broke from the river lands and traveled across the grassland. Brave Eagle's body was drenched in sweat, but his trot never varied. Kallie struggled in the hot sun. Her dress was soaked with sweat and crusted with dust. She could no longer endure her insatiable thirst and fell hopelessly behind.

Brave Eagle lifted her onto Wind Racer. Unable to remain hidden in the grasslands, he unrolled the buffalo robe, making her crouch down under it. Kallie's protests did no good, for Brave Eagle insisted. From a distance, she would look like a buffalo roaming the prairie. Leading the way, Brave Eagle ran for the rest of the day. He did not break his stride until the setting sun gave way to a huge moon on the horizon.

When the moon was high in the sky, the weary travelers stopped to rest behind a small knoll where they would be hidden. The prairie night chill was more forgiving than the blazing sun. Brave Eagle covered himself with the robe, drank from the water pouch, and devoured half-dried meat. Kallie eagerly drank the water until Brave Eagle took it back and shook his head no. They were in dry, hot country now. Too exhausted to eat, she collapsed in Brave Eagle's arms.

Kallie's body ached. She noticed that, although Brave Eagle looked tired, he did not sleep. She realized he was trying to remain alert in case the formidable enemy still stalked them. Closing her eyes for a moment, she unintentionally fell asleep. She awoke to Brave Eagle's strong embrace. She felt better after sleeping and gently massaged his neck to wake him. Brave Eagle responded with shock at his carelessness. He helped Kallie leap on Wind Racer. He began to run alongside them. Brave Eagle's body glistened with sweat as he kept a strong, fast pace throughout the day.

Kallie dreaded the day's hardships, for it was a continual battle against the sun. The meal of dry meat caused her to retch. Despite the rock Brave Eagle had placed in her mouth, her throat was dry, and her continual thirst raged. Kallie rode with trepidation, fearing their arrival. His calloused hands lifted her off his horse. Smiling, he pulled out the water pouch and let her drink the last of their water supply. When the last drop rolled down Kallie's chin, he pointed to the silhouettes of tepees off in the distance.

Caressing her, Brave Eagle brushed his lips past her neck and cheek, lowering himself to give her a full, endearing kiss. Kallie exploded with passion as her lips craved his. Holding Brave Eagle tightly, she surrendered herself to him, desperately hoping he needed her too. Brave Eagle held her tightly against the backdrop of the wild prairie. The sun dropped low on the horizon, and colors of the sunset streamed against the billowing clouds. A soft breeze blew Kallie's long wavy hair. Brave Eagle broke from her embrace, and she felt as if he was being pulled to his home. As they made their way to the village, he motioned her to walk behind him. He tried to explain something, but she did not understand.

Barely breathing, Kallie tried to match Brave Eagle's fast pace. She could not keep up and felt threatened by his obvious excitement. They passed the young boys who were watching the herds of horses. Kallie faced their curious stares. The sentries crowded around Brave Eagle and talked while completely ignoring her. She took this distraction as an opportunity to look around. The village was a large one. Curious children stood back while the adults ran to greet Brave Eagle. Her heart filled with terror, and she could not feel her breath. As the crowd engulfed them, she was truly in his world.

Chapter 7: *The Village*

Tiyata: At Home

The massive settlement of tepees was located in a sea of short grasses. A river ran along one side of the village and meandered past the outer tepees. Willows, alders, and cottonwoods grew on its banks. On the other side of the waters were rolling hills and cliffs dotted with small green shrubs. Gentle hills turned into dark mountains that extended to the horizon. They seemed to go on forever.

Dogs ran wild and barked with excitement as Brave Eagle and Kallie approached. She walked closely behind him with her head slightly down. As they passed several tepees, one stood out because of its colorful decorations. Layers of red, black, and blue stripes covered the whole tepee. Kallie recognized Bear's horse tethered to a stake just outside it but did not see Bear anywhere.

Huge painted shields hung from cottonwood trees. Wind chimes clanged from branches, making magical sounds. This would have fascinated her if she weren't so terrified. Buffalo meat hung from huge racks. Big rib bones stood against the fires as they walked by. Pungent smells of fresh blood and skins were everywhere. Circles of buffalo hides were stretched out on the ground, their edges pierced by wooden stakes.

A crowd gathered around Kallie. She tried to keep her head down and focus on the dark-haired children who shouted at her. Naked, they started touching and pulling at her clothing. Brave Eagle, smiling at the younger ones, shooed them away.

Kallie peered into the crowd and searched for Elizabeth. That is when she met the fierce glare of a beautiful young woman. Kallie

48

instinctively sensed the woman was trouble. Perhaps this woman was in love with Brave Eagle. Kallie knew she was her enemy.

It was obvious that much talk had preceded their arrival. Everyone lined up in a procession to observe Brave Eagle and his captive. Gossip whipped around the crowd like a snake, and the sounds of whispering were everywhere. People were pointing to the four long scrapes on Brave Eagle's face and Kallie's discolored black eye. Brave Eagle seemed happy to see his friends and family. He embraced them affectionately and shouted cheerfully as he walked toward the central tepee. Old men, grinning, welcomed Brave Eagle.

A man who appeared to be chief stood outside a large tepee entrance. He wore a headdress of eagle feathers, trimmed with a beaded band, and a fringed shirt that was open to reveal a strong chest. His quiet, dignified expression broke into a smile of straight, white teeth when he embraced Brave Eagle. The chief looked at Kallie with curiosity, but she did not fear him. Kallie gazed at the chief long enough to realize he had a strong family resemblance to Brave Eagle. Perhaps this man was Brave Eagle's father and could become an ally to her.

Next to the chief stood a woman. The harsh climate had not blown the prettiness from her face, for her skin was smooth and soft. She wore a buckskin dress with a beaded neckline that dangled with shells. Long black braids trailed down to her waist. Her expression was tense but softened every time she looked at Brave Eagle. Her expression turned to anger when she stared at Kallie.

Brave Eagle spoke in front of the gathering. Kallie figured it was about their encounter with Hawk Claw. The chief reacted by motioning some of the men inside the tepee. Every man nodded his head in agreement and hurried in.

Before entering the tepee, the chief pointed at Kallie and spoke to the crowd. She stood in fear as the meaningless language streamed by her. Aware the conversation was about her fate, she stood expressionless. Kallie could not speak one word in her defense. She had to rely on Brave Eagle to save her.

She watched as the confident expression on Brave Eagle's face turned into astonishment. The outcome could not be good. His body language was filled with tension. His eyes shouted out in alarm. When Brave Eagle was composed enough to speak, his voice betrayed him. Speaking above his natural tone, his voice resonated with anger and confusion. During Brave Eagle's public outcry, the chief's woman glared at Kallie.

Confusion ran through the crowd. The chief seemed puzzled by Brave Eagle's outburst and prodded him to the tepee entrance. Brave Eagle shot Kallie a quick glance before turning to enter.

Kallie felt less secure with each passing moment. Her mind demanded she show strength, but she could barely stand. Her knees were buckling. Then their chatter sounded vicious, and people grabbed and pinched her. During this uncomfortable investigation, Kallie was aware of someone reaching out to her. Shifting her eyes, she saw an old man staring at her. An old woman forcefully jerked her head down by pulling Kallie's hair. Humiliated and frightened, Kallie heard the old man laughing at her. She felt angry and ready to lash out, but she controlled her temper.

Suddenly, men emerged from the tepee, and the chief addressed the crowd with some sort of proclamation. He pointed to Kallie and the old man who had laughed at her. The crowd reverberated with hissing whispers. Kallie's throat became so constricted she could barely swallow. Shaking uncontrollably, Kallie waited until the elderly woman tugged at her to follow. Kallie dared to look back only once. Catching the eyes of Brave Eagle, she begged him for help, but he stood defeated. Turning away, Kallie walked behind the old woman, who moved through the curious crowd.

Kallie thought back to her dreams. Was this the danger her premonitions had predicted? Had she been spared her life after the raid just to die a slow, tortured death? Where was her God now? Why did he continually forsake her? Tears welled up. Hysterical by the time she arrived at the tepee, she fell through the entrance. She crumbled to the floor. Holding her sides with her arms, she pondered the hopelessness of her situation. A thought of horror struck her; was she to be the old man's wife? Revolted, suddenly she felt more of a kinship with Elizabeth. No longer pretending to be strong, Kallie crawled to the corner and cried until she fell asleep. No one came to her aid, but no one bothered her either.

Kallie awoke in the middle of the night shivering with cold. The smell of wood smoke hung in the air. In the center of the tepee, remnants of a glowing fire created long shadows. As her eyes grew accustomed to the surrounding darkness, she could see the old man and woman sleeping soundly together. Kallie puzzled over her fate. Was she to be a slave of this old man? He had not touched her. The plants she had gathered while with Brave Eagle lay close to where she had been sleeping. Kallie appreciated the gesture. The tepee atmosphere was peaceful, with many interesting dried plants and strange items hanging from the walls.

Kallie had to relieve herself and did not know what to do. Finally lifting the entrance skin door, she peeked out. A few village fires still glowed in the night. All was quiet except for the howl of wolves in the distance. Pensive, she slipped out of the tepee and walked to a clump of trees. She could hear the gentle current of the river as it flowed by. Making her way in the night, she noticed a silhouette close to the tepee. Apprehensive, a strange resignation washed over her. Sighing a long, defeated breath, Kallie decided there was little she could do to defend herself.

Brave Eagle stepped from out of the shadows. Under the light of the moon, he quickly embraced and kissed her. Looking down upon her, he tried to talk to her. Kallie did not comprehend his strange language and could only grasp a sense of his words. Noticing his eyes were sincere, Kallie held back her tears. She kissed her warrior to show she trusted him. Brave Eagle's body felt so good to touch, and his strong muscles rippled in the embrace. Kallie wanted the encounter to last forever, but it was over in a brief moment. Before turning away, Brave Eagle pulled the arrowhead necklace off his chest and gently placed it around her neck. Kallie nervously unclasped the gold necklace that held her mother's Irish claddagh ring and put it around his neck in return. Smiling at him, she held back tears. Grinning back at her, Brave Eagle turned and departed as quietly as he had come.

Chapter 8: *Lost Buffalo Trades in a Favor*

Pejuta wicasa: Medicine Man
Skilled in Herbal Medicine

The next day Brave Eagle sought out Lost Buffalo, the medicine man, for some answers. Brave Eagle had hoped life would be simpler once he was back at the village. He was ready for a woman and longed for a family of sons. Thinking back to the death of his wife, Two Moons, his heart ached, but he was ready to start life again. In keeping with tribal custom, Two Moons's younger sister, Dawn Star, had been waiting for him. As Brave Eagle walked with Lost Buffalo, he tried to think of a way to bring up the subject of the captive without being disrespectful. Lost Buffalo was now the owner of his white captive, Kallie.

Lost Buffalo told him, "I feel old, and you seem upset."

In the spirit of politeness and respect, Brave Eagle remained silent. Lost Buffalo continued, "It was the crows. They flew over my tepee four times and warned me about the arrival of a white woman. I listened. Perhaps I listened too well, for now I am obligated to protect her. My wife, Yellow Willow, does not question my actions. She is a wise woman and knows the spirits have mysterious ways. She knows it does no good to argue with spirits."

Lost Buffalo stopped for a moment and explained, "This captive came to my tepee at a high price, an exchange for a valuable favor from a prestigious family, your family. It is logical for you to marry Dawn Star. Her family matches your family in wealth, status, and prestige. Many tribal leaders have risen from both your bloodlines. Your own father,

Flaming Arrow, the chief, has encouraged the marriage as soon as your grieving period is over. It now appears over."

Lost Buffalo continued, "I have no plans of keeping the captive as a wife. She would eat too much and cause trouble. However, as Yellow Willow has reminded me, the spirits say nothing about working the white woman hard. For the present time, this is what I intend to do."

Brave Eagle said, "You are a wise man and much respected by both my father and myself."

Lost Buffalo said, "A wise old man needs to avoid troublesome woman issues. The captive is from a strange breed. Relationships are best left up to the older women. They have spirit knowledge that few men develop. Now I am winded and want to sit." The two men entered the tepee. Lost Buffalo sat in his willow chair and began to cough. Brave Eagle worried that Lost Buffalo's lungs sounded congested, and even Yellow Willow's powerful medicine did not help his cough. After his spasm settled, Lost Buffalo studied the captive as she entered with his wife. His eyes widened in astonishment when he glimpsed Brave Eagle's sacred arrowhead dangling from her white neck.

Lost Buffalo handed Brave Eagle a pipe and said, "Have a smoke. You are from a powerful family that expects you to marry Dawn Star." Lost Buffalo took back the burning pipe, used a thin stick to press down the last of the tobacco, and said, "It is strange how sometimes our hearts find a different path … but, Brave Eagle, your power necklace? What will happen when you go on the raid? You will need it. This could be a bad omen!"

Brave Eagle said, "It will protect her. It is a good omen."

Lost Buffalo paused and then said, "It is a powerful combination, that of battle, pride, and love. Be careful. You must focus only on the raid you promoted. The elders are in favor of this raid, but remember you are a leader. The young men follow you into battle. Do not stray from this. You have a voice to speak powerfully. Use it wisely."

Lost Buffalo continued, "Let's not think on this any longer. It seems the spirit world has intentions for the captive. I cannot change my decision even for a decent young man like you."

Brave Eagle saw sadness in the captive's expression and wondered what she was thinking. He pretended not to be interested as Lost Buffalo and Yellow Willow conversed, but he listened carefully.

Lost Buffalo said, "Yellow Willow, the captive has a curiosity about the plants that hang from our tepee frame. I have decided the white woman can help our niece Running Brook train as an herbal apprentice. I can send the white woman out farther to collect plants than what is considered safe for our women to go. No one would question it. While keeping a watchful eye over her, Running Brook can learn the woman's language. This might be helpful in the future."

Yellow Willow smiled at Lost Buffalo while motioning Kallie to serve him and Brave Eagle soup. As Kallie clumsily brought the soup, Yellow Willow knelt close beside her husband.

Yellow Willow said softly, "The woman's name is Kallie." Yellow Willow smiled at Lost Buffalo and said, "That is how Brave Eagle addresses her."

Lost Buffalo nodded his head in acknowledgement while sipping his soup. "We have some time before we decide her fate. I will have to follow my dreams very closely in the future."

As Brave Eagle excused himself, Lost Buffalo reminded him, "Focus on the raid … on Hawk Claw, the enemy. The drums will signal when the raid will begin. Go prepare. It will be soon, and don't be angry with me. It was the crows."

Chapter 9: *White Woman*

Witoka: Female Captive

After Brave Eagle exited, Kallie wondered just what the conversation had been about. It was probably about her fate, and yet she could not understand any of it. She had been left alone in the tepee.

Kallie reminded herself that this was not the bleakest, scariest day of her life. She thought back to the day she and her brother Michael had had to bury her parents. The bright sun overhead had caused muddy sweat to drip off her brow. Her hands had been filthy from shoveling, and she used her dress sleeve to wipe her muddy face. That was the moment when she spotted a man riding toward her on a beautiful chestnut horse. She recognized him as the gentleman who had sold medicine at the revival. Her father had bought several bottles. The gentleman was the most handsome man she had ever seen, with bright-blue eyes and straight white teeth. He was a Frenchman and had been so charming, Kallie had smiled right back. His clean hands were not the callused hands of a farmer, so she had quickly hidden hers. He tipped his hat ever so slightly and said, "Howdy, ma'am. Looks like you could use some help."

The man's name was Armand, and he ended up staying at the farmhouse. At first, he was helpful. But then it became clear that he didn't do heavy work and loved the drink just like her father had. One night Armand sat by the fire and made bullets for his long rifle. As he shaved off the seam left by the mold, he had nonchalantly mentioned he was leaving for St. Louis and then would be going on to Independence by steamer. From there, he'd be leaving for Oregon. He had asked if she might want to come along. She had quickly responded yes, happy to leave her destitute farm life behind.

The next day she had saddled her horse, Clara, rode to Millicent's, and told her the news. Millicent had not shown much emotion. She simply requested that Kallie bring Armand and her brothers to the house for dinner. As it turned out, Millicent had also invited the preacher and insisted they get married.

The wedding ceremony had been a solemn affair because the preacher began with funeral prayers for her parents. It had been hard to act happy after that, but she could tell her brothers were proud of her. They were excited about their sister traveling to Oregon so they could follow someday. The preacher lectured on about being a servant of God. Just when she could barely stand it, he had turned to her and spoke of wifely duties. It had embarrassed her so much that she could only look at Michael, who mocked the preacher behind his back. Finally, when the ceremony was over, Armand had kissed her, and they were officially husband and wife.

Armand and she had left the farm as the sun set on her parents' graves. As they hurried away, she could not wait for the preacher and his tight-lipped wife to leave her sight. Finally, late that night, she and Armand stopped to camp. The preacher couple had pulled their wagon alongside and also stopped. She could not believe their indiscretion, but she said nothing. Then, after another long day of travel together, she nudged Armand and asked about the preacher's expected departure. Armand had grinned. "Oh, I plumb forgot formal introductions. Kallie, I'd like you to meet my sister, Elizabeth, and her preacher husband, Jacob. They'll be traveling with us to Oregon."

She had glared back at the preacher, and a sinking feeling overcame her. Instead of her troubles being left behind, they had come to stay. It was with a heavy heart that she began her married life with Armand.

Kallie's thoughts were interrupted by a swift poke in the ribs. The old woman pointed to the empty water bags. Kallie quickly picked up the bags and scurried behind the woman. Most of the day, Kallie did numerous chores, including making a fire, cleaning the tepee, and collecting firewood along the river. Life was comfortable enough except for constant hunger gnawing at her growling stomach. The pains raged even though the woman gave her bits of dried meat.

She discovered the old woman was stern but not malicious; she expected Kallie to obey her and work hard. The woman's eyes expressed dignity, and her lips rested in an upward position, giving her a contented look. Dark strands still lingered in her long gray braids. Wrinkled by a hard life outdoors, the woman's face possessed a timeless look. Her back was strong and straight, not curved like those of the other older women. Kallie wondered if maybe this woman was younger than she originally had thought.

Outside the larger tepee, a smaller tepee held huge bundles of herbs hanging from the ceiling. It sparked Kallie's curiosity, and she decided to explore it when the opportunity arose. The old couple's door had a huge buffalo painted on it that encompassed the whole skin. A battle scene was depicted on the outside wall of the tepee. Horses painted in many colors dominated the landscape. Many warriors lay dead while the survivors held their bows and arrows. Another scene skirted the tepee's lower border, displaying a series of prominent geometric designs. What their significance was, Kallie had no idea. Pausing to look closer at the designs, she was interrupted by the woman's grunts, demanding she come inside.

Inside, the tepee had a familiar feel to it even though Kallie was a stranger. The tepee had the same feel as Millicent's farmhouse because of the many mysterious concoctions brewing in the shadows. Kallie observed the skin drums, pipes, and rattles with handles wrapped in animal skins and claws hanging from the tepee frame. Several long cases fringed with beads leaned against the walls. Unloading her water bags, Kallie gasped in horror as she faced a rattlesnake head. The old woman laughed at her. Embarrassed, Kallie shyly smiled back. As she looked in fascination at the assorted necklace pouches, stones, and crystals placed strategically around the tepee, she relaxed. It felt like a magical place, and at least someone who collected plants was sheltering her.

Exploring further, Kallie encountered hollow buffalo horns filled with mixtures that emitted strange new smoky smells. When she recognized the rose-colored rocks from the pictured caves where they had taken shelter from the twister storm, she smiled. Painted figures on the inside tepee walls danced around her with the never-ending change of the sun's rays and prairie winds. Drying plants hung from the ceiling, creating an aromatic smell. Learning about her role would require patience, for Kallie knew little about village living. The old woman showed her how to fold up the tepee bottom so stuffy air could be put into motion. Pausing, she listened to the buffalo hoofs hanging above and clanging in the gentle breeze. She thought to herself that the woman seemed nice enough, but what of the old man? Just what were his intentions?

Drums sounded throughout the village and interrupted Kallie's questioning thoughts. The sides of the tepee reverberated with the pulsing vibrations. She moved to get up, but her body revolted, for her muscles were stiff and sore. Hunger carved an empty pit in her stomach, but the old woman did not offer any food. Instead, she motioned Kallie to follow her. The old woman stooped down to unleash the skin door. Kallie peered into the distance where the drum sounds originated. There, many people were gathered in a large circle. Decorated men frantically danced to the percussions. Formidable, with their headdresses of buffalo and eagle feathers, they made her fearful. Their extended arms grasped large poles with tails hanging from them. The women made shrill cries and surrounded the men with their own circle. Children stood back and observed their elders. Sounds of rattles resonated from the maze of moving people silhouetted against the sun.

When the dancing furor reached its climax, the women's circle dispersed, and their wild, shrill cries echoed in every direction. Then suddenly all was quiet, with the exception of a gentle prairie breeze rippling through camp. The old man who had taken her stood in the middle of the men with his head bowed in prayer. After a long silence, he released the men by waving feathered sticks in the air. Next, the men yelled until the ferocious warriors mounted their horses. The painted warriors circled the village before their departure.

Kallie gasped as she spotted Brave Eagle riding by with a war club clenched in his fist. She tried to be obvious, but he never once looked her way. Looking intense and wild, Brave Eagle galloped straight ahead. Her necklace on his slick chest sparkled as sunlight hit it. Wind Racer's hooves pounded the ground as Brave Eagle raced away with the other men.

A desperate, sinking feeling overcame her. She feared he was going after Hawk Claw and the battle would be a bloody one. Shivers ran down her body as Kallie remembered hiding in the bushes. Hawk Claw had frightened her so much she had almost cried out. Luckily, she and Brave Eagle had escaped, but now it appeared that he hurried off to confront this enemy. As the dust cloud from his racing horse settled, she silently prayed for his safe return. If he died, her hopes of survival would die with him. She wondered if he even thought about her now that he had left for battle.

Chapter 10: *The Raid*

Ahikte: To Kill in Battle

Drum sounds still reverberated within Brave Eagle's heart as he rode toward the tribal boundaries. Battle would serve as a distraction from the shock of losing Kallie to Lost Buffalo. He had waved good-bye to Dawn Star, but now he had to focus on the raid. Pretty Shield, his mother, had cried a shrill courage song in his honor while pointing to Speckled Eagle, his younger brother. Her worried look had reminded Brave Eagle of his obligation to protect his younger brother. Brave Eagle had hollered a reassuring acknowledgment to her and then raced ahead to lead the war party.

As he rode, Brave Eagle reflected on the war council meeting that had been held the night before. His father, Chief Flaming Arrow, had smoked the sacred pipe. Flaming Arrow had requested the Great Spirit give guidance to his warriors. When the last thin strand of smoke had dissipated, Flaming Arrow had given Brave Eagle possession of the pipe. It was now Brave Eagle's time to convince the others.

He had told the council Hawk Claw was greedy and an enemy. Hawk Claw's men had been painted for battle and appeared ready to attack any travelers or hunters. The war party had acted like they were thirsty for blood.

Brave Eagle had continued by pointing out to his fellow warriors that the war party had been too close to their tribal lands. Perhaps Hawk Claw was testing the tribe's strength before executing a raid. Even worse, the war party may have been searching for buffalo. This action would have stampeded the herds and left Brave Eagle's people to go hungry.

Brave Eagle had insisted his warriors attack the enemy camp before Hawk Claw returned to prey upon them. Hawk Claw must know Brave Eagle would defend what was rightfully his.

The eldest and most prestigious warriors had sat closest to the fire. They had been first to voice their opinions. One of the oldest men in the tribe, One Buffalo, had spoken so softly he was barely audible above the crackling fire. He had uttered, "Finding the buffalo herds is what we must do. The hunt is more important than any revenge. The summer buffalo herds are late, and the migrations are changing. The hunting scouts have not brought back any good news about the herds' whereabouts. Soon our meat supplies will be gone. This matter with Hawk Claw's tribe can wait. He did not actually raid our village, so why invite disaster?"

Some of the older men nodded their heads in agreement, but it was the younger warriors who had shown their impatience. Weasel Tail had supported Brave Eagle and was ready to fight alongside him. When Weasel Tail had spoken, his strong voice had resonated with pride. "We cannot fear this Hawk Claw. If not this season, then Hawk Claw will strike the next. His men are most likely chasing buffalo away from our traditional hunting lands. We must protect our land by striking back and showing Hawk Claw we are not afraid."

When the last breath of tobacco had been smoked, the inner circle made a decision. Urgency had filled the air as Flaming Arrow pointed his long pipe at Black Hand, the war chief. In a calm voice he had spoken. "Black Hand, you will carry the sacred bundle. Investigate the intruders' destination, and you will have the final say on any retaliatory actions."

The younger men had leaped up with excitement in their eyes. As with all tribal battles, every man was free to decide his own actions. Many younger men had volunteered because it was a chance to raid horses. Good, strong horses brought wealth and opportunities.

Early the next morning, everyone had been busy collecting extra bowstrings, sinew, war paint bags, clothes, food, and fire-making equipment. Many of the men had packed sacred pipes and tobacco as special war medicine. The warriors had not expected to be gone long, only long enough to raid horses and ride back proudly. Dressed for war, they had danced confidently before the people. When Lost Buffalo gave the signal, they had ridden off in a thunderous show of power.

Confident of their combined strength, the raiding party raced across their territory. Brave Eagle decided they should camp at the river site where the intruders had last been seen. Black Hand signaled the men to move cautiously. They snaked around on the ridge and moved against the wind so their enemies would not smell them. Weasel Tail studied the landscape, using his uncanny ability to sense enemies. His keen eyes followed every slight movement in the brush, for there were many possible ambush sites. When Weasel Tail was convinced the area was safe, Black Hand motioned the men to set camp. Soon it would be dark, and there were still defense preparations to be completed.

Black Hand sent out three scouts disguised in wolf skins. He instructed them to travel along the ravines until they found Hawk Claw's camp. After the scouts left, he and Brave Eagle smoked and meditated upon the sacred medicine bundle. As they sent prayers up through the smoke, each man made a vow. If the raid was successful, Brave Eagle committed to giving thanks at the next Sun Dance. This was the biggest celebration in their lands, where men hung from their pierced flesh to pay homage to the Great Spirit.

After making his vow, Brave Eagle continued to prepare for battle. He was ready to exact revenge. But still a forlorn feeling nagged at him, and he needed to be alone. To avoid questions, Brave Eagle said, "Black Hand, I am going to ride out in search of intruders."

Black Hand smiled his approval, but Weasel Tail insisted on accompanying him. As they rode to the place where the ridge turned into grassland, Brave Eagle told Weasel Tail that he wanted to ride alone.

Weasel Tail stalwartly shook his head. "No. It is not safe to venture by yourself. I will go with you. You must clear your head of that white woman. Hawk Claw is a powerful enemy to fight. You cannot be distracted by what is no longer yours."

Brave Eagle shot Weasel Tail a sharp glance. "I will fight Hawk Claw on my own terms. You need not worry. Remember you called me the white woman's dog. I have not forgotten." He noticed the huge silver cross was tied to Weasel Tail's breastplate. "You are the one with two women. I have none to distract me now."

Weasel Tail laughed. "Then it is I who will have all the woman trouble." Pointing at Kallie's necklace dangling on Brave Eagle's chest, he was dumbstruck. "Where is your warrior's arrowhead? It is a bad omen to go unprotected. It is bad medicine to replace your necklace with the white woman's symbol. It was not powerful enough to protect her from you. Why would you believe in its power? Why would you ever trade your power symbol for it?"

Angrily, Brave Eagle said, "You have two women. You tell me."

Weasel Tail generously handed Brave Eagle his prized eagle-claw necklace. "This is powerful medicine. You must take it!"

Brave Eagle was grateful but shook his head no. "I must ask for an omen. To do this, I need to be alone. Do not worry; I will return unharmed and ready to fight alongside you."

Weasel Tail turned his horse and advised him, "Dawn Star is a beautiful spring flower and sweet as the nectar within. You loved her sister as a wife, and you will also learn to love Dawn Star. That is how it should be. Now spend your time gathering strength for the raid. I'll need you to fight with me. It might take the two of us to hack down Hawk Claw." Weasel Tail then rode away.

Wind Racer galloped while Brave Eagle extended his arms outward and lifted his head toward the sky. As he took a deep breath, Kallie's ring bounced upon his chest. Listening and feeling, he searched for an answer. As the sun set into darkness, no visions about the raid came to him. Instead, he could only smell and feel buffalo. Sign of buffalo was not the omen he had expected. Still, he could not shake it. It came strong and clear. Was it possible—were the buffalo finally migrating toward their lands? The tribe would need every young warrior for a large hunt. Unsure of what to do about his conflicting thoughts, he headed for the safety of camp. He struggled with his dilemma and did not know what to think. His heart sank when he thought of Dawn Star and Kallie. Perhaps being involved with the two women was confusing his prayers. He wondered about what action he should take. Should he gamble on his intuition about the buffalo hunt or attack Hawk Claw's village?

Finally, before arriving at camp, he decided to continue with the raid. Since boyhood, Brave Eagle had been taught it was better to die in battle than to wither in old age. Besides, his father had sent their best scouts out looking for signs of the herd. The matter was best left to them.

At camp the men spoke about fighting strategies. They confidently boasted about the number of horses they would steal. Stories of their brave deeds would be told in front of the tribal council. Huge celebration fires would be held in their honor. Slowly, after much discussion, the men retired for the night.

When the scouts returned in the morning, they deliberately tripped the sticks Black Hand had set up for them. This action caused all the waking men to scurry about. They frantically grabbed as many sticks as they could, because each stick represented a horse that could be taken in the raid.

Brave Eagle grabbed only one stick, sat in a circle, and waited for the scouts to devour their meals. His excitement rose when the scouts reported they had followed the war party's tracks back to Hawk Claw's village. Soon everyone would have the chance to raid horses and seek revenge.

Brave Eagle was still troubled. His premonitions about the buffalo herds grew stronger. He could not let them go. His intuition was matched against his desire for revenge. His confusion intensified when Weasel Tail asked him to speak to the men about their mission.

As he looked at the eager warriors, hungry for horses and coup, Brave Eagle groped for a solution. No man would dare call him a coward, but if he revealed his misgivings, his future leadership could be in jeopardy. He could not quit now, after he had instigated the raid. Not knowing what he would do, he stood and spoke in a clear voice. "It must be known that our enemies cannot hunt us on our tribal grounds, so close to our women and children. They must know so others will also know this to be true. As much as I want to fight Hawk Claw, I have received no visions of the raid. My dreams do not aid me. Brothers, instead I have received only visions of buffalo. I smell buffalo and hear the bulls rut in my sleep. The buffalo are so late this year that perhaps my dream is a good omen. It is more important than revenge. We have a responsibility to fill our children's bellies. I believe we need to go back, search out the buffalo, and assist in the hunt."

The warriors were silent, looking stunned. Weasel Tail vehemently responded, "Brave Eagle, are you sure you are not hearing your own spirit rut?"

The group of warriors put their heads down at hearing Weasel Tail's insult. No one said a word.

Black Hand stood up. "We must put our faith in Flaming Arrow and the war council. They have already sent scouts to find the buffalo trails. We have danced the buffalo dance. As we travel forward, we will ask for more omens so we will know what to do. If we see the sign of buffalo, we will know it is an omen to go back. I see only our strength in my visions. As we move closer to our enemy's village, we must use greater caution so we do not invite tragedy. Tonight, when we reach camp, I will ask for an omen. At sunrise, I will decide on whether we raid or not."

Other warriors, including Weasel Tail and Bear, nodded their heads in consent. Brave Eagle sat motionless, in deep thought. He would go along with the raid if that was the final decision, but buffalo still permeated his thoughts. He was certain the herd was close. In the end, Brave Eagle relented, against his better judgment, and nodded in affirmation of Black Hand's decision to move forward.

The men gathered their belongings and hurried off. Riding single file in the gully, they moved closer toward the enemy camp. Careful to make no unnecessary sounds, they spoke in birdcalls and used their buffalo robes as signals. Bear rode alongside Brave Eagle.

Bear whispered, "If I am lucky in battle, this raid will bring me the trophy horses I need. Running Brook's father demands a high price of five horses for his daughter. But if I can do this, her father might see I am a warrior who will provide for her. Two more horses, and then I can finally ask Running Brook's father for his daughter."

Brave Eagle smiled at his friend, but he had become a different man since he agreed to continue the raid. He smelled the air like a grizzly, listened like the mountain lion, and scanned the area like an eagle. He concentrated on finding Hawk Claw and would get revenge on him by stealing his favorite horse. Brave Eagle would pluck the horse staked outside Hawk Claw's tepee. He would have to be careful not to wake his enemy. If Hawk Claw woke, then it would be a fight to the death. There was no other way.

The raiding party rode in the stifling heat until close to sunset, when Speckled Eagle spotted a pile of rocks left by the scouts. This signified the place where they were to camp and construct a field shelter to hold their supplies. The men bent long willow branches and covered them with leaves and bark. Rocks were placed for reinforcement around the bottom to serve as a defense place if plans went awry. After the horses were well hidden and the shelter was complete, they quietly waited for the scouts to return. Black Hand smoked alone and seemed to be in a contemplative mood.

Brave Eagle and Speckled Eagle listened to the night sounds. They were the last to retire for the night. Brave Eagle was in no hurry because of the thoughts churning in his head. He felt enormous responsibility toward his younger brother and wondered how he would protect him during the raid. Brave Eagle was determined to daringly snatch Hawk Claw's prize horse, which would be tethered close to his tepee. To do this, he must strike as an eagle without the burden of his younger brother.

Speckled Eagle whispered, "I would like to talk to you about Dawn Star." Brave Eagle's body tensed with the mention of her name, and he shook his head no. He would not discuss such a matter the night before the raid. He then stared off into the distance. Giving up, Speckled Eagle moved to his buffalo robe and fell asleep.

The next morning, Black Hand unwrapped the medicine bundle for everyone to see. It signaled they should attack at night. During the day the men busied themselves with battle preparations. They checked all weapons as well as their war shields, which held spirit protectors. The men quietly mixed paint in the horn bowls and then painted themselves and their horses. Many of the warriors made personal offerings in case the raid did not go as planned.

Brave Eagle applied red paint to the upper half of his face. Positioning his three-feathered crown securely on the back of his head, he braided the side part of his hair to keep it away from his face. He would wear only his breechcloth and moccasins in combat. Upon his bare chest lay Kallie's golden ring and his war bundle necklaces. The bundle held an eagle claw, a grizzly tooth, and a green rock. These power items gave him eagle vision, swiftness, and strength. A quiver of arrows and a bow were strapped across his back. His left arm held a mighty shield to which seven eagle feathers were attached. In the shield's center was a drawing of an eagle surrounded by a circle of wolf tracks. A sharp knife dangled from his belt. Brave Eagle's other hand clasped a spear decorated with eagle feathers streaming down the red-painted pole. Wind Racer wore the same markings as his master, and he held his head high in the air. Ready for battle, the horse flared his nostrils, and his legs twitched with excitement.

In the late afternoon the men left the camp. Brave Eagle used the tenseness and excitement of anticipation to ready himself. Adrenaline surged in his veins. He rode close to Black Hand, Weasel Tail, and Bear. These men provided a source of inspiration and courage to all the men. Their fate hung in the stillness of the night.

Brave Eagle was surprised to see his brother following so close to him. Speckled Eagle was too young to fully participate in such a raid, and Brave Eagle had assumed that Black Hand would put his brother in charge of the horses. Forgetting his brother, he concentrated on his plans to pluck Hawk Claw's horse.

Finally, in the deep night, they reached the wooded area of Hawk Claw's village. Black Hand signaled his men. Everyone patiently waited while Black Hand stealthily slipped into the enemy village undetected. They crouched in quiet suspense. Brave Eagle's mouth became dry, and he could barely swallow. When enough saliva formed in his mouth, he spat on the ground. He was ready.

Black Hand reappeared as silently as he had left. Excitedly, he motioned the men to form a circle. Their muscular bodies were oiled, and they smelled the strength of one another in their closeness. Together they would succeed in their mission. Black Hand explained the plan through a series of hand motions. Some of the men would cut part of the main herd away in the pasture. They were ordered to take off with the horses as soon as possible. Some men were allowed to capture horses picketed at the edge of the village.

Black Hand spoke out loud only once. "You have one chance. If something does not work, everyone must cut and run. You will fight only when confronted." Black Hand pointed. "The younger boys will guard our horses and await our return."

The men approached the sleeping camp like stalking cougars. Brave Eagle swiftly sent off an arrow with his mark on it and killed an approaching dog that had just caught their scent. They would have to be vigilant not to awaken the enemy. Brave Eagle and Weasel Tail skirted around the camp to reach Hawk Claw's tepee. Bear followed behind, approached a tepee, and cut the tethers holding two horses. Brave Eagle stopped in disbelief as his young brother, Speckled Eagle, who followed behind Bear, tripped and spooked the horse. An alert enemy sentry came to investigate. Brave Eagle ran behind the surprised guard, who turned and shot.

Brave Eagle heard the arrow rip flesh as it pierced his leg. The wound radiated pain. He grabbed his leg but then instantly released it. Gathering strength, Brave Eagle clutched his war club but could not react fast enough. The warrior knocked him down with a furious hit from his club. Brave Eagle's head burst with throbbing, but he instinctively rolled in time to prevent a lance from piercing his chest. As the lance struck the ground, Brave Eagle grabbed his opponent's leg and tripped him. He forcefully landed the blunt side of his war club upon the sentry's head, knocking him out. He sprawled lifelessly on the ground.

Speckled Eagle helped his older brother make a run for it. Brave Eagle hopped with his good leg while dragging the other. He was not panicked, for time had seemed to stop for him. The arrow was still lodged in his leg. It throbbed painfully. Gritting his teeth, he leaped on Wind Racer. They quietly rode out of the enemy camp.

Time was to their advantage, and it was useless trying to obscure so many horse tracks. They ran through the dark night until Black Hand finally signaled to change trails.

The men gathered around as he explained, "Hawk Claw is an expert tracker and can read much in any sign of disturbed vegetation. But remember—I am an expert also. Let's confuse our tracks by traveling in the deep streambed and then switching trails several times."

After traveling a long distance, they crossed a swath of brown that ran alongside a knoll. Everyone looked dumbfounded. Black Hand said what everyone knew already. "A herd of buffalo has passed by without our detection. This is a bad omen. It is too late to follow them now."

This new development tempered the excitement of the raid. When the men arrived at their cache, they were tired. It had been a victorious raid producing some thirty horses. Once the horses were watered, they would pound the earth until they reached home. There the rest of the tribe would be waiting anxiously for the men's safe return.

Brave Eagle's leg had reddened. Bear helped him off his horse and washed the dirt from Brave Eagle's swollen wound. Bear distracted Brave Eagle by telling him, "I've captured two beautiful horses. These two, in addition to the three I already have, should be enough to satisfy Running Brook's father."

Brave Eagle groaned. "You are a generous man. You will make a good husband who can provide for his family."

Another warrior, Short Bull, inspected Brave Eagle's leg wound and said, "Save your breath for breathing." Wasting little time, Short Bull motioned a few men to hold the injured warrior. Without consulting anyone, Short Bull skillfully grabbed the broken arrow shaft and pushed. Brave Eagle's face contorted as he cried out, so the men wrestled him down to keep him still. The shaft slowly moved through the bloody leg tissue until the arrowhead appeared out the other side. Then Short Bull made a jerking movement and pulled the arrowhead through. He held it up as if it were a prize. Quickly, Short Bull rinsed the wound and closed it in a tightly wrapped poultice. As he placed the bloody arrowhead in Brave Eagle's hand, Short Bull spoke in a hushed voice.

"Here, take this. Now the honor of this fight should be enough to satisfy your blood revenge."

Brave Eagle grimaced with pain as he looked at the bloody arrowhead. His leg throbbed, his head ached, and he told no one about his blurry vision. Anger consumed him because revenge had eluded him. He answered Short Bull, "My battle with Hawk Claw is not yet finished."

Chapter 11: *Brave Eagle Return*

Gli: They Have Come

Kallie and Yellow Willow's niece, Running Brook, walked far on the river trail. Lost Buffalo had sent them to collect wood for the planned celebration. Swaying grasses were still wet with dew, and the early morning sun shined upon them. Kallie was grateful to have the worn moccasins the old man had given her. They were too big, but she wrapped rawhide strips around her feet and up to her ankles to help stabilize them.

The river had become Kallie's favorite place. She watched Running Brook gracefully pivot on top of the river rocks. As she dipped her hand for a drink, Kallie's queasiness came back. She was having trouble keeping food down but told no one. Kallie longed for Brave Eagle's presence and yet was confused about her being abandoned by him. He had let go of her so easily. A streak of anger rose as she lamented her situation. But then, with a sigh of resignation, she resumed collecting firewood. A large load would please the old couple.

Kallie's days were an endless series of chores, but she was content under the old couple's protection. Even though most of the tribe was indifferent, some of the women were antagonistic. Collecting wood was a relief because she was spared from their constant jeers and gossip. Running Brook proved to be a helpful companion and patiently tried to teach her the tribal language. Kallie picked up some phrases quickly but could barely pronounce many common words. She learned the old couple's names were Yellow Willow and Lost Buffalo. Kallie was frustrated that Running Brook was quickly learning English while she struggled with this strange tongue.

The warm day passed quickly and lapsed into twilight. The evening sky was lit with stars. Sending a quiet prayer for Brave Eagle's safety, she wished that he would somehow rescue her. Howls in the background sent shivers down her spine, as Kallie imagined the bloodthirsty predators lurking in shadows nearby. Hurrying for the safety of the old couple's tepee, Kallie was glad she was almost there. She suddenly realized that the tepee's location was vulnerable. They would be the first to be attacked in a skirmish.

As Kallie entered, Lost Buffalo lifted off his shirt and pointed to a small bowl of oil. She complied because it was an easy task compared with the job of tediously sewing animal skins. She dipped her hands in the oil and began to rub Lost Buffalo's arthritic back. Lost Buffalo had been a powerful man before disease had gripped him. His back muscles were still strong, but his lungs wheezed with each breath. After massaging his back, Kallie set the bowl down and rubbed her face and hands. Her dry skin soaked up the leftover oil. Its rancid smell made her queasy. Her sickness had come back again. An uneasy thought occurred to her as she prepared for bed.

During the night, fretfulness kept her awake. In the glow of the fire, she saw Lost Buffalo look over at his sleeping wife and quietly rise from his bed. He smoked his pipe. His lungs could no longer take aggravation, so he sucked in the slightest puff of tobacco. He arranged sacred stones in a circle and meditated upon them. Patiently, he seemed to wait for a message. Perhaps he did not receive one, because he went back to bed while mumbling something about spirits.

In the morning, Kallie heard Lost Buffalo tell Yellow Willow, "Dreams have directed me to prepare for the warriors' return. A celebration will be held in two days. I want this quiet for now."

He showed Kallie how to crush flower seeds into a fine powder by using a grinding stone. This powder would be used in a special medicine for dancing. Yellow Willow handed Kallie comfrey leaves and marshmallow root to mix in with the powder. After their preparations were done, they rolled up the bottom tepee flap to draw in a cross-breeze.

This would cool the interior and allow Lost Buffalo more comfort as he finished plans for the ceremony.

Kallie made tea for the couple by using a cooking pouch on their small outside fire. While outside, she hoped for a glimpse of Elizabeth. Oh, how she longed for her company. So far, Kallie had not been allowed contact with her. She had heard from Running Brook that the brave known as Weasel Tail had claimed Elizabeth as his second wife.

She noticed Flaming Arrow, the chief, approaching the tepee. Flaming Arrow moved his arms and walked the same way as Brave Eagle. Brushing past her, he called out for Lost Buffalo, and Yellow Willow motioned him into the tepee.

Yellow Willow emerged and told Kallie to follow. They walked on a path that led to a tepee-like structure close to the river but situated away from the villagers' view. This was the large steam lodge, now in use by the women. It was their turn. A fire-keeper outside the lodge heated rocks to be used in the steam bath. When rocks were thrown into the central container, a billow of white steam engulfed the enclosure.

Kallie sat on a flat stone that served as a bench and undressed. Then she stepped inside the bath. Naked, she breathed in the steam and closed her eyes. There was a steady flow of conversation, gossip, and laughter, although the women ignored her. She suspected that they held back vicious gossip about her out of respect for Yellow Willow.

The heat sensation prickled Kallie's skin, and it felt wonderful. She washed off the dust and dirt with soapwort and water. It was apparent the women in the bath were Yellow Willow's friends or relatives, so Kallie had nothing to fear. Relaxing, her tired body was cleansed by the steam. Her stomach was unsettled again. The thought she might be pregnant alarmed her. That might explain why her skirt felt tighter. She tried not to think about it. Brave Eagle's necklace hung between her breasts. Although his scent was no longer detectable, she had a habit of touching the arrowhead for comfort. As the steam shrouded her body, she again considered the possibility of pregnancy. It unnerved her. Laziness was not tolerated, and she felt so tired most of the time. Many questions ran through her mind. She wondered whether Brave Eagle or her dead husband Armand was the father. If she was pregnant, what would become of her and the baby? Would the baby be taken away from her, or would she be allowed to raise it? Would the tribe shame her and the baby … cast her out, trade her off, or leave her to die? Would Brave Eagle intervene to protect her? Would Yellow Willow and Lost Buffalo come to her aid?

Kallie knew her belly and breasts were swollen and that Yellow Willow also seemed to notice this. Kallie sighed, for now the situation was even more complicated. She needed to hide her condition until she came up with a plan. Maybe she could use her pregnancy to negotiate some deal with Brave Eagle's family at a later time.

Kallie and Yellow Willow went outside to cool off. As the women scooped river water to pour over their heads, Running Brook came hurrying along the path, her face flushed with excitement. Panting, she yelled, "Yellow Willow! The warriors are coming home with many horses. A few of the men are wounded."

Yellow Willow dressed quickly and left as fast as she could. All the remaining women had also dispersed and followed Yellow Willow. In the sudden stillness, Kallie wondered if Brave Eagle was all right and also ventured toward the commotion.

Dogs barked in the distance. Warriors rode toward camp in a formation of success but signaled there were wounded. As their silhouettes became larger, Lost Buffalo ordered a travois to aid the wounded. Everyone seemed deeply relieved that no young men had been killed. Most of the other villagers were already running out to meet their warriors and find out the scope of the injuries. As Brave Eagle rode up to the crowd, Kallie realized he was hurt. His eyes looked dull and lifeless. Flaming Arrow rushed to help his son off his horse and onto the stretcher. Pretty Shield, just arriving, bit her lower lip and held her hand over her mouth to cover her screams. She ran the back of her other hand against Brave Eagle's forehead and seemed relieved. Pretty Shield called out, "There is no fever," and then she added, "He is lethargic, and his head is swollen."

Lost Buffalo ordered, "Take the wounded into the healing tepee."

Kallie observed that Speckled Eagle looked panicked as his mother approached him. Pretty Shield eyed her younger son with suspicion. She asked loudly, "How did your brother get injured? Why do you look so guilty? You were supposed to only watch the horses and not fight. I will definitely talk to your father about the matter."

Dawn Star arrived and looked relieved that Brave Eagle was alive. As Speckled Eagle helped carry his brother into the tepee, Kallie noticed Dawn Star smiled at him. Speckled Eagle smiled sweetly back.

Flaming Arrow and Black Hand spoke loudly enough for everyone in the crowd to hear. Flaming Arrow asked Black Hand, "What kind of reprisals can we expect?"

Black Hand speculated, "There could be trouble. We'd better increase the number of scouts for sentry duty."

Flaming Arrow repeated to the men, "Increase the guards around camp. Call a council meeting as soon as the wounded are attended to. If the injured warriors survive, there will be a celebration dance." And then he added, "It would be prudent to honor the buffalo as well. Our best buffalo scouts are not back yet."

Flaming Arrow then spoke to everyone. "Without a successful hunt, we cannot feed our children's bellies. Winter will be a miserable season of illness and starvation. I care less for the feats of battle and more about our children. The buffalo migration is late, and there is no news on the herd's location. We must prepare anyway and be ready when good news comes."

Kallie listened and interpreted as best she could until Running Brook interrupted, "Let's help Yellow Willow."

Kallie followed Running Brook into the healing tepee. Brave Eagle was conscious and groaning. Lost Buffalo had examined Brave Eagle's leg wound and said to Yellow Willow, "Short Bull has done a good job treating the leg, and there is no fever. It is Brave Eagle's head wound that worries me. The swelling and discoloration are dissipating, but head wounds can be troublesome. Yellow Willow, make up a poultice to put on Brave Eagle's head, and keep watch. I need to go to the council meeting. It will be starting soon."

Running Brook handed Kallie a used poultice and whispered, "Bear has delivered horses at my father's tepee door. There, with the horses safely tethered, I hope Bear will watch to see if my father accepts them. I am so excited."

"What does it mean if your father accepts them?"

Running Brook said, "It means my father proclaims Bear is worthy to marry me!"

The young women were instructed to leave the healing tepee. As they stood outside, Running Brook explained, "There will be a celebration dance to honor the warriors and thank the Great Spirit for their safe return. This celebration is set for two sunsets from this day. This will also serve to call in the buffalo to the tribe's hunting grounds."

Chief Flaming Arrow seemed worried. Before he entered his tepee, he encountered Pretty Shield, who looked angry. Ignoring her, he told both her and the crowd, "I do not want to be disturbed."

Kallie asked Running Brook, "What is going on?"

Running Brook explained, "Bear told me the council began with the warriors' accounts of the raid. The elders listened and cross-examined the raid participants to determine truth from boastful claims. It is important to award honors according to acts and not exaggerations.

"Flaming Arrow said he was distressed to hear about Brave Eagle's buffalo omen and then the discovery of buffalo tracks after the raid. He asked the young men what good were horses if the summer buffalo hunt did not take place. His comments set off a heated debate."

After the council meeting, even Lost Buffalo seemed in a bad mood. He curtly ordered Kallie away from the healing tepee and away from Brave Eagle. It infuriated her to see others going back and forth to the healing tepee. Pretty Shield protected the entrance and pushed her away every time she attempted to enter.

Kallie decided to bide her time collecting firewood. With everyone distracted, she enjoyed the precious freedom. Walking until sunset, she returned only as darkness settled into blackness. Running Brook, excited with news, was waiting for her. She said, "Brave Eagle is feeling better. He insisted on getting up even though Lost Buffalo told him not to. Not even Pretty Shield could convince him to stay put. I am sure you know head wounds cannot be trusted. The good news is that Brave Eagle can walk even though he has a limp from the arrow wound."

Running Brook looked around and then continued, "Brave Eagle seemed upset. He asked Dawn Star instead of Flaming Arrow to help him get to his tepee. Lost Buffalo yelled at me. Flaming Arrow and Pretty Shield argued. Everyone except Bear seemed agitated from the council meeting." Shrugging her shoulders, Running Brook slipped away into the night.

In the morning, Lost Buffalo had calmed down and was busy preparing for the celebration. Kallie helped the couple as much as she could by working steadily from the moment the sun came up. The day proved to be scorching hot, and there was no escape from the blazing sun. She accompanied Yellow Willow to an open area. There, women were treating a buffalo hide for the celebration. They busily worked on the skin, which was stretched out and held with pegs. Kallie tried to help but felt dizzy every time she bent over. She felt like she was going to purge her meal.

Yellow Willow seemed worried and sharply directed, "Kallie and Running Brook, come help me." Walking into the tepee, Yellow Willow brushed past Lost Buffalo and commanded, "Kallie, rest." Kallie, feeling very queasy, immediately drifted to the corner.

Yellow Willow informed Running Brook, "I must go back to the women's circle to control the gossip." Running Brook looked confused. "Kallie is with child. The less the others know, the easier it will be to negotiate our family's position." Yellow Willow looked directly at Running Brook and whispered, "This is our secret for now. Tell no one."

Kallie watched Lost Buffalo as he sat in his backrest. He ignored the commotion and seemed to enjoy the moment. The tepee flaps were open to let the prairie breezes through, making it very comfortable even in the midday heat. The old man seemed excited about the upcoming activities and had been making preparations.

Flaming Arrow and Brave Eagle entered the tepee, interrupting the quiet. Kallie was elated but pretended to be asleep. The men talked about the details of the celebration. Then as best as Kallie could understand, the discussion turned to buffalo, leadership issues, and upset elders.

Flaming Arrow said, "Brave Eagle, final decisions should always reflect what is best for the tribe."

Lost Buffalo added, "A good leader learns from his mistakes. You must remember my many stories on this."

There was no response from Brave Eagle. His swollen eyes focused on Kallie. She had looked up for a moment and found his eyes gazing into hers. Giving him a soft smile, she pretended to drift back to sleep. Her eyes barely open, she could make out Flaming Arrow staring in her direction. Lost Buffalo said, "She is a good worker and helps us. She is sick today. She is with child."

Surprised, Flaming Arrow said, "Lost Buffalo, you have fathered a child quickly."

Lost Buffalo laughed. "You need to ask Brave Eagle about that."

Brave Eagle did not speak but only stared at Kallie.

Chapter 12: *Celebration*

Ecaca: Fun as a Diversion

Kallie noticed the entire village buzzed with excitement as preparations for the celebration were made. Sage was readied for burning and smudging. Firewood was collected from every direction and stacked for a huge communal fire. Painted skins waved in the wind. Horn bowls held pigments used for body painting, and dance outfits hung from branches. Ceremonial drums and rattles were strategically placed around the central fire pit. Special blends of tobacco were distributed for pipes. Herbal concoctions were being brewed. Great portions of stews, using the last of their buffalo meat supplies, were being prepared, and with luck, the spirit of the buffalo would return to them soon. It was that or starve during the cold winter.

As tribal medicine man, Lost Buffalo returned to his tepee and meditated into a trancelike state. His long necklaces clanked together as he unrolled his sacred medicine bundle. This bundle was the heart of his power. Examining each item, Lost Buffalo held its essence to gain spiritual insight for the ceremony. His tasks were both a special honor and a vital one. Tonight he would not only honor the brave young warriors but also appeal to the buffalo spirit to aid them. The buffalo scouts were long overdue. People were anxiously waiting for sign of the great herds so they could migrate for the hunt. Gophers, antelope, and rabbits could feed them during summer, but only buffalo could sustain the tribe during winter.

As evening approached, Lost Buffalo dressed in a shamanic outfit of animal skin to start the ceremony. Burning sage, he waved its purifying smoke with an eagle feather to cleanse himself. He instructed everyone in the tribe to follow his example so prayers would float faster to the Great Spirit. He called the guardian spirits from all directions, including above and below him. With dramatic rattling, he called in the mighty spirit of the buffalo. When he felt all the spirits were present, everyone, including Kallie, paused with respectful silence.

When the timing was just right, he began to chant and rattle. Soon the elders began to dance in a large circle, slowly drawing in men wearing buffalo heads. Each of the dancers rattled and drummed until as one, they re-created the spirit of the buffalo. Sounds of bells and rattles filled the people's hearts as they hoped buffalo spirits would reveal their location.

The entire village gathered at the huge fire. Vibrations from drums traveled toward the stars. The participants from the raid proudly collected into a circle. There the council awarded various feathers, depending on individual feats. The warriors displayed these eagle feathers in their war bonnets. Observers rattled and yelled.

Brave Eagle and his companions looked spectacular in their dancing clothes. Their bodies pulsated with strength. Flowing from the dancers' backs were huge bustles of eagle feathers extending outward. Most of the men wore their personal medicine bundles. Some men held special lances decorated with magical feathers, bells, and rattles.

Each warrior told his story through movement. Brave Eagle's dance was short because of his injuries. His feather was split at the top, indicating he was wounded but had successfully rescued another. Kallie stood in the background and studied Brave Eagle's dance, but she did not understand it. What was obvious to her was that he should still be resting to recover from his wounds. Kallie observed Dawn Star as she eagerly applauded the dances of Brave Eagle and Speckled Eagle.

The men had been drinking the special tea Lost Buffalo had prepared, and it made them bold. Now all the men came into the circle wearing outfits designed specifically for the buffalo dance. Buffalo horns protruded from their war bonnets, and eagle feathers and buffalo hooves flowed from their garments. Some men held their lances to show their hunting prowess.

Their faces were painted in honor of the buffalo spirit, and the buffalo dance began. One by one, they fell into a trance. This was vital if they were to bring the buffalo toward their land. The dance was spellbinding. It was hoped the great buffalo herds would present themselves to the scouts.

After the dancing, the mood turned lighter. Laughter, love, and gossip flowed through the crowd. Yellow Willow said, "Kallie, serve food and drink to the elders." After doing what she was told, Kallie poured a portion of stew for herself. Before she tasted the first mouthful, Elizabeth charged toward her.

Kallie jumped up. "Elizabeth, it is good to see you! How are you?"

Elizabeth gave one of her disdaining looks but could not hold it for long. She seemed relieved to see Kallie and quickly took an enormous helping of stew for herself.

Elizabeth looked over her shoulder to make sure no one had noticed her large portion and said, "We'd better eat while they're too occupied to noticed we're eating all their food. Kallie, you've practically been in jail, the way that old woman watches over you. I don't see that warrior boyfriend of yours defending you! I told you that your scheme was crazy. And, Kallie, you've gained weight. That old woman must be feeding you. You're going to grow right out of your outfit, and then what will you do—start wearing a buckskin dress like the Indian women?"

Nothing about Elizabeth had changed, but it was wonderful to see her anyway. Smiling, Kallie said, "Now, Elizabeth, what has happened to you? I hear that strange Indian man claimed you as his second wife."

Responding with her mouth full, Elizabeth explained, "I'm living with his family now. They treat me fairly ... and yes, that heathen has taken a liking to me. He was one of those savages who killed my poor husband—the big fellow, that one they call Weasel Tail. I'll just play along and bide my time until I get rescued from this savagery. Kallie, I keep hoping and praying to our Lord Jesus Christ to show us mercy. I have faith he will come down from the heavens to rescue me himself if need be."

Kallie laughed, noting Elizabeth had not lost any of her fiery spirit. Then she inquired, "Do you know anything about Brave Eagle?"

81

Elizabeth's eyebrows shot up, "Yes, I do. I happen to know he has a young female named Dawn Star whom he is expected to marry. She is the younger sister of his wife, who died in childbirth. Did you even know that he had a wife before, Kallie, an Indian wife? Now, I can see the disappointment on your face, but my Lord, it is for the best! You must stick to your own kind. I'm even sure it is in the Holy Book somewhere. You would do well just to tough this situation out and pray to survive! When we get rescued, then you can build your life again. You can marry a stern white missionary husband more suited to your needs."

Kallie could not bear to hear any more. Even if what Elizabeth had said was true, she could not believe it. She spun to see couples dancing around the fire. Running Brook looked radiant as she danced with Bear. She twirled and twirled until her shawl seemed to come alive with the sounds of jingling bells. Everyone was laughing as couples snaked around the circle. Her happiness for Running Brook was clouded when she noticed another couple.

Brave Eagle was dancing with the beautiful and supple Dawn Star. He looked magnificent in his war clothes. His long muscular arms were holding her waist tightly. Even though he was limping, he held a proud posture. Dawn Star was laughing softly and won approval from the people who were observing.

Kallie poured herself a large portion of the bubbling tea mixture Lost Buffalo had concocted. It tasted bitter and gave her a strange sensation that traveled all the way to her stomach. She did not care. In her lament, she drank another cup in a hurried gulp. Deeply upset, Kallie realized Elizabeth was probably right. It had been foolhardy to have any feelings toward the warrior. It seemed her dead husband, Armand, was looking down upon her and laughing at her misery. Although she was angry and hurt, a small voice rose from within Kallie. It told her to fight for Brave Eagle. Feeling confused and light-headed, she decided to wait a bit longer before talking to Brave Eagle. She busied herself with serving the elders and tried not to faint from dizziness.

The merriment was contagious for everyone except Kallie. Even Elizabeth joined in for some awkward dances with Weasel Tail. While the couple was dancing, Kallie thought she saw Elizabeth flash him a reserved smile. Jealousy burned inside her, for even Elizabeth had a suitor. Kallie had only a ghost of a man who haunted her in the shadows. Brave Eagle could not or would not reciprocate any feelings of love or commitment.

Standing alone in the midst of celebration, Kallie was lost in thought. Suddenly, the hairs stood up on the back of her neck. Turning around, she met Dawn Star's dark eyes and twisted smile. Kallie revealed nothing about her insecurities and boldly stared back into Dawn Star's cold eyes. Kallie broke the awkward encounter by offering tea to an elder. Feeling strange from the ceremonial tea, she drifted off and floated through the crowd. People were indifferent to her as she wandered aimlessly. She inadvertently bumped into Brave Eagle.

Standing before him, Kallie did not escape Dawn Star's jealous eyes. Brave Eagle politely asked her how she was feeling. Answering in his language for the first time, she beamed with pride. Kallie, however, could not escape Dawn Star's jealous eyes. Dawn Star, gracefully but forcefully, grabbed Brave Eagle's arm and escorted him back to the dance circle. Kallie observed that Dawn Star was indeed beautiful. Tall and strong, she possessed a beautifully shaped face and large, dark, almond-shaped eyes. An intricately beaded hairpiece held her long black hair. As she passed by victoriously, Kallie stuck her foot out to trip her. Dawn Star fell to the ground, creating a hush in the crowd. Brave Eagle looked puzzled but quickly helped Dawn Star and escorted her to the dance circle. Kallie smiled with satisfaction.

The strange brew was having an impact. Kallie felt light-headed and could not mask her feelings. Seeking refuge, she walked past Elizabeth and toward the river. Close to the village, but away from prying ears, she released her emotions. Sobbing, she pounded her fists on the ground until she was drained of all energy. Dizzy and cold, Kallie tried to get up. After several attempts, she could not do it. Her head was spinning. After one last try, she collapsed.

In the distance, she thought she heard Elizabeth say, "Kallie is over there somewhere in those bushes."

Brave Eagle said, "I'll look for her. You go back before observant eyes notice you are gone."

She heard Brave Eagle limp toward her. He softly called out to her. She could not reply, even though she tried.

He shook her, but still she could not speak. He checked her breathing and then smiled down upon her. He called out her name again and gently lifted her close to him. As he embraced her, she felt him touch her swollen stomach. Kallie felt Brave Eagle lift her, but when he put the extra weight on his injured leg, he fell with her. Then she heard him limp away.

When Brave Eagle returned, she heard him talking to someone. "She's over here. I am glad you came, because I need your help."

She heard Bear say, "What has happened?"

Brave Eagle asked, "Will you carry Kallie to her tepee?" Kallie felt Bear scoop her up into his arms. She was limp, nearly unconscious, and did not stir.

As the men walked with her, Bear said, "I did not see you at the last couples dance. Dawn Star had to dance with your brother, Speckled Eagle. I think you are in trouble, my friend."

Brave Eagle replied, "We must get ready for the grass dance and buffalo dance. I will worry about trouble later. It will still be here tomorrow."

Bear said, "Did you know your father has proclaimed the buffalo herds will come? He told everyone to make preparations for departure. He said the scouts would soon return with good news. He is sure of it."

Brave Eagle said, "That is good news. Let's drink more of that tea and go dance."

Both men laughed as they laid Kallie under a warm robe. She could hear village drums vibrating in the prairie night. Kallie thought she felt a kiss on her cheek and smiled to herself before falling into a deep sleep.

Kallie awoke clutching Brave Eagle's arrowhead necklace and wondered how she had found her way to bed. She couldn't remember. The tepee was empty. Drums droned in the background. Running Brook poked her head into the tepee and sighed. "Here is some tea. I'm tired from dancing all night, but Flaming Arrow has decided it is time for the tribe to prepare for a move. Hurry. Get up. We need to go to the medicine tepee and prepare the plant bundles my uncle requested."

Confused, Kallie quickly downed her tea. Had she understood Running Brook correctly? Did Running Brook mean the whole village was moving? Where would they be going? All anyone ever talked about was the buffalo hunt. Suddenly she remembered Brave Eagle and Bear's conversation from the night before and knew it to be the reason. Fear overtook her. Kallie had grown accustomed to this place and resisted the thought of being forced into a new situation. Soon enough, the brutal winter winds would beat against the tepee walls, and where would she be? What about her baby?

Following Running Brook's example, Kallie worked hard preparing healing supplies. Most of the potions were divided according to need. For the next several days, the village was alive with activity.

As the tribe prepared to move, the prairie changed from summer gold to autumn reds. Grasses became dusty brown as they whipped in the unrelenting breeze. During the day the sun was warm and refreshing, but there was an unmistakable chill in the evening air. Lost Buffalo seemed restless and had predicted an early, ferocious winter. He said, "I am afraid the buffalo herds are sparse and are not following normal migration paths. We need food. I am worried about the winter and bone-chilling cold. Great amounts of meat are needed to sustain our tribe over a long, brutal winter. Although we are prepared for a hunt, we are forced to sit. The buffalo scouts have not returned."

While Lost Buffalo was consumed by his thoughts, Kallie left him alone. The sun was shining, so she gathered sand cherries along the river. She always went farther than any other woman dared go. All tribal women knew anyone wandering too far would be first to be killed by predators or invaders. Kallie did not care. She enjoyed being alone and away from prying eyes. She reached for berries, and each movement strained her cotton skirt. Her clothes were impossibly tight, even though she had tried to reshape them and had taken out stitches where she could.

Hearing a noise, Kallie hid behind vegetation. She was relieved to discover it was Brave Eagle. He did not scold her like the others but only ate some berries from her bark container. While savoring their sweet taste, he explained, "We have a saying. If a person gathering cherries moves in the direction contrary to the wind, the cherries will be sweet. If you move with the wind, the berries will be bitter." Looking at her with a shy smile, he gathered more berries from her container and said, "These are sweet."

Kallie and Brave Eagle sat together watching insects dance in the sun. He put his fingers through the rips in Kallie's skirt and poked her bare skin. As he pressed on her stomach, she felt the baby's slight movement. A big smile appeared on Brave Eagle's face as he looked into her eyes. He tugged at her clothes. They would not last much longer. He stretched out on the ground and, in no apparent hurry, held her close. Kallie wanted to ask him about their relationship, but something stopped her. Questioning would surely chase him away. As if he sensed her uneasiness, Brave Eagle got up and motioned for her to follow him. When they arrived back at camp, Brave Eagle flashed a smile at her. Kallie watched him ride out of the village with his brother, Speckled Eagle, and wondered where they were going.

Chapter 13: *To Obtain a Favor*

Anakiciksin: To Come to One's Aid

Brave Eagle and Speckled Eagle hunted along the draws of the river searching for food. They were successful in securing only a few jackrabbits. As they rode back to the encampment, Speckled Eagle cautiously inquired, "Brother ... about Dawn Star."

Brave Eagle gave him a sharp glare and then looked straight ahead and said, "Speckled Eagle, you have become mother's spokesman. I will not hear it. As a younger brother, you have no right to tell me what to do."

There was no more talking between the two brothers as they approached the camp. Brave Eagle left his brother and rode to his aunt's home with a rabbit in hand. He planned to ask a favor. His aunt, Silver Reed, was a strong, likable woman who had treated him like her own son.

Silver Reed welcomed him with a big hug and said, "My nephew, what is on your mind today? You look troubled."

Brave Eagle handed her his rabbit and said, "Kallie needs a new dress."

Silver Reed said, "Such a strange request for Lost Buffalo's woman. This could cause me trouble, but I will help my favorite nephew." After an uneasy silence she added, "I must mention this to your mother, and she will not be happy."

Brave Eagle nodded at Silver Reed and cringed at the thought of his mother's reaction.

Together, they walked to his mother's tepee. Pretty Shield said, "Brave Eagle, stand up straight. Silver Reed, my sister, it is good to see you. What do you bring in your backpack?"

Silver Reed pulled out an old buffalo skin dress and explained, "Pretty Shield, I plan to give this to Brave Eagle so he can take it to the white captive."

Pretty Shield reacted, saying, "I cannot understand how my own loved ones can betray this family. Brave Eagle, every opportunity has been given to you. Now your leadership will always be questioned because of a scrawny, ugly captive."

Silver Reed handed the dress to Brave Eagle. Pretty Shield said, "I pray that Dawn Star's family will not find out about this indiscretion. It would be a disgrace. It is time for you to marry. Your father must help me resolve this." She stood up. "I will have my way on this."

Brave Eagle said, "Kallie is not ugly," and hurried to Lost Buffalo's tepee. He was disappointed that only Yellow Willow was at the entrance. He gave her the other jackrabbit and then handed over the dress.

Yellow Willow said, "We are very grateful for the rabbit because Lost Buffalo is feeling too ill to hunt. Please come inside."

Brave Eagle bent over to enter but heard a sound far off on the horizon. He cocked his ear and said, "The scouts are back!" The scouts were riding toward him in a formation that could mean only one thing: they had found a herd of buffalo!

The village drummer pounded out a message. The big hunt was on! Brave Eagle rushed out to greet the scouts and wait for more news. Children ran around cheering, and even the boys watching the pony herds raced into camp to see if they had heard the drum's message correctly.

The excited scouts explained they had found a large herd that could sustain the tribe throughout winter. The journey to the buffalo would take them several campfires. They would have to travel beyond their traditional winter camp. After hearing from the scouts, Brave Eagle waited for Flaming Arrow to give the go-ahead.

Flaming Arrow announced, "Elders will be left at the wintering grounds. Those who can no longer keep up with the rigors of the hunt will stay on their own. This will save the tribe desperately needed time. The best time to hunt is as soon as possible, while the cows are fat and before the bulls have left the herd. The time to go is now. Bear, Flying Crow, and Short Bull will stay until our other scouts signal them to follow."

Brave Eagle did not question his father's decision, because a successful hunt was crucial for the tribe's survival. He became part of the camp's excited movements. He was eager to move before winter winds dominated and hunger set in. Most of the autumn days still offered warmth for traveling. The nights had frosted, and the ever-present prairie winds had already turned cold.

The people quickly worked in unison. The tribe moved in a systematic order. The strongest scouts went out first, soon followed by the hunters on horseback. Families with horses pulling their belongings on travois went next. Tepee skins lined the frames overflowing with belongings. The rest of the tribe, young and old, walked. The young girls constantly tried to keep the dogs from fighting. At the rear of this mighty formation, selected boys herded the remaining horses. The tribe's procession moved steadily and never seemed to stop for any reason. Everyone was expected to keep up, and Brave Eagle knew this would be hard for Kallie. He quietly left his family group and began to search for her.

Brave Eagle found her with Yellow Willow's family. They walked alongside a pony drag that carried their belongings. The women were busy gossiping. Brave Eagle had always marveled how the gossip flowed before returning back to the original speaker. His family traveled close by, but Brave Eagle managed to stay clear of Pretty Shield's reproaches.

After days of constant travel, the tribe arrived at their traditional wintering grounds. At this spot, the river had cut a deep valley now covered with trees. It offered a refuge against the winter winds, which could stab like a knife. Brave Eagle knew it to be a comfortable spot where winter days were warmed by tepee fires and the stories of elders.

Brave Eagle avoided his mother's sharp gaze and helped Yellow Willow set up the old couple's tepee. Kallie looked beautiful and seemed excited about having a warm home again. But then she must have just realized the rest of the tribe was going on without her, because suddenly her expression changed to a fearful one. After a short, tearful good-bye, Yellow Willow's relatives hurried to rejoin the others

Running Brook held something in her arms as she ran past Brave Eagle. He watched as she tried to catch her breath while asking, "Kallie, could you take this one? He will not make it. I do not have the heart to kill it. Please hide it. This puppy limps badly."

Kallie took the dog, nodded her head, and asked, "What is its name?"

Brave Eagle observed Running Brook's quizzical expression as she replied, "Name? Why would you name a dog? I saved it from my father's hatchet. I call it using this sound." Running Brook made a clicking sound with her tongue on the roof of her mouth. "I must catch up with the others. Don't worry, Kallie. We will be back after the hunt and butchering. Just think, we'll have food again."

Brave Eagle shot Kallie one last glance as she held the young dog in her arms. It was past time for him to catch up with his family, and he moved on as Kallie just stood looking at him. As he rode toward the dark hills, he glanced back one last time.

Chapter 14: *Kallie's Story*

Wayasni: Talk until the Fire Goes Out

It now was obvious to Kallie that she and the oldest, feeblest people were staying behind. She would be held captive in this lonely place while the others moved on cheerfully in chase of the buffalo. Soon, the last group of young, healthy men were to leave. These included Bear, who announced that he had received a signal from scouts. His group would be gone by the next day.

Anxious for company, Kallie searched for Yellow Willow. She found her placing additional skins along the tepee bottom while Hawk Woman and Buffalo Woman visited. Their arthritic hands sewed with grace from years of experience.

Kallie gathered the shirt she was sewing for Lost Buffalo. She was proud of it. The seams were strong and neat, but she dreaded displaying her clumsy beadwork. To make matters worse, she had no desire to improve, even though Yellow Willow insisted she practice. All the older women expected her to enjoy beading as they did. Besides, everyone knew a woman's reputation depended on her beadwork. Everyone's belongings glittered with treasured bead designs and patterns. Resigned to the fact that she must try, Kallie patiently sewed her beads as straight as possible.

The women's chattering intensified until someone thoughtlessly mentioned Dawn Star. This was followed by an awkward silence. Quickly changing the topic, Yellow Willow said, "Oh, Kallie, you know nothing. You must practice beading, or you will never get a husband."

The old women giggled, and Hawk Woman joked as she pointed at Kallie's enlarged belly. "Oh, she knows one thing, and it is about men." Everyone, including Kallie, laughed. The distraction caused her to prick her finger again, which caused the women to laugh even harder. Kallie was saved when the thin stew began to steam. Jumping up, she served meager portions. The women ate in silence, each missing family members and hoping for their safe return.

That evening at dusk, she and the old couple went visiting, which always included telling stories. Kallie tried to decipher the language, but many of the words lost their meaning. Bored, she thought to herself, Dawn Star, the huntress, would study her prey, Brave Eagle, closely. Dawn Star would watch his every move. Providing him with food, she would watch him swallow as he ate his meal. She would know he silently thanked her by the way he ate. Fidgeting, Kallie could barely keep her jealousy under control.

Bear nudged her. "Kallie, tell us about your travels. The elders want to hear it, and I can interpret. Tonight is the only opportunity. Tomorrow, at daylight, I will join the scouts and be gone."

Kallie felt self-conscious because everyone was staring at her. There would be no getting out of the situation. She started, "After days of hard traveling, our group arrived at St. Louis. It was a grand city, better than any picture book. Its waterfront street had all types of stores, inns, billiard parlors, and gambling saloons. Horses and buggies filled the streets with motion. Women wearing the latest fashions walked upon boardwalks. Huge steamers barged supplies, wagons, rifles, army equipment, and farm tools. The docks were crowded with traders, Indians, mountain men, slaves, and settlers, all seeking passage to Independence, the start of the Oregon Trail.

"My husband's eyes sparkled as he looked upon the city's commotion. Excited, he let out a holler and twirled me around. He told me he felt lucky because there would be fresh people in town and money to be made at cards. Elizabeth and Jacob slipped away toward the other end of town to set up their wagon for preaching. This was the first time Armand and I had been left alone. Armand drove our wagon to a fancy hotel called The Waterfront.

"A beautifully dressed woman greeted Armand with a kiss and spoke to him in French. It was like she knew him already. A huge crystal chandelier hung from the center of the ceiling. Colors of the sun danced through the prisms and were reflected in a full-length mirror. A table covered by green cloth held decanters of cigars and jars of red-and-orange candied fruit. Packs of cards and backgammon games were laid out on tables. Across the room, a crimson calico curtain with a fluted opening exposed a counter holding more liquor bottles than I had seen in a lifetime.

"Armand started drinking shots from a bottle of whiskey. After several swigs, his cheeks were flushed and his eyes took on the same look as my father's when he drank. I had a sinking feeling when I realized that Armand had the same crazy desire for liquor as my father.

"Later that night, Armand left me alone in our room while he went downstairs to the saloon. He forbade me to follow him. That was fine at first, but then I grew curious about what Armand was doing. I heard all sorts of noises in the hallway. There was banging against the walls and the sounds of women laughing and men's voices.

"When the hallway cleared, I ran down the stairs and hid behind a curtain until the barroom door opened. This exposed a huge saloon that was crowded and noisy. A man at the piano played dancing music. Dancing girls in bright low-cut dresses with long red feathers danced on a makeshift stage. The girls kicked their legs up high, exposing black lace stockings and red garter belts. The air was filled with smoke and laughter. My husband, Armand, was sitting at a long oak table and playing cards with fancy-dressed gentlemen. The atmosphere of the game was serious and tension-filled. The card table was enveloped in cigar smoke, and the poker chips flew about.

"At the card game, Armand won four tickets from St. Louis to Independence on a steamer named the *Ohio*. We were excited because Independence would be our starting point for the Oregon Trail. Armand sold all the horses except Clara, my horse. He had made arrangements to keep her even though we would have to pay at least one dollar for her passage. In exchange for Armand's one act of kindness, I worked hard at selling liquor from the back of our wagon. Armand had bought me a fancy saloon dress to wear while selling our fake medicine. This selling technique proved very successful because many men stopped to buy from me. I sold so many bottles of Miracle Cure that I started keeping some of the money without informing the others.

"Finally, the time came to depart on the boat. The *Ohio* had a tall painted chimney. The steamer's decks were crowded with heavy cargo and filled with disassembled wagons, draft animals, and plows mixed in with all types of merchandise consigned to frontier stores in Independence. The ship labored against the Mississippi River's mighty current. Every day we'd get hung up on snags or sandbars, causing long delays. Finally, after eight days of constant struggle, we saw signs along the riverbanks of wagons making their way toward Independence.

"At last the steamer blew its landing whistle. We anchored on the upper bluffs just outside of Independence. It took two days to unload all the cargo from our steamer. Jacob left for town on my horse, Clara. Later that afternoon, he returned with six scraggly mules. I scoffed at his lack of knowledge about beasts of burden. We pushed on past Independence Square and settled into a camp that other travelers had set up. We needed to get the rest of our supplies. Together, we hurried through the town's muddy streets until the men located the gunsmith's shop. Elizabeth strolled on to the millinery shop, where lovely dresses that were already sewn fluttered in display windows. I ventured to the apothecary's shop, where a skeleton was displayed in the doorway. Inside the store, bundles of pungent herbs hung from the ceiling. A doctor weighed out herbs for me. These were plants that would help cure catarrh and ague. I also bought additional herbs and tonic bottles with pretty labels. The doctor and I conversed until Armand came in and told me to hurry. Our last stop was the general store, where Armand helped me post a letter to my brothers. He was careful to write small so we'd use only one sheet of paper. That way, upon receiving it, my brothers would not have to pay much for postage. The storekeeper folded our letter and sealed it. It would be the last letter I would ever write them.

"Back at camp, Armand never did a lick of work except peel skins off a few potatoes. He bragged that his hands were soft and flexible for his work. His fingers could feel the slightest vibration of each card. His card shuffling had to be fast as lightning so he could cheat but look like an honest man. He explained that I had to do all the chores, work with the horses, and fix the wagon when it was needed, or it wouldn't get done. In addition to all the chores, he made me polish his boots every day.

"Spring rains made our camp cold and dreary. Since everyone had to wait for the weather to change before departing, Armand decided to keep on playing poker. He won money every night. During this time, I made good earnings selling medicine. I also made a popular potion that the ladies bought when their menfolk weren't looking. It was my love potion. It had a lovely essence of lilac, combined with a drop of harebell to bring love through the heart, three drops of foxglove to relieve any heart tensions, one drop of sweet gale, and monkshood to help interactions with others. Mixing the essence with brandy and some of Jacob's holy water formed a sweet-tasting potion. I used it all the time, but it didn't seem to work on Armand and me. We continued to drift apart. As I said before, I held back some of my earnings and secretly saved several coins in a leather pouch. It started out as a small amount, but over time I grew bolder and accumulated a good sum.

"In a couple of weeks, both wagons were well stocked for our western journey. There were bags of coffee, beans, flour, and dried fruit. Clay jars held vinegar and molasses. Bacon was stored in a barrel of cornmeal. Spare harnesses, wagon parts, and guns filled any unoccupied space. Armand and I planned to camp in a tent most nights, but we also had a mattress full of hay in the middle of the wagon. A false bottom in the wagon held cases of forty-five-caliber guns that Jacob and Armand had bought. Each gun would fetch at least ten dollars once we cleared the fort.

"The rains finally quit, and grasses greened up. Taking advantage of the sun, I washed dirty laundry. Jacob, Armand, and Elizabeth had gone to town, and I had been left alone. It was a warm, beautiful day, and we'd be leaving soon. But what I couldn't know was there was trouble in town. Here is what Elizabeth told me.

"The sheriff had set a trap at the saloon. He had a wealthy stranger from New Orleans announce a high-stakes card event. Armand took the bait. As the game progressed, Armand started winning all the poker chips. The rich stranger tapped his finger on his Sharp's Pepper Box pistol as he watched Armand play. Even he could not find evidence of cheating until it was Armand's turn to deal. When the stranger heard the sound of the card shuffle, he knew it didn't sound right. He drew his pistol on my husband and demanded to see the bottom of the card deck. Armand protested, but the other players did not defend him and, instead, waited for him to comply. Armand turned over the deck, displaying a couple of aces wrong side up. Armand tried to act indignant, but once he realized that he wasn't fooling anyone, he pushed over the oak table. In the turmoil that followed, a fight broke out, and Armand managed to dodge the bullets meant for him.

"Jacob and Elizabeth heard the commotion and cowered in the driver's seat of their wagon. Armand leaped into the back. Jacob snapped the reins and fled out of town. Arriving back at camp, the three of them were drenched in mud. Armand leaped out of Jacob's wagon and hitched the mules to our wagon. He was clearly out of his element, for his fancy hat was gone and his ruffled French shirt had been ruined. Frantically, he whipped the mules, and off we went. I was in the back of the wagon when Armand yelled, 'Kallie, darling, we're going to Oregon.'

"That was the moment of my fateful decision. As I sat on the edge of the wagon's back, I debated whether or not to leap. But I asked myself what kind of a situation I would be jumping into. I had never attended a hanging before, and I didn't know if they hung women, but I didn't want to find out. In that brief moment, I decided to stay put in back of the wagon. After that, I could only hope for the best."

Bear motioned for Kallie to keep telling her story. He asked, "What happened next?"

Kallie continued, "We traveled through the rainy night as fast as we could. Jacob took the lead, and I scoffed at his decisions. It made no sense to me to ruin our mules in endless travel during the cool, wet night. If the sheriff had sent out a posse on horseback, it would have caught up to our wagons in no time. Rain made the trail so muddy it was almost impassable. The wagon wheels creaked as they pushed through the muddy ruts. Huge oak branches swayed just above our wagon cover. This was a concern, because a tear would leave us defenseless against the sky's torrent. Every time our axles bottomed out in a deep rut, the exhausted mules strained until they were close to collapse. Armand was splattered with mud but stayed confident of escape, until we turned a corner. There in the middle of the trail was Elizabeth's and Jacob's wagon stopped by a broken wheel.

"Elizabeth's bonnet was so limp it covered most of her face. She cupped her hands and shouted, 'God has unleashed the great flood over mankind again. It wouldn't surprise me if it rained for forty more days. We will have to camp right here until help comes along.'

"The next morning, Armand kissed me on the cheek and proclaimed, 'Our luck has changed. Get up and make breakfast. There are men here who are helping us.'

"Peeking out from the canvas, I saw that Santa Fe traders from Independence had stopped. An older driver fixed our broken wheel and advised Armand, 'If you hurry to Alcove Springs, you'll catch up with a moving company. The sooner you folks hook up with them, the safer you'll be.'

"Alcove Springs was a beautiful place. Water gushed over a ten-foot ledge into a deep pool below. The leader, named Captain Henry Brown, saw our fire and came out to inspect us. Henry wore buckskin clothing, rode a painted horse, and looked wild. Recognizing us from the camp in Independence, he explained that he'd been voted leader of the moving company. He was a seasoned traveler, and now he would be leading the way to Oregon.

"Captain Brown explained that we were welcome to join up if we were willing to follow certain rules. The morning bugle went off at 4:00 a.m. sharp, and everyone was expected to help with the cattle whether you had livestock or not. They would travel until noon. A midday break would serve to rest the beasts and allow for the main meal of the day. At 2:00 p.m. sharp the train would head west again until nightfall.

"If folks were lost or sick, it was up to each wagon to decide whether to continue on or stay behind to help. The company would keep going at a steady pace so as to clear the mountain passes before winter. The captain put his head down and said, 'No drinking; no gambling.' Then he laughed. 'At least don't get caught. No setting off by yourselves unless you mean to break off for good. It takes too much time to find lost wagons.' Armand and Jacob shook the captain's hand and drove our wagons into the company camp.

"Next morning, the bugle rang out at 4:00 a.m. The air was chilly for springtime. My body ached and I felt nauseous when I woke up. I wore my light cotton dress and shook the dust out of my apron before tying it on myself. My bonnet was ragged and dirty, but I dared not be without it. Clara was restless until I let her graze freely. Jacob hitched up the mules while Armand went to help round up cattle. Elizabeth and I made breakfast.

"As we drank the last of our coffee, Elizabeth scoffed, 'It'll take forever to collect all these cattle every morning. Imagine thirty-eight wagons and all these loose cattle.'

"With his mouth full of porridge, Jacob preached, 'Elizabeth, we're part of a company now. Different people, different needs, and different dispositions all brought together under mutual dependence. We all have the same intent, and that is to reach the Promised Land. Everyone has to work together. And besides,' he showed his wicked smile, 'we will not go hungry. These folks may help our mission with gifts.'

"Elizabeth reprimanded, 'Fine, you do the collecting of cattle every morning. I'll not be part of it.'

Armand laughed. Winking at Elizabeth, he promised her, 'We'll move up toward the lead; that way, it will be less dusty.' Our wagons were in front by noon, and then it was time to rest the herd. We ate our big meal of the day. It was always the same—beans, bread, and coffee.

"The prairie was beautiful. Tall grasses grew everywhere, and delicate flowers dotted the landscape. As we walked behind the wagons, Elizabeth groaned about mosquitoes that were as big as flies. Sometimes the people walking would take cutoff paths that ran parallel to the main trail and many times were bordered by shady creeks. It was a pleasant change from the perpetual and choking dust created by the wagons. We had fun wading in the streams.

"We followed the Platte River until finally we had to cross, and it turned out to be particularly treacherous for us. Captain Brown determined that we should take the wheels off and use the wagon beds as rafts. The current was swifter than it looked, and the riverbanks turned into muck like quicksand. Several of the travelers, including Elizabeth, refused to move. Jacob patiently coaxed her by reminding her that missionary work was the work of God. A trusting servant of God could not refuse. How would it look to the others?

"After traveling a few more days, we encountered hilly country. Bad luck started. A wagon wheel gave way and ran over a man's leg. It festered, and a fever took him. It was the first funeral, and Jacob said a comforting eulogy. Soon after, another man complained of an aching head in the afternoon, and by evening he was dead. Many people became sick and died. We buried them in shallow graves and kept going.

"The wagon train was planning to resupply at Fort John, where there was a trading post. This country proved challenging. As we climbed higher, the soil turned sparse and yucca plants covered the hills. As the barefoot children walked, they had to watch for rattlers. We were excited when we spotted tepees outside of Fort John. The fort was set on the confluence of Horse Creek and the North Fork of the Platte. The captain led us on a trading trail used by Indians and trappers. Just outside the fort we found a good camping spot with firewood and water.

"We set up camp while Captain Brown and a group of men, including Armand, rode off to visit the trading post inside the fort. Just as Armand had anticipated, plenty of traders wanted his guns. Even with the exorbitant prices of supplies, Armand was able to trade for anything we needed. Also, he procured a large barrel of whiskey and shared it freely with the traders and Indians alike. That night drunken fights broke out and careless shots were fired. The next morning the wagon train company left in disgust. Armand in his drunken stupor yelled, 'To hell with them. They were moving too slow with all those cattle.'

"One of the fur traders slurred, 'Them fools! They'll never clear the passes in time. There's a cutoff on the north side. From there, your two wagons could meet up with other companies moving faster. It is a safe enough trail to travel; just watch out for rattlers and Indians. I'll sell you a map. It'll cost you only a couple of drinks.'

"We took the trader's advice and traveled the north cutoff trail. After a few days, we came upon a swollen river that looked angry and fast. It swept over a huge area. No one had mentioned this was such a hazardous crossing. Armand unfolded the map. Thankfully, the map showed another lesser tributary that was narrow enough to cross safely. The spot had an *X* right on it. Armand led the way and told us to look for a wooden sign put up by trappers. The sign said Sweet Grass Crossing.

"Just like Armand said, we found the sign hanging from a tree. It was a beautiful spot with sweetgrass and flowers dotting the riverbanks. Butterflies fluttered about. The sun was out, and we decided to cross before evening. Sweet Grass Crossing looked much easier than passage at the main river branch. Before actually crossing, we stopped to organize our things and fix a meal for the day. While we rested at the crossing, Armand found another, older sign that had fallen facedown. It showed a carving of a rattlesnake and seemed like a warning.

"Jacob and Elizabeth started in with their wagon first. We followed right behind them. Everything was routine until I spotted rattlers in the water. They were gliding horizontally and made little waves as they propelled forward. A group of rattlers swam right toward the lead mule. Elizabeth screamed, and the terrified mules veered wildly off course. Our wagons caught a strong current, which pulled us into the main channel. The wagons swirled out of control in dark, deep waters. I clung to the wagon sides until wood splinters covered my hands. Suddenly our wagon hit a huge tree snagged on the river bottom. It kept Armand and me dangling. The wagon became stuck and bobbed up and down in the rushing water.

"Jacob and Elizabeth sped by us. Elizabeth desperately clung to Jacob while he tried to push her away! They were lucky. Their sturdy wagon was still intact when they landed on the other side of the river. The running water was pounding our wagon, but our belongings were still in place. We sat, hung up on the tree, mangled but still alive.

"Finally, the massive tree broke free, and our wagon tipped and was swept down the river. When we landed onshore, there was little left. We took stock of what we had. My horse, Clara, was gone, and only two of the mules had made it. There was little to provide us warmth, shelter, and food. Jacob said we needed one more mule to pull the wagon. I volunteered to go search for the missing beasts and walked a long way downriver. I kept calling for my horse, Clara. I knew she would come if she were able. I did hear a horse's neighing, but it was not Clara's whinny. It gave me shivers. The queerest feeling overcame me. I felt I was being watched. I hid in the bushes for the longest time but saw no one. Hearing no unusual sounds, I hastily retreated back to our wagons.

"We struggled to set up a meager camp. I kept calling for Clara. Eventually, she came limping into camp. I was overjoyed.

"As we huddled together by a small fire, everyone was worried. I was exhausted and went to sleep under the lean-to without even a blanket to keep me warm. The next morning, I felt much better. Elizabeth and I cleaned and dried out what was left of our tattered belongings. No one spoke about our terrible dilemma."

Kallie smiled at Bear and continued, "As you know, a group of warriors quietly stepped out of the vegetation. They were streaked with war paint, so I knew they were not friendly. As they approached us, Elizabeth screamed. Jacob rushed toward Armand, who was fumbling around for his gun. The war party did not attack until Jacob grabbed the gun and fired it carelessly at them. This brought a shower of arrows upon both men. Soon Armand and Jacob were sprawled out in the mud, scalped and dead, with numerous arrows piercing their bodies.

"Screaming, Elizabeth crouched with her back to the wagon, armed with an iron skillet and a long knife. At first, the warriors laughed and taunted her. As they tried to grab her, the swipes from her long knife kept them away. Soon, a hush of respect came over them.

"While the braves were occupied with Elizabeth, no one was focused on me, so I slowly stepped back, one step at a time, toward the woodland cover. I tried to remain calm so my motions would not be detected. I took more steps and then darted into the brush. I did not get far. Strong arms grabbed me. In a swift motion, Brave Eagle gripped me tightly against his body while his other hand covered my mouth. He then said something I could not understand. With his breath, he blew into my nostrils, scaring me into stillness. My eyes were open wide in terror, and I could smell him. In moments, I was bound by rope and thrown sideways on his horse.

"Brave Eagle leaped upon his horse. With a high-pitched war cry, he signaled you and the others. I suppose you know the rest of the story."

As Bear prepared to leave, he told her, "I made the horse call. I had told Brave Eagle that I could lure you into a trap. When you weren't fooled, Brave Eagle started to follow you. He respected your spirit. He said you were of the horse totem."

Lost Buffalo spoke to Bear, in front of everyone. "Yes, and he caught her like one of his wild mustangs." Bear nodded with agreement and left. Kallie did not see Bear leave the next morning. She was left with a woman from Dawn Star's family, Walks Far, who Kallie knew, was her enemy.

Chapter 15: *The Journey Within*

Awacin: Meditate

It was so quiet. Alone and hungry, Kallie shivered with cold. The older ones could provide precious little food or protection. She felt her baby move as cold, lonely winds stabbed at her protruding belly. She resolved to stay strong. She and her baby would survive at all costs.

Days stretched by. Kallie, clutching her ragged buffalo robe, continually searched the horizon for any sight of the others. Chilly winds blasted through the valley, and the threat of snow hung in the air. Hunger stalked her, for the meager portion of watered-down buffalo stew was never enough. Lost Buffalo had consulted his stones and predicted an early winter with many storms. As the baby kicked, Kallie wondered if it was a boy or girl, light or dark. Feeling vulnerable, she prayed the baby would survive the winter. She was so hungry.

Camp was lonely, although Kallie enjoyed a newfound freedom. There was no one to avoid, and most of the elders accepted her in their circle. She split her time between collecting wood for elders and scrounging for prairie turnips. The older men hunted birds, hares, or an occasional antelope, but they barely subsisted on the meager supplies. Patiently, everyone prayed the rest of the tribe would return with rich buffalo meat to nourish them before it was too late.

While the women chattered on, Lost Buffalo signaled Kallie to leave with him. She sheepishly lagged behind him, afraid she might have done something to cause him to be upset. After they arrived home, Lost Buffalo unrolled one of his sacred bundles, revealing a buffalo drum and beater. Large eagle feathers hung from beaded rawhide seams. He waved the drum over the fire. Lighting sweetgrass in a bowl, he used an eagle feather to motion the smoke to surround him. This would purify the sacred space and send his prayers upward to the skies.

Lost Buffalo showed Kallie a special prayer feather he had used since before he had married Yellow Willow. He questioned, "You are usually the first person to rise. Do you pray in the early morning?"

Puzzled, Kallie cautiously answered, "No, I never think of prayer so early in the morning."

"It is a shame, but I am relieved," he said, chuckling. "The prayers that rise with the sun are the first ones heard. There is much power in this, being the first," he said with a twinkle in his eye. "Being first is good for special requests. I will say no more about this, since you may not have any special concerns to ask about. Kallie, when is it you pray?"

Kallie looked down and said, "I pray when I'm in trouble or upset."

Lost Buffalo laughingly advised her, "If that is the only time you pray, then you will find yourself in trouble all the time. Now take this. Smudge yourself, and purify your space."

Kallie accepted the smudge bowl and motioned smoke with the feather. Its sweet smell was exotic to her senses.

Together, they held hands while Lost Buffalo called in special guidance for her spirit journey. Kallie thought Lost Buffalo was a fascinating man when he displayed his powers. It was strange that he would call this ceremony a journey. Were they actually going somewhere? Lost Buffalo handed her a beautiful gourd rattle. Its wood handle was carved into a buffalo shape. She followed his lead and shook the rattle as close to his rhythm as possible.

A sense of freedom filled her as she reflected upon the sweet smell of the summer prairie grasses. Moving in the wind, the grasses made wispy sounds. The rattling abruptly stopped and brought her back. Quickly she lowered her rattle and placed it with the other sacred items. Lost Buffalo motioned Kallie to lie on the buffalo robe. Nervous because she did not know what to expect, she did as he commanded. Relaxed in his chair, Lost Buffalo laughed at her and lifted his drum.

Beating it softly, he whispered, "Close your eyes. Follow your heart where it wants to go. Do not question the spirit world, and try to be respectful. See what they tell you. If spirit tells you to fly like the crow, then fly is what you must do. The guides are not used to a white woman and will not understand your abrupt manner. Let your spirit soar where it must go but, again, be respectful. "Now the journey begins. Your spirit protector will come to you as a mountain lioness. Kallie, do you feel its presence?"

Kallie, sensing the cat spirit, barely nodded her head yes. Steady beats of the drum lulled her into a dreamlike trance.

Lost Buffalo continued, "You must find your way to the lower world by using an earth opening. The lower world is deep within Earth Mother. This is where your guides will greet you. Introduce yourself. Then ask a question of the spirit world. It must be from your heart; you must be honest. Ask it three times. If you are sincere, then the answer will come. However, it may not be the answer you are seeking.

"Breathe deeply, and let your spirits guide you. They may take you to the middle world, where it is much like here, or to the upper world, where the winds play with the clouds. Spirit territory is endless. When you are done with your spirit journey, I will call you back by beating on the drum with four long strokes."

Listening to the steady drumbeat, Kallie felt herself falling through a hole in the ground. She landed near a cave sheltered by boulders and dense vegetation. Peering into its opening, she discovered green eyes glowing back at her. It was her lioness spirit protector. Remembering Lost Buffalo's advice, Kallie asked the question that was burning inside of her: "What is to become of me and my baby?"

As if in a dream, an owl magically flew above her. She followed it as best she could. Her vision became very clear, and she could see in the dark. Approaching the eastern direction, she saw her parents' dilapidated farmhouse. Her brother Michael was sitting at the table drinking a cup of his brew in the glow of the fireplace. The fields were producing, and it was close to harvest time. Sadness stirred within her when she viewed the crosses marking her parents' graves. It all seemed like a lifetime ago.

They flew to the south, and Kallie's heart jumped at the sight of Millicent's cabin. Herbs and concoctions still lined the shelves. Kallie called out to her, but the owl pulled her sharply westward.

They hovered above a steep canyon wall of red stone. At the bottom of the cliffs flowed a green river. A hawk called to look below. Kallie saw a woman with a baby and a man paddling a canoe. Landing the canoe, they ascended up the red rocks of the canyon. Several dragonflies darted past Kallie. Straining, she could not see and splashed into the waters. A beaver circled and blocked her travel. The mysterious couple and their child slipped away undetected.

The river's current swept her to where the rest of the tribe was hunting. Many buffalo carcasses were on the ground, and people were fed and happy. In another area there had been an accident. A hunter trampled by a wounded bull had severely broken his leg. Another warrior held a gaping hole in his chest as blood spewed on the ground. Kallie could feel his intense pain and started to gasp. She could not breathe. The drumming slowed into four long beats calling her back from her dream.

Kallie sat up and foretold, "There has been an accident."

Lost Buffalo insisted Kallie calm herself. He carefully listened while she explained her journey. Lost Buffalo looked surprised at her prediction.

Finally, he said, "My rocks have also indicated some type of disturbance has occurred. We will ready ourselves for possible wounded, but we will wait until dawn. Things sometimes look different in the morning light. If what you saw is true, we will have time before they arrive. That is, if they arrive."

Lost Buffalo interpreted Kallie's vision. "Most of your journey makes sense. Your totem, the mountain lion, is a difficult one for a woman to have. It makes you a target for other people's problems. The owl is a seeker of unseen truths. It is a great gift, the ability to see in the dark. Dragonflies signify winds of change, and the buffalo represents reconnecting with life."

Lost Buffalo sat up. "Messenger hawk appears to caution you. Hawk's message is the baby will survive, but your life is another matter.

It also troubles me the beaver appears in the seventh direction, the space within." Lost Buffalo looked directly into her eyes and said, "This can mean only one thing: something dangerous lurks in your life. Spiritual protection will be needed to keep you safe."

Kallie wanted to ask him more, but Lost Buffalo said, "Now leave me. I must be alone." He fell into a deep sleep, and she was left to hear the howling wind and wonder about what lurked in the darkness.

Chapter 16: *The Hunt*

Igni: Stalk Game

Brave Eagle was excited. His leg wound from the raid had healed, and he felt strong enough to hunt again. Roaming over the expansive prairie, he observed the winds kicking up dust. Dark clouds cast shadows on the flowing grass. In his heart he felt generations of spirit ancestors traveling alongside him. Life on the buffalo hunt was less complicated and provided a reprieve from the decision he would eventually be forced to make.

As he contemplated hunting strategies, he could almost hear the thunderous explosion of great bulls. As he guided Wind Racer with just the pressure from his knees, they would approach a ferocious bull so close that a bow length separated them. This proximity could be achieved only because of Wind Racer's superior racing ability and stamina. Maintaining this precarious distance, Brave Eagle would shoot two fatal arrows. One would pierce behind the last rib, and the other would go through the left shoulder and into the heart. These vital spots were crucial targets; if they were missed, the wounded animal might run away and be lost. If he had to use more than two arrows to bring the massive creature down, he would quickly do so. But then he would risk his life to remove the extra arrows before the women in his family found out and criticized him with their endless jokes.

As Wind Racer shook his mane, Brave Eagle shifted his attention. He could not forget the feel and smell of Kallie. Remembering their time together, he smiled at the irony of his situation. It seemed that she had captured him and not the other way around. Wrestling with the question that haunted him, he wondered if the child she carried was his son.

Dawn Star, who brushed past him on her horse, interrupted his thoughts. Her beauty and soft laughter brought him back to reality. Everyone, especially his parents, expected him to marry Dawn Star. His quiet but intentional avoidance of her had only escalated the situation. He was expected to do the right thing, but somehow he could not accept what he must do. Sheepishly smiling at her, he moved up the line with the other men.

Observant scouts led the way downwind because the bison sense of smell was strong. The scouts interpreted game signs along the way. Smells that came with the breeze, animal sounds, and cloud movements all told a story. Watchful warriors followed the scouts' lead, while outriders guarded the flanks. Long processions of families quietly snaked along grassy hills. Long poles from their travois stuck high in the air. Dogs and children moved about hunting rodents and ground squirrels.

Finally, after days of travel, the buffalo scouts returned. Their news was good; fresh buffalo tracks had been spotted. Brave Eagle's father, Flaming Arrow, signaled with his hand to indicate it was again time to prepare for a hunt. Excited women set up small temporary willow shelters, for there was no need to establish family circles. After the hunt ensured a winter supply of meat, they would return to their traditional winter camp.

Brave Eagle looked forward to that day. He knew the elders would be anxiously waiting. The buffalo provided all their life necessities. Much would be made from the harvest. Hides would be transformed into moccasins, clothes, and almost impenetrable medicine shields. Sinew taken from the large tendon close to the backbone would be used for sewing. Bones would be made into clubs, eating utensils, and glue. Even the buffalo's hair would be woven into rope.

Soon excitement and trepidation filled the men's hearts as they formed a circle. Lighthearted discussion turned serious as they carefully planned their coordinated hunting strategy. Buffalo hunting was dangerous. Flaming Arrow declared that Flying Crow would be the main strategist. Even though it was his first time being leader of the hunt, his word would be law. Anyone not obeying would be severely punished. This discipline would ensure that every man and family would receive a fair chance at obtaining needed food.

The cold northern winds stabbed Brave Eagle's skin as he checked the notches on his arrow shaft. Satisfied his weapon would bring lightning speed and power, he relaxed. A good bow determined whether a man lived or died on the hunt. Brave Eagle watched Bear prepare his hunting equipment. He was proud to have such a loyal friend. They would work as partners on the hunt and be successful in providing food for their families.

Stars twinkled as nightfall arrived. People spread out hides of buffalo bedding and slept in the grass. Soft glowing fires fueled from buffalo dung lined the countryside. This was a deeply spiritual time. Anticipation of the hunt caused Brave Eagle to grow restless. He walked toward Dawn Star, who was drinking tea by her family fire. She looked beautiful in the moonlight, her black hair flowing flawlessly. Her almond-shaped eyes shone with vitality and excitement as she flirted with him. All the women of her family had the same beautiful eyes, and Dawn Star was no exception. They could be traced through generations. She looked so much like his first wife, Two Moons, now that she was grown. It was as if his dead wife stared up at him.

Although Dawn Star acted shyly, Brave Eagle knew she possessed a strength that was to be respected. He signaled her to meet him out in the darkness. Once they were on the prairie, Dawn Star slipped her hand in his. Gazing at the sky, Dawn Star cooed, "I cannot wait for the hunt. How good it will be to have fresh meat. The winds make me shiver."

Brave Eagle gently placed his robe around her. He closed his eyes as his chin rested upon her. His arms encased her strong and youthful body. She reminded him of a common childhood experience, and they both laughed. Brave Eagle turned to look at her.

Dawn Star's laughter ceased. She said, "You are wearing a cross? That is not our way. Things were as they should be until that captive came along. That is a bastard child she carries." Dawn Star paused to look lovingly at Brave Eagle. "Perhaps my aunt Walks Far will help her; she knows all the herbs for every problem, and she is so careful." Brave

Eagle looked at her waiting for more explanation, but Dawn Star just smiled. He gently kissed behind her ear and moved across her neck until he found her lips.

They shared a long passionate moment in the night. As the buffalo robe slipped down to the ground, Dawn Star moaned, "You are a strong and honorable man. I long for the time when we will be together."

Brave Eagle eagerly responded to Dawn Star. They kissed and spoke of promises of love. When they came back to camp, Bear walked past them. He said, "You two are a handsome pair," and winked at Brave Eagle.

The next morning the sun gleamed ribbons of reds and oranges over the land. Purple hues lit up the hills in the background. It was very quiet with the exception of the children, who ran around playing with small bows and arrows, pretending to hunt. The men prepared for the next buffalo sighting.

Brave Eagle finished painting the upper portion of his face black. He dipped his fingertips into the paint bowl and added four stripes over Kallie's nail marks on his cheek. With this simple gesture, he turned his original humiliation into honor of her catlike spirit. He could use the stalking skills of the mountain lion in addition to his own animal totems.

With rope of braided buffalo hair, he tied three eagle feathers onto Wind Racer's tail. He painted yellow lightning bolts that extended from Wind Racer's rump to his hooves. These marks would impart the speed and power needed to chase down many bulls. Brave Eagle tied a secure knot on Wind Racer's hunting bridle. Coiling the excess rope, he tucked it under his belt. The extra rope would give him a chance if he were toppled from his horse. There would be danger of being trampled by bulls in a stampede. Feeling excited, Brave Eagle stood tall and strong. He was ready.

The hunters followed the scouts to a canyon. When they reached the edge, they saw a herd of buffalo grazing below. A group of young bulls attempted to join the herd and skimmed along the outer edges. Bulls surrounded cows that nervously picked up their heads to listen and smell.

111

Everyone smiled in jubilation at the tremendous hunting opportunities. The men grouped together according to plan. Flying Crow said, "Brave Eagle, take a group of men on the sunrise side of the canyon. When the signal is given, you and your men rush the herd. Get them running in circles." Flying Crow waited for every man to give him a sign of agreement, and then he looked at the other group. "Short Bull, you and the others surround the herd as it stampedes toward the sunset side of the canyon. The older men and younger boys will follow Short Bull. Wait for his signal."

Flying Crow warned the eager younger hunters, "Hunt only the young buffalo—the orphans or the two teeth. Stay clear of the bulls." Then scanning the herd formation, Flying Crow concluded, "When the herd has dispersed and run away, stop to check that all wounded animals have been killed. Only after that will I signal the women to begin the butchering."

Flying Crow jumped on his horse. "Remember—the spirits of our forefathers accompany us. Let's go."

The hunters descended into the canyon. Before the dust had settled, each group had secured its position. Adrenaline pumped through every hunter's veins, and their excitement could barely be contained. Flying Crow gave the signal by waving a buffalo robe.

A sea of brown stampeded in the planned direction. Brave Eagle clamped down on his horse's flank. Dropping back to the edge of the stampede, Brave Eagle took his first shot at a mighty bull. He released one arrow and then another until the wounded creature collapsed. Acting on raw instinct, Brave Eagle leaped from Wind Racer and shouted, "Yahoo."

As Brave Eagle slit the animal's throat, he offered prayers of gratitude to the Great Spirit. He wiped the bloody knife across his leggings and extracted his arrows from the carcass. The wind was cold, but sweat dripped from his body. Most of the herd had dispersed and was stampeding north as planned. Buffalo carcasses were scattered everywhere, but his remaining arrow clearly marked this carcass. His catch, in addition to the kills of his father and brother, would feed their extended family through the winter. Flying Crow signaled the younger men to pursue wounded stragglers. Brave Eagle ignored this opportunity and instead searched for Bear. It was unusual that Bear was not close by his side. Brave Eagle cleared the knoll. His feelings of triumph quickly turned to panic. A wounded buffalo had toppled Bear off his horse. The horse was running wildly in circles, dragging Bear by its tether rope. The massive bull was charging, its hooves landing perilously close to Bear's head.

Brave Eagle rode frantically toward the raging bull. His throat constricted as he yelled out Bear's name in anguish. Sweat mixed with war paint dripped into his eyes, making them burn. Stretching his bowstring, he released his last two arrows. One entered just under the buffalo's eye and wedged in its skull, but it did not kill him. Instead, the frenzied bull stopped and snorted at his new opponent.

It was an impressive bull with a height of at least seven feet. Its broad shoulders were mountains of muscle. Tensed from rushing adrenalin, its huge head was down; its eyes were bloodshot with anger. Its nostrils were enlarged and steamed vapors as he exhaled. Aroused, the wounded animal was an awesome sight as it charged. Even though Brave Eagle's last arrow had pierced its heart, the great beast's body continued forward. With astounding tenacity, the creature turned under Wind Racer and toppled him. As Brave Eagle fell, the bull's large horn gouged him through his rib cage.

Brave Eagle yelled out in pain. As he lapsed into unconsciousness, he saw visions of Kallie. Her pretty eyes shone as she sat cross-legged at her lodge fire. A burning sensation soon brought him back to a painful reality. He grabbed his stomach and felt warm blood gushing out over his fingers. Struggling, he eventually managed to slide out from underneath the bull's massive head.

Dazed, Brave Eagle crawled over to the immobile Bear, who grimaced in excruciating pain. When Brave Eagle surveyed the extent of the damage, he knew the situation was grave. He spoke a few words of comfort to Bear but realized that Bear's contorted leg was badly broken. It hung in a most unnatural position. The femur was poking through swollen, purplish skin.

Weasel Tail took one quick look at him and Bear and then immediately rode away to summon help. Women came quickly with travois. Struggling, Winter Grass Woman finally caught up to the other women. An elder, she was skilled with medicine and immediately assessed the condition of the wounded men. She said, "I cannot set Bear's leg. This is a complicated break. Even a small error will cause him to be crippled for the rest of his life or, even worse, kill him."

A woman asked, "What can we do? There must be something."

Winter Grass Woman said, "Lost Buffalo and Yellow Willow have the experience to provide the best treatment. I can only hope Bear will survive the trip back to winter camp."

She then approached Brave Eagle. Calmly, she applied pressure to his wound to stop the profuse bleeding. She said, "This is a gaping wound and your ribs are broken, but the organs seem intact and are not severed. You should heal if fever doesn't set in."

Winter Grass Woman turned her attention to stabilizing Bear's broken leg. Brave Eagle heard the old woman instruct Pretty Shield to finish cleaning and bandaging his wound. He saw his father and Black Hand rush upon the scene. Flaming Arrow said, "They are still alive, but we cannot stop the hunt for anyone's injury, even my own son's."

Black Hand agreed. "Timing is crucial. We must harvest more buffalo while the hunting is good. Time is short before the herd scatters. What do you propose to do?"

Flaming Arrow answered, "You will assist Flying Crow while I transport Brave Eagle and Bear back to the wintering grounds. There they will have the best chance for survival."

Black Hand replied, "That is a dangerous thing to do. We need you here."

Flaming Arrow said, "Yes, but this is my firstborn son. You must lead the hunt without me. I will discuss this no more. It is time for the women to butcher." Flaming Arrow addressed Pretty Shield. "Make the needed preparations."

Lost Buffalo's son Short Bull said, "I will go with you to winter camp. I can help with the wounded."

Black Hand nodded in agreement and shouted, "Women, go back to your harvesting. Men, continue to hunt strays and make sure all of the wounded animals are killed. Brave Eagle and Bear will be well cared for."

Brave Eagle felt Flaming Arrow and Short Bull lift him onto a travel travois and, under Pretty Shield's supervision, rope him securely into place. Dawn Star covered him with an extra-thick buffalo robe and grasped his hand. Brave Eagle knew injury from the seasonal hunt was a reality that every generation had experienced. Hunting buffalo was exhilarating but could turn deadly.

As Dawn Star gazed down at him, a tear rolled from her cheek and fell on his face. He saw that the other women had quickly and efficiently continued with the huge task of butchering. Although saddened by the accident, they spoke out loud and thanked the Great Spirit for the bountiful harvest. After throwing large pieces of the rich meat into fresh skins, the women sliced off chunks from warm, steaming livers. Now they could eat.

Every breath caused Brave Eagle searing pain. He tried to smile at Dawn Star and his mother to say good-bye, but he could not. Then Flaming Arrow and Short Bull guided the horse that pulled him toward winter camp. Every jerk and oscillation sent him into pain until unconsciousness granted him relief.

Brave Eagle regained consciousness when the men stopped to care for Bear or feed the horses. They traveled throughout the night and following days. Flaming Arrow and Short Bull did not slow the pace. Brave Eagle knew expediency was Bear's only hope. He looked to Short Bull or Flaming Arrow for some sign of reassurance, but he received none. Flaming Arrow mercilessly drove the horses toward winter camp and kept telling Bear that Lost Buffalo and Yellow Willow would know what to do.

Negotiating the terrain was difficult. Every jerk of the travois sent Bear into spasms of severe pain until he was too weak to react. Brave Eagle shivered endlessly. Short Bull had tried to force Brave Eagle to swallow medicinal drops, but he had spit them out. Impatient, Flaming Arrow shouted, "Short Bull, we are wasting valuable time. We must drive on."

Brave Eagle went in and out of consciousness but was elated when he saw a glow emitting from Lost Buffalo's winter lodge. It signaled the end of their long struggle. Competing with the wind, Short Bull shouted, "Father, Mother, come help us! Quick, we have wounded." Brave Eagle rejoiced at seeing Lost Buffalo and Yellow Willow emerge ready to help, as though they had been waiting for them. Other elders had heard the commotion and gathered, but Brave Eagle did not see Kallie. Walks Far eagerly grabbed the fresh meat packed on the horses, announcing she would prepare a meal.

Lost Buffalo pointed to the medicinal tepee and commanded, "Move the men in there. Yellow Willow, hurry and stoke the fire."

Once Brave Eagle was inside, he heard Yellow Willow say, "Kallie's premonition came true. Just as Lost Buffalo said, she possesses a magical gift. She can see in the darkness."

The other women did not react to Yellow Willow's statement but turned to help him and Bear. They cut away the men's bloody clothing and bandages. Next, with steaming-hot water they cleansed the gaping wounds. They applied yarrow poultices to relieve swelling. For the first time, Brave Eagle felt relief and comfort.

Under Yellow Willow's directions, a decoction of sweet flag and purple coneflower tea was administered to Bear. Brave Eagle knew this would lessen Bear's fever. Bear grimaced and yelled out. Shock waves of pain seemed to pulsate throughout Bear's body at the slightest touch. Brave Eagle waited for Lost Buffalo's diagnosis and prayed Bear would survive and be able to walk again.

Brave Eagle could barely swallow drops of a tincture made from willow bark and valerian that Yellow Willow administered. She anxiously watched his reaction and explained, "This tincture will relieve the pain if your stomach can tolerate it." Brave Eagle knew that if he could not keep the medicine down, the wound was deep and had ruptured his stomach. He would soon know the prognosis.

Brave Eagle stared at his father but did not respond to any spoken word. His father, Flaming Arrow, warmed and shook his bare hands as if to restore feeling to them. His father looked old and deeply concerned. Brave Eagle wanted to ask about Kallie and her whereabouts, but he could not speak. His eyes had gone blurry, and he felt dangerously fatigued. His usual fighting spirit had vanished.

Chapter 17: *Caring for the Wounded*

Pikiciya: To Make One Well

Kallie woke and heard a commotion. She followed Yellow Willow's voice and entered the healing tepee. Her premonition had come true. Brave Eagle and Bear were injured. While women irrigated Brave Eagle's wound to remove any debris and contaminants, Kallie assessed his condition. He was breathing from both sides of his chest evenly, so his lungs were not punctured. The skin around the wound showed no sign of rot or significant tissue loss. Besides broken ribs, there didn't seem to be any structural damage, although the gash was opened and bleeding. Tricky stitching would be needed to properly close the nasty cut. It wasn't the wound but Brave Eagle's blank expression that alarmed her. There was no sign of life in his eyes. Was it possible he had sustained another head injury?

Bear's grotesque leg caused her to despair. The leg's swollen bend was colored with an angry shade of purple. She had helped Millicent set leg bones before but never one of such distortion. Helpless, she hoped that Lost Buffalo or Yellow Willow could set it properly.

Lost Buffalo consulted with Yellow Willow and Hawk Woman about what to do. Standing beyond Bear's hearing, he whispered, "I can set Bear's leg, but he will have a bad limp the rest of his days. His warrior days will be over. However, there is a chance I could try twisting the leg to make the broken bones match better. It is riskier and more painful. It might take several attempts. We would need everyone's strength just to hold him still. I am not sure about this."

Breaking the uncomfortable silence, Kallie said, "Bear would want us to try to make him walk without a limp." Lost Buffalo looked at her, unconvinced, so she explained, "Bear wants to marry Running Brook. There is no other way."

Lost Buffalo inquired, "Kallie, have you ever fixed such a break?"

Kallie reported, "No." She remembered that, back home, her neighbor Millicent had fixed a similar break once. It had been a tremendous risk since the sharp ends of the broken bone could have caused internal damage. Millicent had twisted and pulled the leg back into its natural position while several men held the victim. The struggle had turned out to be worth it, for the young man barely limped after the break had healed.

Lost Buffalo knelt down to examine Bear's leg once more before making a final decision. Closing his eyes, his outstretched hands scanned Bear's entire body. His hands remained above the skin, never touching the leg. He paused over the fracture site for several minutes. Then, troubled by his rheumatic back, Lost Buffalo stood up. He commanded, "Get Flaming Arrow and Short Bull. We will need more women to hold him down."

When everyone was assembled, Lost Buffalo began. He instructed Yellow Willow, "Gently pull Bear's leg while I position it so the bone ends match. This will take both strength and gentle guidance. You will feel when the leg offers the right resistance. I will be moving it this way, and you will move his leg down. It must be fast, and we must work as one." Then Lost Buffalo paused and inquired, "Kallie, can you assist Yellow Willow if she needs help?" Kallie nodded yes.

Bear was delirious but managed to bite on a stick. Flaming Arrow, Short Bull, and several women steadied him. Bear was a strong man, and it would take all their strength to contain him. It helped that he was losing consciousness. Looking tense, Lost Buffalo began the procedure. Grimacing, Yellow Willow pulled while Lost Buffalo expertly twisted the leg. Bear cried for mercy while others struggled to stabilize him.

Obviously shaken, Lost Buffalo was not successful the first time. Drops of perspiration ran down the old medicine man's wrinkled face. Strands of his gray hair stuck in sweat on his forehead. Powerless, Kallie stood behind Yellow Willow and tried to block out Bear's screams. Yellow Willow's steadfast determination gave Lost Buffalo no chance to surrender. He attempted to set the break a second time. Amid Bear's screams, Yellow Willow coaxed Lost Buffalo, "Just a little more. It feels right. Yes, we have it!"

After they bridged the bone, they made a strong, temporary brace. The women lifted themselves off Bear as his tremors calmed. Compresses were immediately applied, and Hawk Woman forced drops of purple coneflower and willow bark down his throat. Lost Buffalo chanted healing songs while moving smoking cottonwood bark around the tepee. His song allowed Lost Buffalo to combine the spirit of the wood with Bear's natural strength. This would enable the leg to become strong once again.

When the excruciating procedure was done, most of the elders left for a meal of stew. Yellow Willow, shaking from fatigue, showed Kallie a container. Tiny bone needles and sinew thread were soaking in a hot green liquid. Yellow Willow said, "Brave Eagle's lungs are not punctured, but his wound has been opened many times. Stitches will make it heal faster. My hands are shaking. I will help Flaming Arrow hold Brave Eagle steady. Can you do this?"

Kallie nodded yes. Millicent had taught her how to sew up people, and she had done so many times. Kallie threaded the needle and tied the proper knot to facilitate healing. The wound was irregular and jagged, so the corners needed to be secured.

She drove the needle in. Brave Eagle grimaced with each stab of the needle but was immobilized by his father's hold. The gash was deep enough that she needed to match layers of muscle and skin. She avoided the temptation to place numerous closures, which could pool up with blood and cause festering.

Ignoring Brave Eagle's gasping, Kallie worked steadily, never taking her eyes off the wound. When the inner cut was closed, she sutured a new set of stitches on the surface. Stitches were placed so that no gap appeared and the skin edges just touched each other. It was a nasty jagged rip, but she expertly made a corner stitch to hold it. Kallie sewed several clean stitches that had little tension. This method would preserve blood flow to the wound edge. The rest of the cut was angular, and it took several sutures to cover the full length of the wound.

As she stitched, Kallie thought about her complicated relationship with Brave Eagle. Her internal thoughts began with distrust. His lack of spirit meant he had turned away from her. He had left her completely. He had not fought to keep her. Kallie's hands were red with blood, so she could not wipe her tears away. As she tied a square knot using two throws, anger washed over her. She pulled up more tightly than needed, causing Brave Eagle to cry out. Shocked at her own carelessness, she avoided Yellow Willow's stare.

Soon there was nothing left to do but let the wounded sleep. Kallie, Yellow Willow, Short Bull, and Flaming Arrow left for Walks Far's lodge. Walks Far welcomed them. "Come in. Come in. Have a warm meal."

After they finished eating, Yellow Willow said, "Kallie did a good job of stitching."

Caustically, Walks Far replied, "The captive might be good at sewing a wound but is even better at eating up our precious food supply."

Light-headed, Kallie sat down to sip her tea. Walks Far pointed at her belly and asked, "Where does the baby come from? How can you take care of a baby? Aren't you afraid someone will take it from you?"

Shaken, Kallie shook her head. "I don't know."

The other women broke into nervous giggles at such an embarrassing confrontation. Subdued, Kallie clutched her belly and moved closer to Yellow Willow. She did not trust Walks Far. The woman had quickly found Kallie's weakness and had used it against her. Apprehensive, she began to wonder whether the tribe would take her baby if it turned out to be Brave Eagle's.

After a long silence, Yellow Willow politely explained that they needed to leave. Kallie escaped Walks Far's wrath by quickly following. Yellow Willow's tepee was a refuge for Kallie. She sewed on Lost Buffalo's shirt until she was sure no one was approaching. Then in secret, she opened the rawhide bag containing her meager possessions. She shook out a precious vial from the hem of her old dress. Its clear glass revealed the last drops of her mother's perfume. The sweet lavender scent reminded her of her ma and memories a lifetime ago. Trembling, she smeared the last drops upon her neck and breasts, breathing in the precious vapors. Her baby kicked. Kallie prayed that somehow Lost Buffalo and Yellow Willow would protect her. She hid in the tepee until Yellow Willow instructed her to check the wounded.

When she entered the healing tepee, she noted that Bear was sleeping peacefully. Flaming Arrow sat in the corner, his stalwart expression revealing nothing about his feelings. He would not look up. Finally, he left, and she concentrated on Brave Eagle. His cool, clammy forehead revealed his worsening condition. He was growing colder. As Kallie bent over to place a warm compress on his forehead, Brave Eagle opened his eyes. He grabbed her arm. Shocked, she awkwardly tried to turn away, but Brave Eagle pulled her down toward him. His strong hands would not let go of her. Instead of resisting him, she closed her eyes and gently massaged his neck. His breathing remained shallow, and he became very still. Frightened, Kallie closed her eyes and prayed he would survive. Maybe if he survived, then she and the baby would too.

Kallie fell into Brave Eagle's arms. She felt so comfortable. A soft glow from the fire illuminated the tepee walls while the prairie winds blasted outside. She felt the baby move. The low hum of Bear's snoring filled the last sounds of the evening. She drifted back to peaceful slumber.

Early in the morning, a piercing wail woke them from their sleep. Brave Eagle appeared panicked but became calmer when his father said, "It is just the sound of the wind. The cold air is blasting underneath the tepee underskirt. It smells of snow, although it is too early for a blizzard. No wonder the buffalo are acting strange this season." Bear snored in the corner. Flaming Arrow said, "Ah, my son, you are breathing better, and your skin color is healthier."

Brave Eagle held her tightly underneath the robe, and she heard him say, "Father, I had such a bad dream. I was struggling in blackness. My spirit was unprotected as I walked. I was not of the living. There were no problems and no pain. I rested because my body felt so tired; I could not resist the pull of black stillness enveloping me. I drifted deeper and deeper into the abyss until I caught the slightest scent of lavender. Startled at the scent, I opened my eyes to realize there was no color to the earth and sky. The wind held no sensation; I could not feel even the gentlest of prairie breezes. I was in the Valley of the Dead. My mind fought its way back to the living guided by the smell of lavender."

His father replied, "You are here with us now. Save your breath for breathing." Then Flaming Arrow lifted the buffalo robe where Kallie was hiding. His eyes grew large when he discovered that Brave Eagle was holding her. He asked his son, "Why are you so protective of her? Do you not understand your obligations to Dawn Star and her family? Dawn Star's relations have been more than patient in waiting for you to marry again. You cannot turn your back on tribal traditions."

Kallie watched Brave Eagle try to say something, but instead he closed his eyes. Flaming Arrow continued to ask questions out loud. "Why would Lost Buffalo allow this situation? None of this makes any sense to me, and yet nobody else seems confused. No one can know what has happened here. If Pretty Shield should ever find out, there will be no peace in my life."

Bear's moans interrupted Flaming Arrow's musings. Flaming Arrow turned to Bear and said, "I will go get Yellow Willow and Lost Buffalo to help you."

Chapter 18: *Feeling the Closeness of Another*

Wo canteiyapaya: With a Beating Heart

Kallie hugged Brave Eagle until she heard Yellow Willow's demands to dress. She was startled, but not even Yellow Willow's anger could destroy her happiness. Brave Eagle's coloring had greatly improved, and her spirit soared because of it. Yellow Willow pointed at the exit and said, "Go far and collect firewood by the river. Say nothing about this to anyone! Leave immediately."

Kallie looked over her shoulder before running to the river path. When she was clear of Yellow Willow's angry eyes, she whistled for the young dog Running Brook had given her. Kallie had named him Fella. The dog had become a constant companion to her and yelped for attention. Kallie quickly hushed him.

Crusty ice had formed at the river's edge, and the current bumped against it. More leery of scornful gossip than of cold winds, Kallie stayed outside and collected a huge pile of sticks from the icy waters. The brisk wind rushed through her hair, and she smiled. Finally, she trudged back to Yellow Willow's tepee to deliver a bigger load than usual as a peace offering, but only Lost Buffalo and Flaming Arrow were there. Flaming Arrow said nothing but openly stared at her. This made her feel strange because he had never paid any attention to her before. The situation became uncomfortable until Yellow Willow returned. She invited Flaming Arrow to stay and commanded Kallie to make tea. Kallie, happy to escape their attention, gladly prepared it.

Lost Buffalo sheepishly avoided Yellow Willow's angry looks by explaining to Flaming Arrow, "I am not feeling well. My back is acting up, so I couldn't help my wife this morning. Flaming Arrow, come, sit, and enjoy some tea." Lost Buffalo coughed and asked, "How are the wounded?"

Yellow Willow answered, "As well as can be expected. I got there in time. It was before any of the other women had come."

Lost Buffalo smiled. "Then it is a good omen indeed."

Accepting tea, Flaming Arrow looked confused. There was an awkward pause in the conversation. Then he asked, "Lost Buffalo, are you to be a father once again?"

Lost Buffalo choked on his swallow of tea and said, "My friend, you give me much credit on my abilities, but I am an old man. The white woman is like a daughter to me. I look out for her. That is what the spirits tell me to do. After the child is born, I will find a husband for her. It will not be easy, but Yellow Willow and I are too old to raise a child. Kallie must be matched up." As he laughed, Lost Buffalo shook his head. "The child is not mine."

The uncomfortable silence was broken by the sounds of chattering women coming their way. Entering the tepee, Walks Far commented, "Flaming Arrow, what has happened? You look ill. Is it something Yellow Willow has fed you?"

The other women pretended not to hear the sarcasm in Walks Far's voice and immediately left for the healing tepee. Yellow Willow instructed, "Kallie, come with me. Bring the medicine of willow bark mixed with dried cornflowers. Bear will be needing this soon. Let's go give it to him."

When they arrived, Kallie diluted the herbs with water and then told Bear, "Drink this. It will help the leg pain subside."

To help him relax, Yellow Willow rubbed Bear's tender shoulders. Pouring oil steeped in dried marigolds and yarrow onto her hands, Yellow Willow pressed into his tense muscles so vigorously that Bear politely asked her to stop.

Brave Eagle sipped a nourishing broth. He grimaced and told the gathering group of women, "This churns in my stomach, but I have to eat in order to gain strength."

Walks Far said, "Yes, the sooner you regain your vitality, the sooner you can ride back to the hunt."

Brave Eagle looked at Flaming Arrow and Short Bull and asked, "Can you help me up?"

Yellow Willow cried, "No, you'll rip out your stitches."

Brave Eagle ignored her and addressed the men. "Help me stand."

The men steadied Brave Eagle as he took his first steps since the accident. Grimacing in pain, Brave Eagle limped outside to relieve himself.

Flaming Arrow watched his son walk and said, "He is getting stronger." Everyone in the tepee agreed.

The next morning, Yellow Willow instructed Kallie to accompany her to the sweat lodge. Kallie could tell by Yellow Willow's looks that she was still in trouble. But even though Yellow Willow's anger hurt, Kallie's encounter with Brave Eagle in the healing tepee had been worth it. She vowed to herself that next time she would be clever and not get caught.

Once they were safely inside the lodge and away from prying ears, Yellow Willow scolded, "There are eyes in camp waiting to pounce on you. It is not wise for a woman who is carrying a child to disobey. If you break tribal rules, people will blame you or your child when things go bad. And something always goes wrong. I will not be able to protect you. Now take a bath. I will tell the other women the steam is ready."

Kallie sighed with relief. Maybe now the matter could rest.

In the evening, elders gathered in the healing tepee and passed the smoking pipe late into the night. When Kallie inhaled the smoke, it caused dizziness. The baby kicked frantically, so she politely passed it on. It was enough just to be fed and be close to Brave Eagle. She watched the men's expressions. Flaming Arrow looked worried and distracted. Bear seemed content listening to the elders' stories. Brave Eagle rested quietly and appeared to be in a good mood. He told everyone, "I soon will be well enough to hunt with the other men." Then he paused and looked at her with eyes that sparkled in the fire's glow.

Bear sipped his tea, cleared his throat, and said, "I have a story to tell. Seven summers after the winter of the Star Showers, during the Red Strawberry Moon, my mother and I traveled to the Peace Council. My blood tribe, the Arapaho, all had gathered there."

125

Bear continued, "My main job was to watch our band's horses as they grazed along the river. Each horse was identified by a mark, but there were thousands of horses at the height of the council gathering. Several other boys shared this task, and we bragged about our riding abilities. All of us had learned to ride even before we could walk.

"It was there that I met Brave Eagle, whose name at that time was Little Wolf. He was a few winters older than I. He was from the tribe my mother and I would soon be joining.

"Little Wolf and I debated our prowess and challenged each other to a horse race. The other boys gathered to watch our race. I tied my bridle with a strong knot and looped it around my favorite horse's lower jaw to form a bit. We gathered willow branches for whips, but there really was no need, for our horses loved to run. Little Wolf and I led our ponies to a clearing.

"The race would include a side gallop, which meant hanging off the side of our horses and reaching down to swoop up a buckskin bag placed close to the riverbank. Little Wolf wanted to gamble on the race, but I refused. This confused him, but I did not know how to explain that gambling would never become a habit of mine.

"A flag was waved to start the race. Off we rode at a pounding pace as dust clouds obscured the spectators' view. Circling the course several times, I followed Little Wolf's lead and hung by my horse's side, catching just a fringe of my bag but enough to grab hold. Little Wolf also made a successful grab on his first try. It was apparent we were equally matched in skill, so we decided to stop to prevent unnecessary stress on our horses.

"Then, to show off, I grabbed my horse's neck, hung from the other side, and placed the bag on the original spot. Making a quick pass around the circle, I attempted to grab the bag from the other side. My horse broke his stride, threw me off like a swatted fly, and sent me plunging into the river. The slap of my body entering the water was nothing compared to my embarrassment. The whole crowd ran to the bank, staring in disbelief. Little Wolf, completely covered in sweat and dust, jumped in. After learning I was okay, he extended his hand to help me up. Together, we broke into laughter and climbed up the bank. It was a story we shall tell for years to come, the story of how our friendship began." Bear smiled as he finished.

Kallie tried to look interested in the stories, although she did not understand them. She politely laughed when the others did. After stories, music of flutes, rattles, and drums filled the space. Brave Eagle played his flute. As she closed her eyes, his tender notes made her blush inside. She knew the song was hers even if others listened to it. Even though Walks Far scrutinized their every move, Brave Eagle subtly brushed by her in the midst of everyone. Kallie did not care about disapproval and would risk everything just to be with him. She smiled at him in front of the older women.

Brave Eagle sat near her and told the last tale of the evening. "The morning after the big race, Bear and I slipped away from camp. We rode south, embracing the morning sounds and enjoying the cool breezes. We stopped at the place where the prairie grasses met the trees of the Dark Hills.

"We climbed up to a protruding rock ledge that served as a lookout. We waited, and after no game appeared, we devised a plan. We would bring the game to us. I had mastered the cry of a wounded rabbit. It was so convincing we decided I would mimic the cries of a jackrabbit to bring in a predator.

"While I called, Bear hid in the tall buffalo grass and prepared his bow with arrows. His bowstring and the arrow shaft rested upon his hand. His eyes were focused, and Bear was ready.

"Feeling confident, I continued with rabbit calls. I changed the intensity of the high-pitched mimics and then sometimes remained silent. Both of us were very patient, and the winds were working in our favor. A predator would not catch a scent of us.

"By late afternoon, we were tiring, but we heard a rustle in the bushes; something was moving toward us. I intensified my calls, and Bear steadied his bow. Imagine … out of the vegetation came a huge black bear searching for the wounded rabbit. A male bear that had come from the hills was going to attack … me!

"Bear stood his ground, but he was shaking so the arrow he released only grazed the bear's shoulder. This action caused the beast to roar with anger. The bear stood on its rear legs, making him appear twice his original size. His gaping mouth revealed dagger teeth, and his sharp claws were like knives. It was an amazing sight. Bear shot off his arrows, one right after the other, into the bear's chest. At first they had no effect, but then, in a mighty crash, the bear came down on all fours. It landed close to me. I had been knocked down in the confusion and was trapped underneath one of the black bear's arms. I heard a combination of Bear's yelling and the bear's deafening roar as he shot off the last arrows in rapid fire."

Brave Eagle paused until Bear took over the storytelling. "One of my arrows had pierced the bear's neck artery, and it was bleeding profusely. Relief washed over me until, in horror, I realized I had not only killed my first bear but also had shot Little Wolf, the chief's eldest son, in the behind. Little Wolf was moaning as I ran up to him. There were bloody claw marks all over his back, and the arrow shaft with my marks was protruding from his buttocks. He was not bleeding too badly, but he was in pain.

"Before we made it back to the village, we pulled out our hunting knives. Little Wolf dipped his blade and drew blood from my finger, and I did the same to his. Merging our red, dripping blood, we vowed to be blood brothers forever.

"The guards spotted us and yelled to the others. Little Wolf's mother, Pretty Shield, had been worried and hurried to help her son. Many of Little Wolf's relatives gathered and observed my Arapaho arrow lodged in his butt."

Then Brave Eagle passed the pipe and finished. "After the people heard our story, the tension of the moment dissipated. Our uncles accompanied us back to the hunting site. There we skinned the bear and carried the meat, skin, and claws back to camp. The next night, Bear and I were invited into the warriors' tepee to tell our story and smoke among the men. Later that year, during a vision quest, my friend was given the name of Bear. Lost Buffalo said the name represented a great hunt and becoming a man. And so this is how Bear came to the land of his adopted tribe and became a man and also a blood brother."

After the story, everyone left for the night, including Kallie. Kallie shot a passing, longing look at Brave Eagle. He slightly nodded his head. So, when Lost Buffalo and Yellow Willow were sleeping soundly, Kallie made her move. She was sorry about losing Yellow Willow's trust, but she longed for Brave Eagle. Leaving her sleeping robe so it looked like she was still there, Kallie sternly made Fella lie on her bed. Sliding under the loosened tepee lining, she was free and left undetected. Brave Eagle sat in a makeshift chair as if he was waiting for her. He embraced her, and she reciprocated, holding him close. Kallie applied sage oil to her hands and, being careful not to aggravate his injury, kneaded the tightened muscles along his neck and around his shoulders. Playfully, she tickled the back of his arms. She loved his lean arms of hardened, sinuous muscle. Her massage ended with soft touches converging on his lower back. She ran her fingers through his hair and affectionately pulled his earlobes.

Picturing his wound perfectly healed, she placed her hands above him. The heat from her hands penetrated his back. She thought about how wonderful life would be if only he would claim her and the baby. Brave Eagle held the power to make both her and the baby's lives safe. It was as if her thoughts broke the romantic spell, for Brave Eagle became fidgety. But then his gaze met hers, searching lips found each other, and they kissed passionately. Kallie was totally enthralled, wanting more, wanting all of him. She held on to him as he slowly moved to her. They were lost in time until Brave Eagle jumped. Kallie quickly looked at the entrance, expecting Yellow Willow's wrath.

Instead she saw Brave Eagle's moccasin trim smoking from the fire coals. He awkwardly stood and stomped it out in the dirt. They both shook with quiet laughter and collapsed onto the buffalo robes. Brave Eagle played with the ties on Kallie's buckskin dress until it fell, revealing her swollen breasts. Her loose hair rested upon her shoulders.

Brave Eagle knelt down, drawing her close. She felt his pulsing desire. His eager hands caressed her, and her swollen belly protruded against him. His lips ravished her body as if tasting her. She closed her eyes as sensual feelings engulfed her, and she pushed against the hardness of his body. She felt protected by his strength. The baby stirred inside of her, nestled in between them. She relaxed only after his heavy breathing subsided. His lips brushed lightly past hers. If only, she thought, every night could be like this.

In the dimming glow of the fire, Brave Eagle's kisses caressed Kallie's throat. His power necklace rested between her breasts, and she imagined it protected both her and the baby. As he held her close, she prayed he would never let her go. The tepee wall reflected their merging silhouettes until the first hint of dawn.

Kallie quietly slipped back into her tepee just before the sun's first rays rose upon the horizon. She squirmed under her robe, tired but ecstatic. Brave Eagle's embraces still warmed her. Every part of her felt alive, passionate, and ready for more. His scent lingered on her body. Soon it would be time for her to start morning chores, so she needed to stay awake. If she were not the first one up, Yellow Willow would be suspicious.

Morning arrived, and Kallie woke to Yellow Willow having to repeatedly shake her. Avoiding Yellow Willow's questioning eyes, Kallie grabbed a water container and rushed out. Billowing clouds streamed colors of yellows and purples upon the land. She took a moment to absorb the sight and compose herself for any probing from Yellow Willow. On the way back from the river, she encountered Brave Eagle standing against the rising sun. He acknowledged her by a simple nod as he walked her home. Kallie hurried in to make tea.

Kallie relaxed when nothing was discovered about the night before. Yellow Willow was busy storing cattails in the healing tepee. Kallie could not image what Yellow Willow was doing with so many cattails. The other women, deep in conversation, ignored her. She sat in the corner and finished the skin shirt for Lost Buffalo. Although the shirt was plain without beads, the stitches were straight, and it would function well. She proudly folded it and placed it prominently upon Lost Buffalo's bed.

Desperate to be away from the gossiping women, Kallie escaped them by collecting wood. Walking with Fella, she laughed at his perpetually wagging tail. Finally, away from prying eyes, she replayed the memory of her night with Brave Eagle. She fantasized about her next meeting with him as she threw sticks for Fella. Clutching her robe, she twirled in circles. Perhaps as the night approached, she could escape into his arms once more. She could not wait for another opportunity. As she looked back, she saw Flaming Arrow enter her tepee and wondered if Brave Eagle was also coming.

When Kallie entered the tepee, all was quiet except for the fire's crackle and Lost Buffalo's persistent coughs. Flaming Arrow said, "Lost Buffalo, I am restless. Now that Brave Eagle and Bear are gaining strength, I can think about rejoining the hunt. Tomorrow, I will travel. It is time to go back, and Short Bull will accompany me."

Lost Buffalo asked, "Are you sure it is wise to travel? The weather is changing. It feels like an early blizzard is coming, and traveling during the first storms can be deadly."

Flaming Arrow nodded his head yes and mumbled something Kallie could not make out. Whatever was said, Lost Buffalo seemed to agree.

Lost Buffalo said, "Traveling this time of year can be dangerous, so let us prepare for your journey. Cleanse yourself with sage smoke." Then Lost Buffalo beat away evil spirits with his powerful drumming and sang a song of protection.

Afterward, Lost Buffalo told Kallie, "Give the shirt you have made for me to Flaming Arrow. He can give it to Brave Eagle. It has no beadwork and I, as a medicine man, need many fancy beads. Do this as a favor for me."

Flaming Arrow took the shirt, rolled it up, placed it under his arm, and departed. Upon the news of their impending departure, the elders huddled in the healing tepee to share a last meal with the men.

Kallie was happy that there was food and entertainment. She was elated that Brave Eagle would be left behind in winter camp. She knew his injuries were not yet healed enough for him to leave. The gathering lasted late into the night. Brave Eagle played his flute, and the notes flowed to Kallie. She closed her eyes, remembering their lovemaking the night before, and smiled. In the refuge of her dreams, she prayed he would proclaim his love for her.

After his music stopped, conversation and laughter filled the void. The elders seemed to enjoy the beauty of the night and the warmth of one another's company. Drinking her tea, Kallie pretended to be unaware of Brave Eagle's proximity and was pleasantly surprised when he sat by her. He seemed not to care who was watching, because he boldly squeezed her shoulder. Yellow Willow looked away, but Walks Far glared at Kallie.

The next morning, Yellow Willow instructed Kallie to collect more wood. Kallie did as she was told. It was almost noon before she brought back a cumbersome load. She stacked it outside the tepee and carried a few pieces inside to stoke the fire.

Noticing only Lost Buffalo and Bear in the tepee, Kallie inquired, "Where is everyone? Why is it so quiet?"

Lost Buffalo answered, "Flaming Arrow, Short Bull, and Brave Eagle left this morning for hunting camp."

In disbelief, Kallie said, "What?! Brave Eagle is gone? He left without saying good-bye to me? Why did you not tell me?"

Lost Buffalo said, "They rode this morning before the weather turns bad."

Angry screams raged inside her. Kallie could not believe it. Brave Eagle had left without a word to her. Each beat of her heart pained with frustration and indignation. Tears welled up and rolled down her burning cheeks. She exhaled with furious passion that shook her entire body. Seeing that Kallie was blocking their only exit, Bear and Lost Buffalo exchanged nervous glances. Trapped, they did not utter another word.

Chapter 19: *Fever and the Broken Heart*

Canteonsika: Heart Is Low-Spirited

Kallie was inconsolable. Brave Eagle had deserted her again. He was now with Dawn Star. Without Brave Eagle, the dullness of her existence intensified the torture in her heart. Yellow Willow pleaded, "It is not good for the baby to feel sad all the time. You must not cry. It is a bad omen, especially if you carry a son. He will grow to be weak in a woman's way. Do not cry."

Kallie fought back her watery eyes. Every chore turned into drudgery, and the sharp pain in her heart had dulled into weariness. Bear tried to please Kallie by eagerly gulping down the diluted stew she served him.

Lost Buffalo told her, "Look, Bear's appetite is coming back. This is a good sign. He is lucky that no fever has come."

Lost Buffalo had brought in several arrows and said, "Bear, these need repair and will keep you occupied." Kallie knew Bear was considered a master at making both arrows and bows and watched him enthusiastically begin his task. Bear's cheerful disposition seemed to lighten everyone's day except hers.

Bear said, "Maybe today I can try to stand on my good leg and start to walk with a crutch."

Lost Buffalo said, "Let's do it another time when the women are away. Then you can yell if you need to and still keep your respectability intact."

Lost Buffalo looked closely at Kallie. "You do not look well. Your eyes have dark circles under them. I will do the yarrow poultices for Bear. Go. Enjoy the chatter of the others."

Kallie lifted the tepee flap and exited. The cold prairie winds blasted through her thin, worn robe, but she didn't care. She felt only the dullness of her existence and the emptiness of her tortured heart. Escaping to the expansive prairies, she watched the buffalo grass whip in the wind. Tan-colored grasses blended with winter browns and made a rustling sound that comforted her. Retreat into nature had always been her refuge in bad times. Kallie stepped into the windswept plains. There was nothing between her and the Creator except a sea of prairie grasses. Walking aimlessly, she watched a hawk overhead circling around its chosen prey. The rest of the world lay dormant, frozen against the backdrop of the sun and blue sky. Wrapping her robe around her, Kallie resolved to be strong for her baby. She vowed to outwit Dawn Star and Walks Far. Somehow, she and the baby would survive. Kallie observed their camp in the distance; it was so small and vulnerable to attack. Conditions would become better when the others came back to fill the camp with life again.

Returning in the afternoon, she found the tepee filled with elders laughing and gambling. They had been waiting for Kallie to feed them and stoke the dying fire. Bear was sitting up and laughing with the others but did not partake in their gambling. Kallie wondered why Bear, so congenial, never joined in games. This behavior set him apart from the others. But the atmosphere was light and relaxed now that Bear was healing. He had passed a critical point in his recuperation and soon would be walking with a crutch.

Kallie was relieved, for now he and Running Brook could resume their romance. At the thought of her young friend, Kallie smiled slightly. To her amazement, as she looked down at Bear, he returned a friendly smile. Embarrassed at his unusual attention toward her, Kallie grabbed the bladder water bags. Yellow Willow came up behind her and whispered, "Go check on Hawk Woman." Kallie gave a slight affirmative nod. She left the tepee with water bags hanging from her shoulders. After gathering water from the river, she collected sticks of wood and walked to Hawk Woman's tepee.

All was quiet, so Kallie called, "Hawk Woman, are you there? Hawk Woman?" She heard a faint, guttural reply and quickly entered. Hawk Woman was on the ground, obviously sick with a fever.

Kallie immediately started a small fire to warm the freezing tepee. Taking Hawk Woman's frail hands, Kallie blew her heated breath on them. Then she placed her robe on the old woman. Wetting a soft skin with the cool water, Kallie sponged Hawk Woman's face and throat. This action seemed to soothe her.

Kallie made a tea for the thirsty old woman. As she waited for Hawk Woman to finish her drink, Kallie studied the woman's wrinkled brow. The old woman's skin had been weathered by many hard years of blazing sun and ice-cold winters. Her teeth were so worn down she could only drink broth and gum the smallest portion of tender meat. Then Kallie's thoughts shifted to Brave Eagle and Dawn Star at buffalo camp. It made her stomach muscles tighten as the baby kicked. Kallie's insides burned with anger, and she could not shake the haunting feeling of being abandoned. This feeling of insecurity was always present now.

Hawk Woman focused her bloodshot eyes on Kallie and said, "Thank you for the tea. The buffalo chips and twigs that you gathered will provide a warm fire for me."

Kallie replied, "Here, drink some broth. I will sit with you until you fall asleep."

Hawk Woman said, "I will offer you payment."

Kallie shook her head no and added, "Yellow Willow would never approve of it."

As Kallie walked home under the dark prairie night, the constellation of the great hunter stalked his mighty prey. The star hunter's arched bow sent diamond arrows across the sky. The night sky was breathtaking in its beauty and immensity. Wolves howled in the distance, and Brave Eagle's absence made her feel vulnerable.

Kallie lowered her head to enter the tepee. Fella wagged his tail while the others just stared, waiting for their evening meal. In continual motion, Kallie served stew and added fuel to the fire.

Yellow Willow asked, "Is Hawk Woman feeling better?"

Kallie explained, "She is sleeping, and her fever is gone. We should visit her first thing in the morning."

Kallie dove under her buffalo blanket at her first chance. Bear, who had been moved to their tepee, was already asleep. He snored as loudly as the crying wolves just outside their camp. Fella softly whined with each wolf howl, nervous that they would dare come so close. Kallie was too tired to care. Her tattered, musky buffalo robe provided some warmth.

Yellow Willow tended to the late-night chores and then stood clutching a pair of small moccasins. She commented to Kallie, "You are so sad, but it is good you have a calm, strong manner. We must be careful. Dawn Star's aunt, Walks Far, is ready to attack. For her it is about protecting her family's prestige. Brave Eagle's mother, Pretty Shield, would let no politics pass by without her knowledge of it."

Kallie knew her pregnancy was a complicated matter, but she didn't understand what Yellow Willow was trying to tell her.

Yellow Willow continued, "If Brave Eagle makes a claim to the baby, his family could by tribal conventions take the child. Lost Buffalo has already disclaimed it as his."

Yellow Willow lay down and pulled up her cover because the night had grown colder. She placed her arm upon Lost Buffalo's chest as he snored contentedly. She told Kallie, "He is a good husband, and maybe he will know what to do when the baby is born. But first we all must survive the winter." Sighing, Yellow Willow confirmed, "I am lucky to have him. I worry about his cough. My first husband died early, leaving me with Short Bull, who was young at the time."

Kallie said, "You are lucky to have each other, and Short Bull is a good son."

Yellow Willow said, "My marriage to Lost Buffalo has been most fortunate, but we too have experienced sadness. Our babies all died in infancy with the exception of one little girl."

Yellow Willow began to cry. Kallie asked, "What happened?"

The old woman explained, "The river was strong that year." She looked away and added, "Now, only Short Bull survives, and he shows no eagerness in taking a wife and having children."

Closing her eyes, Yellow Willow said, "It would make our life so much more secure if you could find a husband." And then she drifted into sleep.

Kallie's protruding belly made it difficult for her to get comfortable. She was restless and sensed danger. Bear tossed and turned and kept her from sleeping, so she decided to tend the fire. She wrapped her robe around her, petted Fella, and poked a stick into the glowing embers. They dispersed into many fractured pieces, and sparks of orange shot up into the air. She stared into the fire, trying to quiet her sobs before she woke the others. Thoughts escalated into fears about her baby's fate.

Bear opened his eyes. For a brief moment she locked onto his gaze. Kallie knew that she had been caught crying but then stared back at the fire. She did not care that he watched her, and she was not worried about what he thought.

The young warrior whispered, "I am not tired. I've slept most of the day. Get the gambling bowl. I'll teach you how to play"—and he eyed her with suspicion—"unless you already know the rules."

Deciding to appease Bear, she agreed to play.

Bear instructed Kallie. "As you know, the acorns are painted white on one side and black on the other." He shook the bowl and said, "Tell me how many light or dark you will pick." He had a line of small sticks to keep track of each of their correct guesses.

Kallie discovered, when she concentrated, she could use her inner vision to make correct guesses. Bear managed to make Kallie laugh with his exaggerated responses to her winning streak. They felt more comfortable with each other, laughing quietly while the fire slowly dimmed. Bear smiled as he finished his turn. His eyes sparkled, and his white teeth glistened. Kallie observed how handsome and strong he was. She wondered why he had not married long ago.

The next morning, Kallie went for her daily walk. She did not have much choice, for Yellow Willow insisted she get fresh air for the baby's sake. The weather grew colder, but Kallie was expected to go out and stack firewood so it was ready to be used against the bitter winds. Afterward, Kallie escaped to the river. She noticed it still flowed, but sheets of ice had collected along the bank. She dropped willow leaves into the current, intent on sending messages to her lost warrior. She pretended the golden leaves would pass him and stir pleasant memories of her. Kallie dropped in as many as she could gather before the water and wood she packed on her back grew too heavy.

Kallie spotted wolf tracks on the other side of the river. Their proximity sent shivers down Kallie's spine and ruffled Fella's fur along his back. Her dog growled even though they were close to the tepee, reminding the pair just how vulnerable they were. It worried her that even the predators sensed the fragility of their camp. There were only elders, women, and weak ones who could no longer make long journeys in the winter. Bear was too immobile to be of help.

As they reached the village, only a few dogs ran beside Fella, and they fought over leftover bones discarded in the waste pile. On this otherwise quiet morning, anger burned inside her. Kallie pictured Brave Eagle, happy to be with his family and Dawn Star at the hunting camp. She could not escape this thought no matter how fast she walked.

She stopped to invite Hawk Woman for tea. When Kallie returned to her own tepee, Bear, exhausted from the late-night activities, slept soundly on the floor. The visiting elders moved and chatted around him. Kallie heated water and placed lemongrass herbs in the water to steep. When the liquid was ready, she poured the concoction into the horn cups that lined the floor. As she passed the cups, Yellow Willow grabbed Kallie and said, "Hawk Woman still has not come, so we must go and get her."

Walking, their bodies rubbed against each other until they entered the old woman's tepee. Hawk Woman seemed glad to see them and motioned Yellow Willow and Kallie to sit beside her.

Hawk Woman's hands moved up and down, aggressively exploring Kallie's swollen belly, and she said, "Baby will come in late spring, maybe after the last big blizzard." She gestured to Kallie, "Who is the father? Do you have a white baby?"

Kallie could only shrug her shoulders, offering no reply.

Hawk Woman prodded further. "Do you know about birthing babies?"

Kallie replied, "Yes, I've delivered babies before, but I've never had one myself." Both Yellow Willow and Hawk Woman looked at each other, saying nothing.

Hawk Woman said, "You must find a husband who will protect both you and the baby. It will not be easy to find such a man."

Kallie nodded her head in agreement. She dared not speak the words that had been on her tongue for so long. And besides, Kallie didn't know if the baby's father was her dead husband, Armand, or Brave Eagle. Taking a gamble, she mouthed the name, "Brave Eagle."

Yellow Willow looked down at the ground like this was bad news. Hawk Woman seemed less upset and said, "This will not be easy because of his family." Then, adding the smallest afterthought, she mentioned, "But all negotiations can be done very discreetly so as not to lose face. I am old but respected, and I will try to negotiate a solution for you. Tell me, besides your healing, what are your skills? Can you sew?" Kallie and Yellow Willow nodded their heads yes in unison. "Can you bead?" And they both shook no. Hawk Woman hesitated. Finally, after much thought, she said, "Brave Eagle no longer wears beads in his clothing. This has been his way since his first wife died. Perhaps he has grown used to dressing in such a dull manner. But you must try harder to learn the ways of the people, for you know nothing. It is good, though, that you are a healer. Yes, that will be helpful for negotiations."

Kallie had an ally in Hawk Woman. This was important, because the other women respected her. When Hawk Woman entered any tepee, everyone tended to her every need. Hawk Woman was even allowed to use Lost Buffalo's backrest. No other woman would even dare to think of such behavior. As she and Yellow Willow helped the old woman walk to their tepee, Kallie felt Hawk Woman's strength coming back.

When they arrived, Bear was awake. Displaying his friendly disposition, he gave Kallie a smile. She offered him tea and a bowl of stew, which he gladly accepted. He had been waiting to be served for a long while.

Hawk Woman motioned her to sit. While Hawk Woman sucked a piece of meat, she said, "Kallie, you are like the cedar tree. You are withdrawn into a lonely place but rooted strong. You can communicate with higher powers. You are a strange white woman who possesses a kind heart and a fiery temperament. Brave Eagle is like a cottonwood tree in the draws. He is tall and strong like the first cottonwood a person sees when approaching a river valley. Self-reliant, Brave Eagle can withstand diverse conditions. He is always in motion like the leaves of the cottonwood.

"Dawn Star is like the willow, always found with the others, for they are like water to her, the source of her life. She needs and loves her family. I think Dawn Star is a better match with Brave Eagle's brother, Speckled Eagle. They would make a more balanced couple. Dawn Star always responds to Speckled Eagle with lighthearted comments. The serious Brave Eagle would wear on her over time."

Hawk Woman continued, "This situation will be difficult, but I will do what I can. I will bargain so skillfully that the others will know nothing. This I can do with my years of matchmaking experience. It will be a new idea for Brave Eagle's family and an interesting challenge and …" As Walks Far approached them, Hawk Woman muttered, "Watoga." Kallie had never heard the word before and vowed to remember it, for there was no time to ask about it. Walks Far had an empty cup in her hand and was demanding more tea.

Chapter 20: *How to Get One's Way*

Gmunka: To Set a Trap

The next morning, Kallie woke to find Yellow Willow was already moving around. She said, "Kallie, help us get Bear up. He needs to strengthen his legs by using crutches today." Bear grimaced in pain as the women helped him. Determined, Bear hobbled outside, and soon he was joking with the older men standing around the outdoor cooking fire.

While doing her usual chores outside, Kallie passed the men. As instructed by the older women, she did not look at them. Fella faithfully accompanied her and never seemed to mind the cold winds. Kallie was too hungry and cold to go far and returned quickly after collecting wood.

When she entered the tepee, Hawk Woman was visiting with Yellow Willow. The women were cutting pieces of hide to be sewed together with a bone needle and sinew. Hawk Woman placed a skin piece on Kallie's lap. Kallie looked at the unfinished slippers and asked, "Who are these for?"

The old woman said, "They are for you; sew your best. But remember—never give my pattern pieces to anyone. These have been in my family for several generations. This you must promise me."

Kallie said, "I will not give them to anyone. Thank you."

Hawk Woman moved in closer and whispered in Kallie's ear, "Tell no one I helped you with these."

Drawing up the needle, Kallie asked, "Why?"

Hawk Woman laughed. "If people see your work and mistake it for mine, they will think I am too old to sew." And then Hawk Woman grew serious. "Kallie, be wise. It is time to get a husband. You must be careful around Dawn Star, Walks Far, and Brave Eagle's mother, for they are formidable enemies."

Hawk Woman continued, "Look down at the ground when a man addresses you, and never under any circumstances mention your sewing. We will pray that Pretty Shield does not discover your lack of skills. Now go get a pipe from Lost Buffalo. I feel like smoking."

When Kallie returned with a full pipe, Hawk Woman drew her near again. "You must not laugh with Bear. People are talking. He is healing just fine and does not need you to care for him. Do you understand? Walks Far watches your every move, and she is Dawn Star's aunt. She will hurt you to protect her family. Bear has nothing to lose, while you have everything to lose." Hawk Woman drew in the smoke and coughed.

Kallie brought her more tea, knelt down, and said, "Thank you." Then she left the tepee. She ached for Brave Eagle and had to get away from the others to think about Hawk Woman's advice.

Outside, Lost Buffalo crouched before the fire. He seemed deep in thought, even though the winter day was cold and windy. He looked up at her and said, "Soon the rest of the tribe will be back, and decisions will have to be made. Kallie, you are a curious woman with strange ways, but you are strong and helpful. Most importantly, you are a healer, and the tribe always needs healers. If I can partner you with a strong warrior, it will also protect Yellow Willow. My time on earth is passing. Yellow Willow could live with you and your husband. That is, if I can find you a husband. It is time to put a plan into action, to set a trap. The question is, how do I get to Brave Eagle without any information going through Pretty Shield first?"

Kallie looked over at Bear. Lost Buffalo smiled and said, "Exactly. Let's go see what project Bear is working on."

They moved closer to Bear, and Lost Buffalo said, "You have bent the green willow to just the right arc. Now it is ready to dry. Once you wet it again, it will stretch to the perfect strength and flexibility for a great bow. I have some sinew you could use for a bowstring."

Bear replied, "I could use the sinew, thank you. After I'm done, I plan to paint a new pattern with brilliant reds to mark this bow."

Lost Buffalo replied, "It seems you are feeling better to make such a strong weapon."

Bear nodded yes and kept steadily working on his bow. Lost Buffalo dismissed Kallie, and she pretended to be working behind a skin while she listened.

Lost Buffalo said, "You are walking better with your crutches. Your leg is healing nicely."

Bear sounded excited. "Yes. I am determined to heal so I can marry Running Brook. By this time next year, I hope to be living with Running Brook and be returning from a successful hunt."

Lost Buffalo said, "That is a good vision, and this perfect bow is a good omen. So, my friend, since you bring up the subject of marriage, I need advice. If you were me, what would you do with Kallie and her child?" Bear said nothing, so Lost Buffalo continued, "Do you think Brave Eagle or someone else from the tribe would marry her?"

Bear cleared his throat in a nervous fashion while Lost Buffalo continued with a little lie, "Kallie has asked me to trade her away to another camp or to white traders after the baby comes. This is such a burden for an old man to deal with. Yellow Willow tells me, 'No, make it a man of the tribe!' But I wonder if maybe it would be better to trade her away." He paused and waited for Bear's comments.

Bear quietly replied, "She is your captive to do what you see fit. You are a fair man. I do not know what my friend will do, but I will discuss this with him as soon as I can find the right moment."

Lost Buffalo spoke while turning away. "You should practice walking some more. I must go in and rest."

Bear left his bow to dry and hobbled toward the river path. Kallie came out of hiding and walked after him. Fella ran beside her, barking and leaping in the afternoon sun. The wind began to pick up, and the winter sun cast shadows. Kallie caught up with Bear, and they walked as swaying buffalo grasses whipped in the wind. Cloud formations filled the sky. Bear scanned the horizon in search of the others arriving back at winter camp, but all was quiet.

When morning came, Kallie was surprised fresh snow covered the ground. She was instructed to gather fuel for the sweat lodge fire. As she gathered wood, Kallie looked forward to bathing in warm conditions on such a cold morning. Maybe she would even dive into the icy river before the heat sensations left her body. In the sweat lodge, Kallie planned to sit close to Yellow Willow, whose very presence protected her from the long, cold stares of Dawn Star's aunt, Walks Far.

Kallie walked farther than usual, since winds had hardened the snow. Her moccasins slid on the top, never sinking down below the crust. The river moved slowly, slushy with ice. Kallie made it to the hills and explored the crevasses. Climbing high and looking at the pitted landscape, she spotted a low-lying cave. It was well hidden from the trail and just big enough. Isolated, it offered protection from the brutal winds. She knew this could be her hiding place. Fella explored it, while Kallie gathered tall brown grasses that stuck out above the snow. These would suffice for a bed until she could find an extra buffalo robe.

Kallie started back before others would begin to wonder about her whereabouts. She and Fella hurried along a river trail, enjoying the sun and solitude. Kallie sang quietly the songs of her childhood while walking the miles back to the village. Suddenly, Fella became agitated. His neck fur flared out, his ears went back, and he growled low and deep. The dog's behavior caused Kallie alarm, but she did not detect anything wrong. She saw nothing on the trail, and they traveled around the river bend. There, Kallie discovered four wolves standing on the bank. Three brown wolves and a black one howled. Another wolf farther up the knoll answered back. The wolves loped around one another, vigorously wagging their tails. The tall black male sang a soul-piercing howl, and another started barking. The pack moved toward her. Skittish at first, the wolf pack became bolder with each step closer. Kallie stood paralyzed with fear but then fumbled for her slingshot. An accurate hit might scare them off. She muttered a low warning for Fella to stay put.

The wolves cautiously approached, snarling and showing their sharp teeth. Kallie backed away until she was cornered. She aimed her slingshot, but before she fired, the alpha male yelped and the wolves dispersed. Kallie stood her ground in relief, and Fella whined softly. An older boy from the village rode up to her and simply pointed the way back home. Kallie smiled a thank you, but he had already turned to leave.

Walking behind him, Kallie quickened her pace until tepees were in clear view. There, a man stood by the perimeter of the village. It was Bear. Standing with his crutches, he patiently waited for her. When Kallie arrived, she asked him, "How did you know to send the boy?"

Bear did not answer her question and instead inquired, "Are you all right? Is the baby all right?" She nodded yes. As they headed to camp, she walked behind him as a sign of respect. He looked back at her, explaining, "Brave Eagle made me promise I would protect you." Then he turned around and hobbled toward the men's steam.

Kallie regretted missing the women's steam. Now it was the men's turn. Her tepee was empty, and Kallie wondered if she should search for Yellow Willow. But first she looked around for extra supplies that could be brought to the cave. When she escaped, she would need a buffalo robe, wood, water, and a knife. A weapon would be hard to obtain.

Later that day, Kallie spotted Bear at the water's edge. She left him alone. It appeared he was doing a ritual blessing. Slowly, he dipped his hands into the frigid water and extended his arms as he pointed to each direction. Kallie wondered if it was like her people's baptism but dared not ask. Bear turned around and told Kallie, "Get Lost Buffalo and Yellow Willow. I have prepared gifts for them."

As everyone gathered around, Bear presented the medicine man with a beautiful bow, an elk skin, a special blend of tobacco, and a pipe. Bear said, "I hope these gifts will help repay the healing debt I owe to you. I am walking better every day, and soon I will be able to hunt again."

Lost Buffalo replied, "I am sure this blend of tobacco is mild enough for me. The elk skin is tanned to perfection and will become a history skin to record important events."

Bear looked pleased and told the crowd, "My arrows will claim buffalo in future hunts, and a healthy portion will always go to Yellow

Willow's tepee." Bear lowered his head respectfully as he offered this payment.

Yellow Willow seemed pleased, and Lost Buffalo said, "I accept these offerings."

As Kallie started to leave, Bear followed her. Speaking out of hearing range of the others, he asked, "What would you like as payment for your part in my healing?"

Kallie made an instant decision. She drew a deep breath and blurted, "A buffalo blanket, a fire starter, and a weapon." Bear's eyes opened as if he did not comprehend her answer. The silence between them grew uncomfortable. Kallie knew her request put Bear in an awkward position, but she had to risk it.

He said, "I will think about this strange request. It makes no sense to have these things unless you plan to leave."

Bear entered the tepee, and Kallie followed behind him. Many people were inside, admiring Bear's gifts to Lost Buffalo and Yellow Willow. Everyone enjoyed the evening by eating meager stew and playing drums. Lost Buffalo cleaned his pipe and shared his tobacco, although Kallie noticed Yellow Willow prudently took a large portion and saved it. Kallie tried to stay out of the way, and eventually she rested in the corner. Her buffalo robe provided warmth but no comfort. Every part of her body ached for Brave Eagle to come back to her before it was too late.

Soon heavy eyelids betrayed her, and she fell asleep along the perimeter, oblivious to the cold prairie winds blasting through the bottom lining.

Kallie dreamed of canyon country. A mountain lion moved along a precipitous edge dragging a cub in its mouth. Black crows bothered the mother lion by diving at her. In desperation, she dropped her baby. The crows picked up the vulnerable cub and flew away. The cub turned into her child. Kallie woke, startled. She sat up and tried to forget the nightmare. She looked around.

In this very circle, someone could be plotting to take her baby from her or, even worse, to kill her. Brave Eagle might protect her, but he was unapproachable most of the time. He did not claim her in front of the others, and he might not even help her when the time came. She could trust only Lost Buffalo and Yellow Willow, but even they followed tribal traditions. Bear seemed like a friend and different from the others, but could she trust him?

Frightened, Kallie stayed huddled on the outer perimeter of the tepee. Fella faithfully sat by her side. They both settled into a long, fretful night's sleep.

Chapter 21: *Secrets*

Wawoji: Whisper

Kallie entered her tepee and was surprised that only Bear was there. She took a precious moment to relax and pour them both some tea. Kallie said, "Bear, it is time for you to walk more with your crutches. Lost Buffalo needs to get assertive with you."

Bear laughed. "Let Lost Buffalo worry about me." Outside, the wind was howling, although inside the tepee they were comfortable. Before Kallie stood up with her awkward body and put another log on the fire, Bear whispered, "I have details to share with just you if you sit near me."

Kallie was confused but very curious about his request. She drew her buffalo blanket up to her neck and positioned herself close enough to hear.

Bear used his softest voice to tell his story. "The loss of my father had been such a tragedy. I had been hurt twice: once for the loss of my father and once for the gambling debt he incurred right before his death. We had to sell many of our finest horses to pay his debt. My mother was devastated by our sudden poverty, but my practical grandparents managed to arrange a decent marriage for her. After the Great Peace Council, my mother and I joined this tribe by way of marriage. My mother and I left our people with many teary good-byes, but at least I had a friend when we arrived at our new home. My mother was treated well. We worked hard and did not go hungry. I learned to respect and love my adopted tribe."

Accepting more tea from her, Bear looked around before quietly saying, "As I have told you, my mother and I were treated decently, but

I have never felt completely accepted. It seems I will never be able to obtain status and wealth here."

Kallie noticed the faraway look in Bear's eyes. There was a hint of sadness in them that he could not hide.

He continued, "I am hoping Running Brook's father will accept my offer and I can marry her. I would love to have many children. I will fight and die as a warrior, which is the custom of the people here."

Kallie stared. "Is that the custom here, to fight and die? What was the custom among your original people?"

Bear grew serious. "Among my original tribe, our custom was to defend ourselves when necessary, but we always tried to live with others as cordially as possible. My people liked to trade and learn from others."

Kallie turned to the fire and watched the dwindling yellow embers. Bear had frightened her by talking about warriors and battles, for she had seen enough bloodshed to last a lifetime. She admired him and was thankful that they were on friendly terms. She prayed that she could trust him not to betray her. He was Brave Eagle's friend and someone who could guide her through mysterious tribal history and language. No one else would even try to explain complex tribal relationships to her. Kallie held her protruding belly and wondered if she would be traded off as Bear's mother had been. She pulled her robe tightly around her.

As they sat in the tepee with cups of tea, Kallie thought back to her farm years. It seemed like a lifetime ago. After a few moments she tried to comfort Bear by relating to him, "Our tiny farm was a defenseless place, open to unruly types who drifted by on their way to St. Louis. My father befriended ruffians and traded away our food for liquor. His constant drinking drained my mother. She spent most of her time cooking and drifting off, trying to avoid my father's drunkenness. Sometimes my mother's sadness was lifted by Father's fiddle playing."

Bear added, "You did not finish your story about what happened before we captured you ... the marks on your back."

Kallie drew her robe closer. "After my husband and I started on our journey to Oregon, I realized we were going to live by deceit. Armand would cheat men in cards. Jacob would keep a crowd spellbound by telling Bible stories he didn't believe in. Elizabeth would encourage people to give their hard-earned money to a cause that didn't exist. I too would be expected to sell liquor as a cure-all medicine or read fortunes."

Bear interrupted. "Read fortunes? What is that?"

Kallie took Bear's hand. She explained, "Just looking at hands gives me many clues about the person. There are distinct lines woven into the hands, and if you stare at them long enough, some stand out. The lifeline of a person extends down past the thumb. After looking at a person's life, love, heart, and health lines, I could offer some suggestions. Hand texture gives clues about their line of work. Skin color and temperature show how a person is feeling. Cold, dry hands mean a person is generally cheerful, while hot and wet can indicate moodiness. A person's finger length can also give clues. The grip of a handshake tells me about a person's self-image. Besides, Elizabeth always justified my hand reading to crowds by reciting the proverb, 'Long life in her right hand, in her left hand is riches and honor.'"

Kallie let go of Bear's hand and continued, "One afternoon, back in camp just outside of Independence, the three of them came home much earlier than usual. Armand was in a foul mood. Shouting about missing his lucky piece, he stormed into the wagon and searched for it. The bedding I had just cleaned was carelessly thrown in the mud. I stood there and didn't dare speak to him. Jacob and Elizabeth were arguing loudly with each other but stopped when Armand shouted, 'What the hell is this?'

"Armand's fist popped out of the canvas opening and held my black leather pouch. Numerous silver coins rolled on the ground as Armand spilled its contents. He cursed my name. Then, to my dismay, he grew quiet and walked toward the river. Jacob and Elizabeth scurried to pick up the discarded coins and then joined him. They sat by the river and drank until sunset.

"Miserable, I put things back in the wagon while I waited. Minutes stretched to hours, until finally they approached me. Armand, with his eyes glazed over, was staggering drunk. His throat veins bulged as he cursed me. Jacob smirked his sinister, twisted smile. He seemed happy to stoke Armand's rage, and Elizabeth offered no sympathy toward me. Her eyes were cold.

"Terrified, I turned to flee, but Jacob grabbed my wrists. Elizabeth threw him a rope, and he bound my hands securely to the wagon frame. Fear struck me when I heard the snap of Armand's leather whip. Elizabeth yanked my top down to my waist, so as not to destroy it or give anyone a clue about his madness. The whip cracked and cruelly carved a mark into my back. My torn flesh burned, my knees buckled, and I screamed for mercy.

"After a couple more lashings, Elizabeth calmly ripped the whip from her brother's grip. She exclaimed to everyone, 'It was the wrath of God. That is enough punishment for a thief.' She looked at me and added, 'This time.' Jacob trembled with excitement as his shaky hands untied me.

"Armand stumbled to the mattress and fell into a drunken stupor. I was left to listen to his snores and endure the burning misery in my back. As soon as everyone was asleep, I covered my back with a shawl and rode my horse, Clara, to the apothecary store. It was pitch-black by the time I arrived, but the doctor was in his back office. He gazed at me in horror when he heard my complaint. Gently, he peeled off the top of my blouse and dressed my wounds. He was a kind man, because he took no payment, as I had none to give. When I approached the door, the doctor stood in front of me. With a concerned expression, he confided, 'Folks are getting suspicious of your husband and his two friends. There was trouble at the card table with your husband today. He won a high-stakes game. The losers were rich and influential men. They accused him of cheating and now demand justice. Tell him never to come back if he values his life. There's going to be a sheriff waiting for him at the saloon tomorrow. It would be prudent for you folks to leave at first light. Move on to Oregon with the rest of them, and never come back.'

"I thanked him, ashamed at myself for what I had become. Upon returning to camp, I did not go near my husband. I decided to escape from those three as soon as possible.

"The next morning, everyone acted like the lashing had never happened. The aching of my wounds would not let me forget, for the whipping lasted longer than the initial seconds it took to inflict the wounds. My insides burned every time I drew a breath or tried to move. I could not look at the others; all my thinking went to finding a way to escape. When Armand decided to go into town for one more whiskey and card game, I didn't warn him about the sheriff. I silently bade them farewell and cursed the likes of them." Kallie looked at Bear, "And as you know, my curse worked."

Bear's eyes grew large, and he looked down. Kallie continued, "Then after the fateful river crossing, Jacob and Armand found their whiskey flask on the bank. It was still full of liquor. Elated, they began drinking. Elizabeth and I worked around the camp and tried to ignore them. Armand's mood turned from bad to worse. He blamed me for our desperate situation. Elizabeth's body tensed up at her brother's anger, but she did not try to calm him. Armand demanded that I serve him coffee. While I was pouring it, I accidentally spattered hot coffee over his hand. It sent him into an uncontrollable rage even though the burns were superficial. Armand threw his cup down and grabbed Jacob's horsewhip. He could barely stand as he cracked it. I pleaded with him not to hurt me again. Jacob and Elizabeth ignored my cries for help. I stood frozen in fear, trapped like an animal. I turned to run, but my legs would not move. As I frantically plotted my escape, I looked down the shoreline trying to find a good spot to hide from his wrath. I stood very still. Just at the moment when I was ready to leap into the brush, my eyes met the eyes of another. Intense black eyes stared back at me. Our gazes locked on to each other. I did not move. I had a decision to make on whether or not to warn the others. I remained silent. When I looked up again, I saw nothing. It was like I had imagined it."

Kallie smiled at Bear and continued, "As you know, a group of warriors quietly stepped out of the vegetation.

"While you were occupied with Elizabeth, Brave Eagle's strong arms gripped me tightly against his body. In moments, I was bound by rope and thrown sideways on his horse.

"Brave Eagle leaped upon his horse. With a high-pitched war cry, he signaled you and the others. I suppose you know the rest of the story."

Bear nodded his head and prepared to leave. "Yes, I know it as far as today."

Kallie was desperate to ask Bear for more information, because her mind was cluttered with desperate questions. Would she be traded away? Could Pretty Shield and Walks Far claim rights to her child? Did he see any hope for her and Brave Eagle?

But Bear turned around and left quickly.

Chapter 22: *They Come Home*
Gliyagli: To Go and Come Back

The next morning Kallie and Yellow Willow walked close together. The crisp snow crunched under their footsteps. Kallie was glad Yellow Willow was in good spirits.

Yellow Willow confided, "Kallie, it is time for Bear to move into my son's tepee." Kallie was saddened at the thought of her friend leaving their home, but she knew these matters had already been decided. Yellow Willow continued, "You must be cautious around Dawn Star's aunt, Walks Far. Do not provide her with gossip about your mischief. People are already talking about you and Bear laughing together. Think carefully before you act. Do not give her any information about yourself. She will use it as a weapon against you or your child. And your time is approaching. Walks Far and her family are not to be trusted."

Changing the topic, Yellow Willow asked, "When are you going to tell the others about the marks on your back? The women all have a wager on the reason. Everyone wants to know."

Staring at Yellow Willow, Kallie broke out into nervous laughter. "I don't like to tell about it."

Yellow Willow teased, "Well, you already told Bear about them, but no one needed to tell me why your back wears those angry scars."

Kallie asked, "So tell me, why did I receive those marks?"

Yellow Willow replied, "Disobedience, of course." Kallie nodded yes. Yellow Willow added, "Brave Eagle would not be so brutal. Like his namesake, he can fly with the wind drafts and change his course. He is good at compromise. Even as a young boy he was good at it."

Kallie politely smiled and tried to keep her expression as if everything was normal, but she could barely breathe. Inside, she toyed with a gut-wrenching question and wondered how much she could trust Bear. Had he told Yellow Willow about her plans to escape? Her request for a weapon?

Yellow Willow stood for a moment looking at the sun and said, "The hunters will be back soon. I feel it in the air."

When they entered the tepee, a blast of icy wind found its way in. Bear was there, but Kallie could not look at him for fear she could not keep her composure.

Bear was preparing to leave for Short Bull's empty lodge and slowly stood using his crutch. As he left, Yellow Willow reminded him, "You have forgotten your robe."

Bear replied, "I do not need such an old robe. I leave it for Kallie," and he walked out.

Kallie gathered up the robe and placed it on her side of the tepee. It was a beautiful robe and much thicker than her own. She silently thanked her friend. As Kallie lifted up her basket to get wood, she noticed that it was not empty. Waiting until she was away from the village, she spilled the contents. A large knife and a fire stick fell out. Excited, she decided that she would go to visit the cave at the first opportunity. Kallie quickly collected wood and brought it back to stoke the fire.

The next morning, Kallie hurried to her cave, where she stashed the buffalo robe, water container, fire stick, and knife. Kallie's walk was brisk so she could return to camp before anyone grew suspicious of her long absence. When she arrived at her tepee, Yellow Willow greeted her with kindness. She told her that today they would be going to Hawk Woman's tepee to sew.

The women sewed for most of the afternoon. No one dared to complain about the lack of food, but their growling stomachs reminded them. Kallie felt faint. Walks Far insisted on sitting close to her. This made Kallie even more uncomfortable, although Walks Far acted unusually kindly toward her.

155

When Yellow Willow stepped out for a moment, Walks Far said, "Kallie, here is a special tea I have brewed for you. It is a favorite of Brave Eagle's. You must try it."

Kallie accepted. She tried a sip, but it tasted bitter. She did not want to drink it but did not want to offend Walks Far, who sat motionless and talked about a beading pattern. Kallie noticed Walks Far seemed anxious and pushed her to take another sip.

Kallie tried not to make a face and lied, "Oh, this tea is good."

She swallowed a small sip pretending to like it, trying not to offend her. Walks Far drew in closer. Kallie was about to drink it all down in one large gulp when Yellow Willow shouted through the entrance, "The scouts are coming! The people are coming back to us!"

In the commotion, Kallie hurried out of the tepee, spilling the cup of tea on the ground. She could barely see the horses galloping toward them. Brave Eagle was coming home! She let out an exultant cry with the others. Beating drums let everyone in the encampment know the scouts were coming. It was time to prepare for the hunters' arrival. Fires needed to be readied for roasting buffalo meat. All looked to the horizon with hopeful expectations, but they knew it would be hours before the main body of the tribe would arrive.

Kallie watched Bear and a few other men ride out to meet the scouts. Most of the elders lined up along the river and waited. The winds from the north stung their faces, but Kallie could feel everyone's excitement.

Yellow Willow commanded Kallie, "Pile the wood so they will have a good fire to warm themselves. We must prepare a large stew for the travelers. We will have to use all the food we have left, so be sure to water it down. A lot!"

Kallie was unsure about this, for their meager supplies were almost gone, but Yellow Willow did not change her expression. Kallie knew it was useless to argue about such matters, so she stepped out of the waiting line and got to work.

Kallie had finished preparing the stew by the time the first scouts arrived. She arched her back to relieve her discomfort from stooping over a fire. Yellow Willow's son, Short Bull, rode up along with four scouts.

Loved ones quickly surrounded them. The old women sounded their welcoming cries, and old men hugged the scouts. Everyone laughed in relief, happy the hunters and their families were coming with fresh meat.

Kallie wrapped a robe around her body after unloading the last heap of wood. She heard someone ride toward her. She looked up thinking it was Bear but was startled when she realized it was Brave Eagle. Silently he studied her. She felt her face getting red. A warm smile showed on his face. He leaped down from Wind Racer and stood next to her. Kallie was immobilized by mixed emotions.

Boldly, he grabbed her. As he bent his head downward, he whispered something in Kallie's ear. She closed her eyes and tried to decipher his words but only felt the sensation of his lips upon her ear. In that moment, her frustrations melted away. His long hair covered her face, and she embraced him as best she could with her protruding belly. He broke away and looked down upon her body, expressing amazement at how big she had gotten in pregnancy. He looked very proud and happy. Brave Eagle was reaching out to hold her again when Dawn Star's aunt, Walks Far, interrupted their encounter.

Walks Far said, "Brave Eagle, come to my tepee, now." She spoke with confidence, knowing that he must comply.

Brave Eagle acknowledged her by saying, "Yes. Of course," and he called his horse, Wind Racer, to follow him.

The women funneled the scouts into a warm shelter to feed them. After giving them time to eat, everyone gathered around to hear news of the tribe's expected arrival. Lost Buffalo did not need to hear their report, for he could talk to the crows that continually flew over the village. The birds had already brought him a message that most of the hunters would arrive the next day.

Kallie served stew to Lost Buffalo. He sat, using his backrest, as the scouts gave their accounts. As the others listened, Kallie watched Lost Buffalo observe Walks Far and Brave Eagle. She tried to contain her anger as Walks Far barked orders at her to get more wood. The other women were unpacking the scouts' horses. They carried some of the load to Short Bull's tepee, where the scouts would stay until more people arrived.

Kallie obeyed Walks Far until she was out of her sight. Then she quickened her pace. After gathering the wood, she stood outside the tepee and listened to the men's stories. The wind blew cold, but Kallie felt safer outside away from Walks Far. Kallie heard someone exit the tepee. It was Brave Eagle, looking directly at her. He motioned her to go inside, and not knowing what else to do, she obeyed. Inside, the warm air felt good.

Yellow Willow instructed her to pour the tea while the others enjoyed the conversation. Yellow Willow looked tired and distracted. She stood crouched behind Lost Buffalo and tried to comfort him while he coughed. According to the scouts, the hunt had been successful. All in the tepee thanked the Great Spirit profusely, for their empty bellies would soon be full.

The scouts added that, when the main tribe arrived, there would be plenty of food for everyone. Even as they traveled back to the winter camp, another buffalo herd had been discovered. This herd could be hunted in the late spring when food grew scarce again. Black Hand stated that when he painted the tribal history skin, he would depict this time as the Year of Two Hunts.

After the stories, Kallie distributed wood to other families in the village. Her feelings had been hurt by Bear's abrupt change of behavior. He no longer spoke to her or even looked her way. She did not understand why suddenly he was so unfriendly. Then she heard someone coming up on her. It was Bear. He said, "Kallie, I just threw out an old bow and six arrows by your woodpile. They are no longer mine." He quickly turned and walked toward Short Bull's tepee.

Kallie ran to the woodpile and spied a bow and six arrows buried under the snow. Each of the arrows had a mark of four lines. This was not the mark of Bear. She smiled and realized it was her mark. Bear had not forgotten the four long scratches she had clawed into Brave Eagle's cheek long ago. She did not know how to shoot such a weapon, but if she learned, it would give her some protection. The weapon would have to remain hidden in the snow until she could bring it to the cave. As she turned around, Kallie encountered Brave Eagle and Walks Far, who had silently crept up from behind. Kallie hoped her startled expression did not give her secret away. Walks Far gave her a suspicious look while reprimanding her. "I told you to keep working. Supply our fires. Kallie, come with me!"

Brave Eagle seemed puzzled by Walks Far's hostility and interrupted her. "No, Kallie is to deliver wood to Short Bull's tepee. That is what she was asked to do." He smiled at Walks Far, who tightened her face into a scowl but nodded her approval. Brave Eagle did not seem to notice Walks Far spit on the ground as she hurried away.

Kallie dumped the load of wood and entered Short Bull's empty tepee. She could not resist investigating the bachelors' home. Many drums and weapons hung from the ceiling, and the walls were covered with decorated scenes of great battles. Pipes and small pouches of tobacco, dishes, and half-empty cups lay strewn everywhere. She laughed when she compared the mess to Yellow Willow's cozy and tidy home.

Kallie turned to go. Brave Eagle's deep voice called her name as he entered through the flap. He looked strong and rugged as he stood before her. He was smiling. She immediately looked down, for she was embarrassed at the way he looked at her. It had been such a long time since they had been alone. She meekly offered to get him a cup of tea, which he accepted. Kallie silently poured tea. She drew closer to Brave Eagle and noticed his hand trembled as he held his cup. She pretended not to see this and moved even closer to him. He dropped the cup where he stood and pulled her into his arms. His face moved toward hers until she could taste the salt of his lips. They embraced during this rare private moment. They fell to the ground and crawled under a buffalo blanket. Finally, they were alone and were undisturbed the whole night.

Kallie was surprised when early morning rays hit the tepee. Their solitude lasted only a few moments before Lost Buffalo made an abrupt entrance and kicked the clump of buffalo skins covering Brave Eagle. Lost Buffalo was badly winded but seemed determined not to cough. He said, "Kallie, get dressed." Embarrassed about being naked, she quickly grabbed her dress and covered herself. She tried to shoot off a quick look at Brave Eagle, but Lost Buffalo continued to stare him down.

Lost Buffalo stood before Brave Eagle, who dressed with as much dignity as he could. Lost Buffalo lectured, "If you want Kallie, then you must formally ask and pay for her, just like any other arrangement. Do not taunt Yellow Willow and me. Make the correct decision for yourself, whatever that decision may be. Your family has the right to insist you follow tradition. I have the right to demand you treat me and my family with respect."

Brave Eagle's eyes shifted downward. He said, "Lost Buffalo, you are right. I will discuss this with my father. Flaming Arrow is a fair man."

Lost Buffalo replied, "You are destined to become a great chief. That position comes with much responsibility. Make a final decision about Kallie. If you continue this behavior, as your father's best friend, I will hold no respect or honor for you." Lost Buffalo turned to her and said, "Come with me." As soon as they exited, Lost Buffalo rested to catch his breath and pointed. He said, "Look. There is a new set of footprints in the snow. They are made from a woman's moccasins. Who could be spying on us? This is not a good omen."

Kallie did not answer but suspected Walks Far. She seemed to always be near, following Kallie's every step. Hopefully, Walks Far had not discovered the hidden bow and arrows.

Lost Buffalo and Kallie entered Walks Far's tepee, where everyone had gathered. The scouts were explaining to the elders that the hunters' loads were heavy. Travel over snowy lands with so much meat would be slow. The hunters had planned to stop for the night and wait for the morning sun to warm their way.

Everyone seemed excited except Kallie. She could not endure Walks Far's interrogating stares. Kallie grew more uncomfortable with each moment until Lost Buffalo said, "I am not feeling well, and my coughing spells have drained me. Come, Kallie, walk with me. We will let Yellow Willow bring back all the news." And so, with much relief, she left the gathering with Lost Buffalo.

Back at their tepee, Kallie gently served Lost Buffalo. "Here is some purple coneflower tea for your cough. I am concerned. It is not getting better. You need to fight this."

Lost Buffalo laughed. "Ah, Kallie, you always fight everything. I do not feel like fighting. I have had a good life. I have a good wife. A man cannot ask the Great Spirit for more. I give thanks that I am a contented man."

Kallie obediently answered, "Yes." She kept her feelings to herself while gently rubbing his neck. Although she tried not to, Kallie started to cry. Her tears dropped on Lost Buffalo's shoulders. He pulled her down next to his chest. His grip was surprisingly strong and comforting. Lost Buffalo let Kallie weep. He finally said, "I will never understand your ways. But I am old and do not have to worry about conforming to tribal customs any longer." He squeezed her arm, and her sobs quieted. Kallie became still and listened to Lost Buffalo's wheezing chest. She focused on his buckskin shirt. It was beaded with beautiful patterns Yellow Willow had lovingly sewn for him.

Lost Buffalo spoke softly. "Kallie, bargaining a husband for you has been difficult. I have spoken to Brave Eagle, but his expression provided me with no clues. You must not give yourself to him any longer. Promise me you will not visit him. It is not our way. He must declare his intentions and make a decision, or tribal respect will never be his. It would make my heart happy if he chose you for his wife. However, we do not know what he will decide." Kallie nodded that she understood, but she was feeling too drained to speak.

Lost Buffalo continued, "Acknowledge your pain, and feel it deeply. Then you must make peace with yourself. When you do, offer your peace to the spirit world. The Great Spirit takes such offerings and gives them to those who need them. Use your gifts. In your dreams you talk to the animals, for they tell me about you when I speak to them."

Kallie looked at him. "Do you think I can speak to animals also?"

Lost Buffalo grinned. "Yes. Use your dream visions as part of your healing. Also listen to the plant spirits. They will help you become a powerful healer. You must listen more and talk less. Without silence, how can you hear what the spirits are trying to tell you? Walk a straighter path, and practice your gifts. Tell me, with all your crying, do you feel your baby is in good health?"

Kallie nodded. "Yes, I feel the baby moving." Kallie took advantage of the moment and asked, "What is to become of me after I have the baby?"

Lost Buffalo looked concerned. "I had hoped to marry you off to Brave Eagle and have Yellow Willow live with you as an old one. That way, you could help each other. Brave Eagle would take good care of you both. But now I fear Brave Eagle's indecision must be taken as his final answer.

"I must find you another husband. It might be possible to marry you to another man in the tribe, but this would only bring trouble down upon us. You would disgrace yourself with Brave Eagle at some point in the future. So, if things do not work out as we hope, I have decided to trade you to one of the trappers who come to us each spring. One of them might be persuaded to take you. I cannot say what would become of you when you leave with him. You may be able to return to your own people."

Kallie was dumbfounded, but it seemed Lost Buffalo meant what he said. Accepting this, she whispered the hardest question. "What of the baby?"

Lost Buffalo looked directly at Kallie. "Things could get complicated. What if the trapper will not travel with a baby? And what if the baby looks like a tribal family member? A woman of our tribe, like Walks Far or Dawn Star, may claim it and prevent the baby from leaving with you. I do not wish to scare you, Kallie. Yellow Willow, Hawk Woman, and I will try our best to defend your rights. Most people would look on the child as yours, but you are up against two powerful families—families who are used to having their way."

Kallie clung close to Lost Buffalo. She was glad she had found her cave, a secret place to hide. Her bow and arrows remained buried. Tomorrow, in the morning, she would take them and hide them in the cave before Walks Far had a chance to find them. Kallie felt the warmth and security of Lost Buffalo's body as he held her. Before she fell asleep, she felt she could ask about the word Hawk Woman had used. She spoke as clearly as possible. "Lost Buffalo, what does watoga mean?"

Lost Buffalo, who was almost asleep, looked startled. He said, "It means revenge and is a strange word for you to ask about."

Kallie did not reply, and soon Lost Buffalo was snoring. The fire sputtered its last life. She heard people talking outside the tepee. Yellow Willow said, "Come inside, boys. I will share some of Lost Buffalo's special tobacco."

Following her into the tepee, Brave Eagle and Bear entered. Kallie pretended to be asleep. Yellow Willow told the men, "Leave them be. I will be right back. I need to go get a pouch from outside."

After Yellow Willow left, Bear spoke in a hushed tone to Brave Eagle. "I've been meaning to talk to you. Lost Buffalo recently sought me out and explained he is looking for a warrior to marry Kallie. If none will do it, he will trade her away this spring to a white trapper. She will be gone forever. Brave Eagle, Lost Buffalo seemed serious." The men's conversation was interrupted by Yellow Willow's return. When Kallie peeked out, she saw Brave Eagle staring into the fire. His only movement was offering a pipe to Bear.

Early the next morning, Kallie tried to act as normal as possible. She walked to the woodpile, dug out her weapon buried in the snow, and hid the bow and arrows underneath her robe. It was a cold morning, but Kallie felt invigorated as she walked toward the hidden cave. Fella ran beside her, sniffing the ground and running on river ice. When they were close to the cave entrance, Kallie took a few practice shots with the bow. She was clumsy and would have to practice. She hid them in the deepest part of her cave and left quickly. She looked back, grateful the wind obscured her tracks in the snow.

When she arrived at the village, she found that no one cared about her absence because everyone was scanning the horizon. After a long wait, dark shapes of people and horses dotted the distant landscape. Wind whipped at everyone, but even the extreme bitterness did not cause one person to seek shelter.

First to arrive were the warriors riding their fine horses. The next group of people was also riding on horseback and dragging loads of meat and buffalo skins. Children and dogs ran behind. Waves of people, dogs, and horses came into the winter encampment. In the commotion, tepees were set up, meat was delivered, dogs scurried, and people hugged. The hum of excitement was everywhere. Children shrieked with happiness upon seeing their grandparents. Great stews and huge racks of meat were cooked on outside fires. Many people gathered in the larger tepees, eating hot meals, drinking tea, and sharing tales of adventure.

Kallie watched another group arrive and caught Dawn Star's glare as she rode by. Kallie tried to maintain her composure. The icy moment was interrupted by Elizabeth's voice calling to her. Kallie was shocked to see Elizabeth riding on her horse, Clara. It seemed that Elizabeth now truly belonged to Weasel Tail, because she confidently rode with his other wife. Elizabeth called out, "I can talk when the work is done, so come help me."

Kallie followed along behind Elizabeth until the women stopped to decide where to set up their tepees. She helped carry many poles. Eight massive buffalo skins were stretched over the frame to complete the shelter's exterior. Kallie then set up the two poles that would control the smoke flaps from the outside. A skin curtain covered the east-facing entrance. This was held in place by poles at both the top and bottom.

Seats made of willow sticks were placed in a circle around the fire pit, and Elizabeth proudly pointed to hers. Bedding was laid out, and rawhide parcels containing utensils were unpacked. Many of these were adorned with beautiful porcupine quill designs. Kitchen supplies, clothes, drums, and weapons were all strategically placed along the sides.

Last to be secured was the extra skin lining attached at the back wall to keep out the winter drafts. Elizabeth laughed with the other women, making Kallie envious of Elizabeth's adaptability.

As they went outside, Kallie spotted a smiling Running Brook, who had just ridden in with her family. She had transformed into a beautiful woman during their separation. Running Brook's grandma, Hawk Woman, greeted her granddaughter with elation.

Running Brook's family set up their tepee close to Yellow Willow and Lost Buffalo. Running Brook good-naturedly accepted Kallie's help, even though she had to watch carefully for any mistakes that might be made. Kallie concentrated and soon learned how to properly set the frame poles. She admired the family's collection of containers; all were painted and beaded in geometric designs of blue, red, yellow, and white. Numerous parfleches were stacked along the large tepee's sides. Running Brook soon left in search of her sweetheart, Bear.

Kallie found Elizabeth, flushed from all the excitement. "Kallie," she said, "it seems so long ago that we've had a chance to talk alone. I've befriended a woman named Meadow Grass. She is the first wife of Weasel Tail, one of the braves who had captured us. You remember him, don't you? He is the one who was wearing my silver crucifix." She proudly displayed her cross upon her breasts and beamed with pride that she was able to get it back. "I began to notice that Weasel Tail had a longing look in his eyes, so I played to his advances. At first it was only to get my crucifix off that heathen's chest. Well, soon matters got quite out of hand, and, knowing that security was part of the deal, I was happy. Weasel Tail even gave me Clara as my own horse … as if our wagon horse was his to give away! And the night after our marriage, he presented me with the crucifix. I thanked the Lord."

She seemed happy but then changed her expression and said, "Kallie, I am planning to escape when the timing is right." Elizabeth's blonde hair had fallen out of her tight bun and her dress was faded and torn, but her fiery spirit was still intact. Elizabeth barked orders about the parcels' placements within the tepee. Amazed, Kallie wondered why things came so easy for Elizabeth. When the women were done with their chores, Elizabeth put her arm under Kallie's and exclaimed, "Let's go find something to eat. All this activity has given me quite an appetite."

They approached a big tepee full of people visiting and eating. Elizabeth pushed her way forward and dipped into the cooking container for a large portion of stew while she spoke in English, "Kallie, we are both trying to survive. When I befriended Weasel Tail's wife, I knew, for security's sake, I had to acknowledge her husband's advances. It is a pity, though, because I suspect that it was Weasel Tail's arrows that killed my poor husband, Jacob." Elizabeth's eyes were full of tears as she continued, "Deep in my heart I know Jacob would want me to do whatever was needed to survive, so I didn't give my actions much thought. I played up to Weasel Tail's advances and, since I don't love him, it is not a sin. I'm just trying to survive. As soon as I figure a way out of this mess, I'm going to escape. I advise you to do the same, Kallie. The way you carry on with that warrior is probably making my brother Armand turn in his grave."

Kallie said, "Elizabeth, have you lost your senses? Armand never really cared for me. In the end, he almost killed me. How could you forget that?"

Elizabeth pushed her outside, away from prying eyes, and whispered, "Kallie, you're heading into troubled waters. I'd pray all day on the Holy Book if I were you! Why, you don't even know who the father of your child is, and still you go after the most eligible bachelor in the whole village. He is a powerful man who is from a powerful family, and he is engaged to marry Dawn Star. And she has her claws in him. I always see him right by her side, because his family and hers are close. They are always together. He goes off by himself quite often, but he always returns to her. Always goes to her, Kallie. And what if you have a white baby, my brother's child? That baby would be of my blood and not a savage. What power would you have over him then? Tell me that. Kallie, these people are tighter than a Bible group. They follow every rule set for them. It seems to me, if that warrior fellow married you, he'd be breaking a rule or two. Why don't you find another man, just for the time being? Someone to hold you over until we make our escape?"

Just then Dawn Star and Brave Eagle's mother, Pretty Shield, approached the tepee. Instinctively, Kallie looked down to avoid their hostile glares, and she slowly backed up behind Elizabeth for protection. Elizabeth gulped down the last of her food and warned, "I'd be very careful. Dawn Star has many friends. Everyone seems to like her."

Kallie knew Elizabeth was right. She changed the subject and asked Elizabeth for her hairbrush. When she received the brush, Kallie ran into Yellow Willow's cold tepee and brushed her snarled hair. She struggled with each tangle until her hair was shiny and smooth. She let her long hair remain loose, which gave her a look different from that of the other women.

She heard someone outside the entrance. Expecting Running Brook or Elizabeth, she opened the flap but instead discovered Brave Eagle.

She stared at him, letting in the cold breeze and not knowing what to do. Brave Eagle boldly entered and closed the tepee flap behind him. Stretching his arms outward, he grasped Kallie's shoulders. Smiling, he looked down at her. She did not look up, so Brave Eagle gently placed his hand under her chin and lifted it up until her eyes met his. All Kallie's pent-up anger dissipated in a single second of time. She could not match his intensity, but each time she looked down, he countered by lifting her face toward him again. He pointed to the bedding in the corner, but Kallie shook her head with a strong no. She remembered Lost Buffalo's dire warnings.

Brave Eagle sheepishly felt her swollen belly and laughed when he felt a little leg kick the palm of his hand. He caressed Kallie's shoulders and slipped his hands down her back, feeling her curves. He inquired, "When does the baby come?" Kallie shrugged her shoulders to indicate that she was uncertain. Brave Eagle embraced her, and Kallie enjoyed their closeness. She did not mention any of her feelings about his relationship with Dawn Star, although every fiber in her body wanted to ask about it. Kallie stood enveloped in her lover's arms. She accepted his caresses until it was time for him to leave.

Chapter 23: *Afternoon at the River*

Wokiksan: Friendly Teasing between Male and Female

Kallie enjoyed the morning sun and noticed how the blue skies seemed to stretch on forever. Everything was calm, and the villagers had settled into winter routines. Reunited families were joyous. From outside fires came rich smells of roasted meat. A celebration was being planned to honor the spirit of the buffalo and give thanks for a successful hunt. Happiness echoed throughout the valley, for now the people would not starve. The months of spring would be less threatening. Even Kallie's dog, Fella, appeared less intimidated by the wolves' howls, since the wolf pack had moved farther from camp. The long, cold nights were less lonely. The village was alive with wintertime activities. Men hunted close to camp, young boys watched over horses, and young girls gathered firewood and buffalo dung.

Kallie helped the women prepare hides by stretching skins outside on pegs. The rest of the tanning would be finished during the late winter and early spring. The hides would be tanned with a mixture of buffalo brains and fat rubbed into the skin with a smooth stone. Next, the large skins would be scraped again until they became tender, and then they would be dried in the wind and the sun. The tanned hides would provide leather for pouches, clothes, rawhide straps, and bags.

The women also showed Kallie how to pound dried meat with a skin mallet and mash it with dried berries, pits and all, until it became a paste and then mix it with tallow. This would replenish their pemmican supply of travel food.

The villagers seemed content in winter isolation, but time passed slowly for Kallie. Every day she schemed to encounter Brave Eagle, but she rarely saw him. She suspected it was Yellow Willow's watchful eye that prevented him from interacting with her. So winter passed, and each day the baby grew inside her. She spent her time tending to the old couple.

One morning, Yellow Willow sent Kallie and Running Brook to gather wood. They walked far down the river path, collecting in spots where the other women did not go, for the two longed to speak privately. Running Brook shared gossip about the hunting expedition. This included the courtship of Elizabeth and Weasel Tail in every detail. Kallie listened politely until she could bear it no more. She prodded, "What stories do you have about Brave Eagle?"

Alarmed at the question, Running Brook quickly explained, "Yellow Willow has forbidden me to speak of him to you. Of course, I must obey my aunt."

Kallie felt angry but was distracted by a sharp pain shooting down her legs, making it almost impossible to walk. It frightened her. She could not become immobilized, because she had to be able to escape. Kallie knew this pain was natural and caused by the way the baby was resting. She hoped the baby would move soon.

When they had almost reached the location of her cave, Kallie needed to rest. Running Brook sat close and patiently waited for Kallie's pain to subside. It would be a long walk home.

Running Brook confided, "I hope you win him, Kallie. It would be good for Bear and me to have you and Brave Eagle as friends. We would be strong allies. Did you know that my father accepted the hide from the buffalo that almost killed Bear? It is a change of heart for him. I pray that he will accept Bear's proposal and allow us to be matched." Running Brook began to twirl with her arms extended. Her face was full of happiness at the prospect of being Bear's wife.

Kallie, shivering in her buffalo robe, felt a twinge of jealousy but said, "I hope you will be matched with Bear soon. He will prove to be a worthy husband."

Running Brook laughed at the thought and sprinted to the top of a rock ridge. There she discovered a windswept place where buffalo dung was frozen to the ground. Running Brook was pleased, for dung was a dependable fuel that burned hot and clean. It was an easy way to provide heat and had no odor. She picked up several pieces and put them in her basket.

Before they departed from the ridge top, Kallie glanced up at her cave. She had almost shared her secret with Running Brook but had stopped herself. Remembering Lost Buffalo's stern warning about trading her, she decided that she could tell no one. It would remain a secret. She would keep her baby no matter the risk. Running Brook interrupted her thoughts by making a shrill cry she loved to practice.

They started the long walk to the village. Kallie limped until the baby moved into a position that made it easier for walking. Finally, rising smoke in the distance indicated they were close.

Suddenly Running Brook poked Kallie in the ribs and pointed at two men standing in the tall buffalo grass. Running Brook giggled while she explained her plan. Together, the two women moved in closer and camouflaged themselves in patches of grass. The unsuspecting warriors approached, too absorbed in their conversation to notice them. Running Brook motioned Kallie to follow her lead. Taking a piece of frozen buffalo dung in her hand, Running Brook carefully aimed. Laughing, Running Brook launched her first shot accurately while shouting for Kallie to help. Both women managed to throw several pieces of frozen dung before Brave Eagle and Bear came running. Pretending to be angry, but ducking cautiously, the men stormed toward them. The women took off running while slinging their ammunition over their shoulders.

Running Brook ran a great distance up the trail before Bear was able to topple her. They fell in the snow off the path. Kallie was too pregnant to run far. She put her arms over her face and was quickly bombarded by Brave Eagle's aim. He grinned at her and then collected the dung pieces and put them back in her basket. His eyes were inviting. For a brief moment, he put his arms around her before Bear and Running Brook walked up to them.

Everyone followed Bear, who found a sheltered place and started a fire. Bear embraced Running Brook and covered her with his buffalo robe. Kallie sat directly across from Brave Eagle. He had little protection from the weather, wearing only his winter leggings and a leather shirt. Brave Eagle pulled travel meat from his pouch and offered it to everyone. Wind Racer came from the herd and pranced up to their makeshift shelter.

Bear pulled out an intricately carved pipe. He filled it and gave it to Kallie. She did not partake but desired Brave Eagle's attention, so she passed it to him. Kallie asked, "How did you get your adult name? Bear told me your boy name was Little Wolf."

Brave Eagle exhaled, passed the pipe to Bear, and asked, "He did? When did you two talk about that?"

Bear looked over at Running Brook and said, "Here, let me load this pipe again. It is good stuff, my special blend."

Brave Eagle looked at Kallie and said, "When I was called Little Wolf, I accompanied my great-uncle on a long journey. Our travels brought us to a land of strange and sculpted shapes. The nights were growing cold. It was perfect weather for eagle trapping.

"My uncle showed me how to make an eagle trap by digging a pit large enough to fit me. After the dirt was piled on a buffalo robe, my uncle pulled it away to another location. He carefully compacted the dirt to look like gopher hills to trick the eagles. After much hard work, my trap was finally completed.

"At one end of the pit we distributed sage along the bottom. We tied branches together so they covered the top of the pit; then we camouflaged it further with grass, rocks, and dirt. When we were done, I hunted rabbits.

"The next morning, I carried a rabbit carcass to the pit and climbed into its cold interior. My uncle stacked the branches on top of me. Now my mission intensified. I had to breathe through a small opening, be still, and wait for an eagle to land on my bait. Sleeping was forbidden, so waiting demanded agonizing patience. Smaller birds continually landed, picking at my bait. I occupied my time by using a stick to knock them off.

"Finally, on the fourth day, an eagle landed beside the rabbit bait with a loud thud, a sound I had never heard before. I seized its legs and drew the eagle into the pit as I attempted to twist its neck. Killing the eagle was much more dangerous than my uncle had suggested. Eventually, I succeeded, but the eagle left angry claw marks upon my chest. My uncle said I was lucky, for an eagle's talons could cut deeply and cause profuse bleeding. I was weak with hunger and cramped but elated and proud about my capture.

"That night my uncle gave me my adult name. The name Brave Eagle honors the eagle spirit and guides me always."

Kallie smiled at Brave Eagle. She could not stop staring at him. He was so strong and handsome. She desperately wished he would protect her and the baby. As though he had read her thoughts, he looked over to her and gently touched her cheek. Running Brook and Bear cuddled comfortably in their buffalo robe.

Running Brook passed the pipe and asked, "Did the rest of the journey go well?"

Brave Eagle's look was distant. "No. That journey follows me to this day."

Brave Eagle continued, "On the way home, we encountered a band of hunters. My uncle did not trust them and advised me to keep the eagle feathers well hidden. He reminded me that eagle feathers were very valuable, and two sets of feathers could be traded for a horse.

"In the other group there was a young, serious warrior about my age. His eyes glared at me. Soon his intimidation made my insides boil with anger. Tired from my journey, I left him at the fire pit and climbed under my buffalo robe, depending on my uncle to keep watch.

"In the early morning I awoke to find my uncle sitting in an upright position but sleeping. The men from the other tribe had left, and my precious eagle feathers were gone!

"I pursued them, and soon I reached the group and, just like an eagle, I swooped down and knocked the young man off his horse. In this bold attack his bundle fell and came undone, revealing my feathers. I challenged him in front of the others. There was no way for him to deny his deed. The other men respected us and moved away, leaving the young warrior snarling at me.

"We fought using every ounce of energy possible as we hit, twisted, and threw each other on the ground. We were both bleeding and exhausted. When we stopped, there was no winner, but I was not going to give up my feathers. I whistled for my horse and leaped upon it. I made one circle around the men, who stood watching, and then I hugged my horse's side and extended my arm close to the ground. In one attempt I grabbed my precious bundle. Triumphant, I held the bundle high in the air and made a war cry. As I pressed my horse's flanks to escape, I felt a sharp pain in my leg. The thief's knife blade had cut through my leggings, producing a deep cut. It shocked me that he would resort to such tactics, since this was not a death fight. As I rode off with my bundle, I threatened him that the next time we met it would be a death challenge.

"I rode back to our camp with my bundle secure. Blood from my leg wound dripped until my uncle properly bandaged it. He was thankful I had come back alive, for he was personally responsible for me. My deed earned me my first coup feather."

Kallie smiled as she listened to Brave Eagle's deep, gentle voice. She asked him, "Did you ever see this warrior again?"

He nodded. "Yes, he was the one who stalked us after I captured you. His name is Hawk Claw."

Kallie remembered him and then asked, "When Hawk Claw was stalking us and getting very near, you covered my eyes. Why did you do that?"

"An animal can sense when he is being watched too closely. Your stare could have given him a clue about our hiding place. Hawk Claw is an enemy full of bitterness but a smart one."

Bear coughed as he passed his bear-shaped pipe, and he stated, "He is a lone wolf with mange."

Brave Eagle took the pipe, finished the last of it, and said, "That would be a good name for him, Mangy Lone Wolf." Both Bear and Brave Eagle laughed. Then Brave Eagle said, "It is time to go back before the others wonder where we are."

As they prepared to leave, Kallie strapped the heavy load of wood on her back and picked up the basket of dung. As she started walking, pains struck again, this time radiating through her lower back. She grimaced and began to drag a leg. The others were far ahead of her. She saw Brave Eagle turn around, gallop back, and call out to Bear for additional help. Brave Eagle dismounted and lifted the heavy pack off her back. He extended his arms, intertwined at the palms, to help her step up onto his horse. Kallie was so clumsy that it took both men to help her up, but they finally succeeded. It was uncomfortable for Kallie to ride, but it was the only way for her to make it home.

She thought Brave Eagle looked worried, but he said nothing. When they had passed the boys watching the herds, he helped her down, and she struggled to her tepee. As she opened the skin flap, she turned around and smiled. He had been watching her. He smiled back. She whispered to herself, "I will never let him go."

Chapter 24: *Conversations*

Wakiya: Talk

As Kallie entered the tepee, she was surprised to see Flaming Arrow sitting by the fire. Yellow Willow asked, "Where have you been?"

Startled at Yellow Willow's curtness, Kallie answered truthfully, "I was with Running Brook, Bear, and Brave Eagle."

Lost Buffalo did not look up as he asked, "You have not been alone with Brave Eagle?"

Kallie said, "No." He ignored her and concentrated on the smooth stones spread out before him. He spent much time deciphering the stones' message.

She thought the reading must be for Flaming Arrow. He was wearing an antelope skin shirt his wife, Pretty Shield, had sewn for him. It was meticulously beaded and decorated with long strips of beaver fur. It was a beautiful shirt for a great chief.

Lost Buffalo said, "The stones say it is a good omen. Regardless of the weather, buffalo birthing has already begun."

Flaming Arrow said, "The scouts have spotted a small herd close to our camp. The council has agreed on another buffalo hunt on the condition that only some families will go. It is too early for the village to leave our sheltered winter grounds. There is still bad weather ahead."

Lost Buffalo said, "Tomorrow, I will create a hunting ceremony to take advantage of this good fortune. The rocks agree. It is settled."

Later that day, Lost Buffalo appeared in a formidable outfit of wolf, bear, and buffalo skins. In the middle of the village, the powerful shaman stood facing the lowering sun. He carried an ancient history

cloth to the sacred tepee. Its entrance faced east. Sacred skins hung from
its ceiling. Some of these recorded the earliest times of the tribe. Men
began to play heavy drums. Elders moved close to the sacred tepee,
drawn by Lost Buffalo's magical presence.

Decorated braves entered the tepee to smoke from the sacred pipe.
While each man inhaled, a sacred bundle was held over him to rekindle
courage, regardless of previous hunting misfortunes. All past mistakes
were forgotten. When a man viewed the sacred bundle, only the future
mattered. Each hunter was delighted he had been chosen for the chance
to replenish the village's fresh meat supply.

Lost Buffalo and Flaming Arrow unrolled the sacred bundle and
displayed its contents: an eagle's talon, buffalo tail, human scalps, and
rattlesnake tails. All these items symbolized both bravery and courage.
The hunters huddled around the display until Black Hand, who was the
selected leader of this hunt, gave a signal to disperse. The celebration
was about to begin.

Drumbeats sounded, and their reverberations penetrated everywhere.
A first-quarter moon rose over the village. People rejoiced at the sight of
it because it signified spring. This moon often brought warmer, sunnier
days—a time when snow would melt into puddles and the river would
become a motion of slush.

On this night, huge pouches of stew hung from wood tripods.
There would be feasting now, because after the hunt there would be
replenished racks of fresh meat. Young painted dancers appeared. They
shook their rattles and weaved in and out of the main dance circle. A
group of men played flutes.

Brave Eagle wore a bear-claw necklace and fringed armbands made
from buckskin. His face had a serene expression as he played his flute.
Kallie stood by the men's circle and listened to his seductive song.

Suddenly, Dawn Star pushed her from behind, almost knocking her
down. There was no need for pretense. Their eyes locked in combat.
Kallie coldly stared, ready to defend herself. Pretty Shield, Brave Eagle's
mother, stood behind them as Dawn Star brought out a sewing awl
hidden in her hand. She pointed it at Kallie's belly and hissed at her,
"Go near Brave Eagle, and I will use this."

As Dawn Star stormed toward her, Kallie fell to the ground. This action caused enough commotion to attract Brave Eagle's attention. He stopped his flute playing and rushed to help Kallie. Dawn Star, who wore a beautiful shell dress, moved quickly to his side. She smiled warmly at him. While shrugging her shoulders, Dawn Star explained, "She just fainted. The captive will be fine."

Pretty Shield scoffed, "The white woman must be weak. She is not able to carry her child without getting sick."

Brave Eagle gave his mother a quizzical look while he helped Kallie. He called to his mother, "Get Running Brook." He avoided any possible gossip by quickly joining the men's circle when Running Brook arrived.

Running Brook did not question Kallie about the incident but gently nudged her into the women's circle. As they watched the dancing, Running Brook asked, "Do you feel better?" Kallie nodded yes, trying not to show the anger raging inside.

Flushed with excitement, Running Brook confided, "I have good news. My parents have accepted Bear's offer. We are going to be married. My parents are worried about his leg healing properly, but I know Bear will walk normally again."

Kallie hugged her. "I'm happy for you both. Bear will be a good husband and, given time, his leg will mend completely. When will the marriage ceremony take place?"

"In the summer after Bear and Brave Eagle go horse catching. It will be after that time." Running Brook smiled with a whimsical expression as she spoke about her future.

Songs, drums, and rattles sounded throughout the evening as couples danced and laughed. Kallie felt alone and walked aimlessly through the crowd. Everyone ignored her except Elizabeth, who said, "Kallie, I'm glad to see you. I don't go in for all this foolishness. Let's hide in the shadows so we can sit and drink tea. Thank the Lord! With all the distractions, I won't have to work if they can't find me." As Elizabeth gripped her horn teacup, she whispered, "Kallie, I heard the old man is going to ask Brave Eagle's family about marrying you."

Kallie said, "What?"

Elizabeth laughed at her. "Oh, nothing stays a secret here. Meadow Grass, Weasel Tail's other wife, says it is no use because Dawn Star's family has already negotiated with Brave Eagle's family. Kallie, what are you going to do about the baby? Your time is coming. Do you really think they will let you keep it? I heard Dawn Star telling Meadow Grass how her family is going to take the baby! Imagine that! Bargaining about a poor, helpless baby. But, after all, Kallie, it might be for the best. That way, you won't get all tangled up with these people. I have been praying for a rescue, and one is coming! When they thought I was sleeping, I heard talk about traders coming downriver now that the ice is moving out! Frenchmen! When I heard that, I knew deep within my heart that my prayers had been answered. If you were smart, Kallie, you would be getting ready to leave and put this miserable experience behind you."

Kallie whispered, "I'm going off to have my baby where no one will find me. I found a cave that's perfect. You have to help me, Elizabeth. Please say you'll help me."

Standing up, Elizabeth put both hands on her hips. Her face grew pale as she scolded, "Kallie, running off is not the way to deal with this matter. Why, especially since you have helped birth babies. You should know better. You could bleed to death!"

Kallie stood defiantly, but her insides still quaked from the gossip. She said, "I've attended births, so I'll be prepared, warm, and dry. My dreams have been haunting me again. Premonitions have warned me that I am in danger. This is what I plan to do. I'm not going to let them take my baby away. I'll die first." Kallie's demeanor changed as she lost control and then pleaded, "Please, Elizabeth, don't tell a soul about this. I'm afraid, but I will have the final word on this matter."

Elizabeth pursed her lips to give more advice but just nodded. Pulling Kallie close, Elizabeth whispered, "Hush, or everyone will hear you. Of course you will have your way. You always do. Now, quiet!" Elizabeth, who had experienced Kallie's stubbornness, said, "I might feel the same way if it was my child. I will do my best to keep your secret, Kallie. And in return, I could baptize the baby after it is born. We'll give the baby a good Christian name. If it is a boy, maybe we will name it after my brother Armand or after my dear late husband, Jacob."

Kallie did not react to Elizabeth's insulting comments. She could focus only on how abandoned she felt. It would be very foolish to run off to have her baby alone, but she could not think of any other solutions. Elizabeth's help might be needed, so Kallie decided to make amends and meekly asked her to recite some Bible verses. Elizabeth's face lit up. She let the verses flow from her memory, and words from the scripture smoothly rolled off her tongue.

Elizabeth looked pretty when she relaxed her face and calmed her voice. She recited Bible verses late into the night against a background of music and dancing. Everyone was oblivious to the two white women sitting away from view. Elizabeth's words offered Kallie strength and comfort. Kallie rose, placed her hands on her stomach, and said, "Thank you, Elizabeth."

Elizabeth declared, "Kallie, you are a survivor. If that heathen is what you really want, then fight for him. That's what I would do. I would use the devil himself to keep Dawn Star's claws off him. Fight for him so you have a father for that baby."

Kallie exhaled. "Elizabeth, I'm too tired for fighting. I'm going to have my baby. I don't feel like fighting anymore. I just feel like going to bed. Thank you, and good night."

Waddling away, Kallie entered the cold and dark tepee. Her buffalo robe felt warm and inviting. Just as she was falling asleep, she heard a noise outside. She ignored it until the noise persisted.

Outside, Brave Eagle stood in the shadows. "Shall I play a special song for you?"

Kallie smiled and said, "Yes, please play for me."

Closing her eyes, she listened to Brave Eagle's sweet song. The notes landed deep within her heart. When the song ended, she felt his lips brush hers. She leaned into him. As his arms embraced her, Kallie sighed. For a brief moment he was hers.

Bear and Running Brook brushed past them and disrupted their embrace. Running Brook looked so excited and beautiful. Bear grabbed Brave Eagle's arm and said, "Come. I've been looking for you. Lost Buffalo has something to show you."

Running Brook grabbed his other arm and pulled him along, laughing while she hurried. She looked back at Kallie and shouted, "Yellow Willow says to get some rest. Sleep is good for you and the baby."

Left alone, Kallie returned to the warmth of her bed. She prayed an answer would be found for her. She held the last of the love potion close to her heart. She uncorked the small top, and flower smells permeated the air. Kallie carefully tipped the vial and placed the last drops upon her throat and bosom. Her lips still tingled, and her heart pounded from the brief encounter with Brave Eagle. Kallie listened to beating drums and became so warm that she took off her stiff dress. Finally, comfortable under the robe, she drifted into a deep sleep.

In a dream, Kallie followed a cougar down the river path. Wolves followed her and Fella, but they did not attack and she was not afraid of them. They gathered outside her cave entrance and protected her. Kallie was aware that mysterious traders traveled toward her. She caught a reflection of a hawk overhead and Dawn Star sharpening a weapon. Conflicting thoughts came to her. How could she fight for Brave Eagle? How could she keep her baby even if the birth went normally? How would it end?

The drums' beat droned on steadily. She dreamed that Brave Eagle was next to her. Recognizing his sweet scent, her fingers traced every feature on his smooth face. His embrace felt intoxicating. She pressed herself against him until he became one with her. Sensations rushed throughout her body until she finally collapsed. His presence was so comforting she felt no anxiety.

When Kallie finally awoke, most of the people, including Lost Buffalo and Yellow Willow, were just going to sleep. Groggy but realizing her opportunity, Kallie took dried meat and water containers. She slowly strolled away from the others pretending to be fetching water farther upriver. When she was out of the sight of the villagers, she hurried toward the cave.

The morning was sunny, and river ice had started to melt. The trail became mushy and hard to walk on, but Kallie persisted and finally reached the safety of her cave. Once inside, she rearranged her meager belongings. She buried the dried meat and hid the water containers behind the woodpile. Fella ran around the cave sniffing every corner and claiming the outside area as his own. Kallie unrolled her buffalo skin on the grasses she had collected. The cave was small but comfortable. It was warm, dry, and smelled of sweetgrass. A large stack of firewood stood dry and waiting. Carefully, she dug out her bow and arrows and practiced a few shots. A smile crossed her face when she thought of Bear making the weapon for her.

She had collected moss with Yellow Willow last fall to use as diapers, but she mentally listed two essential items she still needed: a tripod and a cooking bag. They would be harder to obtain because Yellow Willow took account of such things and would become suspicious if these items were missing. Kallie decided to think about that later and sat on rocks warmed by the sun. It felt glorious.

Soon it was time to go. Kallie's moccasins were soggy with mud, and the wind made her shiver. As she and Fella traveled past the wolf site, she heard the river water moving under a thin shield of ice. A beautiful stone sparkled at the river's edge. She picked it up and was amazed at the small purple crystals glistening in the sunlight. Kallie held it in her hand and decided to keep it for good luck. She placed it deep in her pocket.

She collected firewood in case anyone had noticed her long absence from camp. She doubted she would be missed, because everyone was so preoccupied with the celebration. She gathered wood until she heard soft notes of a flute song. Turning, she saw Brave Eagle approaching on his horse while playing his flute.

He stopped and leaped off Wind Racer. Speaking in a calm voice Brave Eagle asked, "Where do you go? Your tracks say you are directed and in a hurry." He gave her a quizzical look and waited for an answer. Kallie wanted to blurt out the truth, but she said nothing. This caused an awkward silence between them. Brave Eagle interrogated her, "Why do you walk so far? It is not safe."

"I like going off by myself. I have a lot to think about. Yellow Willow says it is good for the baby to take long walks, especially if the baby is a warrior." Kallie searched his face for a reaction, but he revealed none of his feelings. A gust of wind blasted through the river valley.

Kallie shivered. She noticed Brave Eagle had no robe and reprimanded him. "Are you not cold? Why don't you dress warmer on such a day? Aren't you concerned about getting a chill?"

Brave Eagle said, "I'm preparing for my vision quest. It is a test of strength. I need to be strong against the cold wind. I will go up on the rocks and ask for guidance." He pointed to the rocks close to her cave, but she revealed nothing.

Brave Eagle changed the subject. "I will miss the spring buffalo hunt. They are so close I can smell them. It will be an easier hunt than usual because there is still snow in the valley where the young have been born. It will be easy to hunt them. The skins of the young are needed for soft things."

Kallie looked at him. "You mean they are going to kill the defenseless young ones?"

He nodded and said, "Yes, so you can make soft skins for your little one. It is our way. We respect the buffalo and the bounty they provide us."

Her thoughts centered on Dawn Star's family taking her baby when she asked him, "So what are you asking guidance for?"

He shot her a look and shook his head. "I do not wish to speak of such matters."

She volunteered, "Well, I do wish to speak of them. I've been praying for help with my situation."

Looking ashamed, Brave Eagle extended his hand and touched her face. He asked in a gentle voice, "Are you fearful?"

She answered, "Yes," catching a slight scent of her love potion on his hand.

Brave Eagle advised her, "Do not be afraid. My mother has birthed many babies, and she will help you."

Kallie reacted strongly and spoke before thinking. "I don't want your mother, Pretty Shield, to help me. She wants you to marry Dawn Star. The two of them plan to steal my baby away from me. Dawn Star stares so coldly and points her sewing awl at my belly. She hisses that she will use it if I so much as talk to you!" She instantly regretted sharing this information when she saw the expression on his face.

"No, you do not have to worry. I will not let them do that to you."
He looked angry. "They are not the bad women you say they are." An
uncomfortable silence overtook them, and Kallie could not think of
anything to say. Her words had only made things worse.

After a long pause, Brave Eagle commented, "The trader called
Henri will be arriving soon. Every year he trades beads and weapons for
our skins before he travels downriver to trade for horses. Then he carries
his heavy load to a trading post. Some years Bear and I have traveled
with him, but not this year."

Kallie could not help but think about Lost Buffalo trading her. She
wondered how Brave Eagle could be so nonchalant in his conversation.
She asked him, "Is the trader Henri a fair man?"

Brave Eagle answered, "He is just a man. Why do you ask such a
question?"

She looked to the ground and then bravely spoke. "I suppose you
already know about Lost Buffalo trading me. Nothing here stays secret
for long."

Brave Eagle acted angry. He leaped on Wind Racer and motioned
for Kallie to follow behind him. Her load was not heavy, so it was fairly
easy to walk on the mushy trail. She did not know what else to say. At
the village path, Kallie left Brave Eagle in silence and walked toward
home.

Before she had gone far, Brave Eagle called out to her, "Kallie, will
you share some of your firewood with our lodge? It is cold, and we are
tired."

Kallie moaned to herself but reversed direction to walk to Short
Bull's tepee. Only Bear was there, and he seemed genuinely glad to see
her. "It was a wonderful celebration, don't you think, Kallie?"

She spoke to Bear. "Yes, it was, but I'm tired, and I'd best be going."

Bear inquired, "Are things going well?"

Kallie shook her head no and wanted to say more, but Bear quickly
whispered, "You should have seen your warrior's face when I spoke of
Lost Buffalo's intentions to sell you off to the trader."

Brave Eagle entered and disrupted their conversation. He said, "It seems you two have a lot to talk about." Bear ignored his comment, and Kallie left in a hurry.

When Kallie arrived at her tepee, she found Yellow Willow packing in excitement. The old woman did not acknowledge Kallie and continued her conversation with Lost Buffalo. "As I told you, Kallie will cook for you. It will be fine."

Lost Buffalo said, "Is there nothing I can do to prevent you from going on the spring buffalo hunt?"

Yellow Willow said, "You know how I look forward to going with my son, Short Bull. Besides, we need soft skins for the baby." Yellow Willow looked at Kallie and said, "I will be back before the baby is born." Then she continued to pack.

The next morning, Kallie and Lost Buffalo stood together and watched Yellow Willow hitch up her travois. Brave Eagle and his mother, Pretty Shield, stopped by. After Lost Buffalo's coughing spell, he said to Brave Eagle, "Only ride a short way, and then turn around. It is time for your vision quest."

Brave Eagle said, "I'll scout for enemy sign with Flying Crow and help with the travois. Then I'll ride back."

Pretty Shield forced a smile and said, "Yellow Willow, now that Lost Buffalo has finally released his grip on you, it must feel good to help with the hunt."

"Yes, I love riding toward the open plains, smelling the buffalo, and experiencing the hunt. After sitting in camp for so long, it will be freeing. And how is it with your family? Are they ready for the hunt? It must be hard to let Flaming Arrow stay behind."

Pretty Shield jeered, "My family is just fine. We have negotiated with Dawn Star's family about her partnership with Brave Eagle." She smiled down at Kallie and Lost Buffalo. "It was expected, of course."

Yellow Willow replied, "Hawk Woman tells me that Kallie would make a good wife for Brave Eagle, and you could fulfill your family obligations by matching Speckled Eagle and Dawn Star. Even you must see how they laugh together." Brave Eagle's mother shot Kallie an angry glance and steered away. Yellow Willow smiled and waved good-bye to them as she rode off.

Lost Buffalo said, "I am sad to see her go, but look, Kallie, over there." Lost Buffalo pointed. "Speckled Eagle and Brave Eagle are having words and appear irritated. Let's move a little closer to hear, since Yellow Willow cannot tell us otherwise."

Kallie and Lost Buffalo snuck behind a tepee and strained to listen to the brothers' conversation.

Speckled Eagle said, "Brother, you are just angry at yourself. You are not hunting because you are troubled and need a vision quest. But I have been thinking about Dawn Star and have an idea—"

Brave Eagle erupted. "It seems everyone is thinking about Dawn Star. It is no one's business until I decide, after my vision quest. Don't you agree, brother?"

Speckled Eagle added, "There is little I can say. You are older and must make the first move. Here she comes now."

Dawn Star looked beautiful as she approached. Her huge almond eyes flirted with the brothers. Dawn Star rode up to the men and spoke about the taste of the warm liver to be Speckled Eagle's when she butchered the young buffalo. Speckled Eagle gave her a glance and flirted. "Dawn Star, I know you will sing your songs to lure the buffalo closer so that I might bring a mighty beast down for you. My marked arrow shaft will lance its heart, and you will know it as a gift to you." Dawn Star laughed loudly, and even Kallie knew this interaction was not appropriate.

Brave Eagle looked with puzzlement at Speckled Eagle and Dawn Star as they departed together. He hurried along, following them until he could catch up.

Kallie and Lost Buffalo wandered to their tepee. The wise shaman had told her not to worry—things would work out—but she was very worried.

Later that evening, Kallie and the old man sat close together chewing on dry meat while they watched the fire. Lost Buffalo told her stories of spring buffalo hunts in the days of his youth. He spoke of his love for Yellow Willow and the sad death of their child. Only his stepson, Short Bull, remained.

Finally, he shared his vision for her. "We must hold on to this night, for time dances around us. Spring brings many changes. We must do the best we can. Your baby will survive, Kallie. But there are many questions. The hawk that appears in your dreams tries to swoop up your baby. He never successfully gathers enough speed to fly away with it, but still, a hawk can do considerable damage. There is darkness, and it is not a clear vision. I cannot make the spirits give me answers until they are ready. I'm tired and must sleep to acquire their guidance." Kallie understood but worried about his premonition until she too fell asleep.

The next day was uneventful until early evening. As Kallie prepared the evening meal, Weasel Tail entered and said, "Scouts report that white men approach our village."

While Lost Buffalo nodded, Kallie noticed how old and sad he looked. He gazed over to Kallie and said, "Well, my adopted daughter, fate has arrived. We cannot escape it now."

Kallie was as terrified as she had been on the first day of her capture. She knew Lost Buffalo had meant what he had said. Everyone in the village expected him to make good on his transaction. When Lost Buffalo got up to go, she could hear some of the young boys outside yelling with excitement about visitors. As she stood, a new sensation overcame her. Her baby had dropped, and she could breathe again.

Chapter 25: *Henri and Pierre*

Itokiyopeya: Trade

It was in the twilight that the two white men came. Quietly, under the rise of the moon, they maneuvered their huge canoe around numerous ice floes. The sentries alerted Flaming Arrow that the white voyagers were approaching.

Kallie joined several people along the riverbank. She knew one of the voyagers, Henri, came to the village site almost every spring. That would be the man to whom she would be traded. She watched him as he paddled toward the shore. Lost Buffalo and Flaming Arrow stood upon the higher side of the riverbank with their arms crossed, while Black Hand remained out of view. Nothing was said as they watched the white men climb up the bank to greet them. Flaming Arrow extended his hand outward instead of shaking the man's hand. Henri shrugged and then mirrored the chief's action and extended his arm and hand.

Kallie noticed the other white man appeared nervous as he stood behind Henri. He was a different kind of man, dressed in black except for a white collar. Golden curly hair framed his youthful face and, although he hung back, he stood tall and strong. He let Henri take care of formalities and did not change his expression or mannerisms.

Henri wore a red knitted hat that was folded on one side and pinned down with a golden cross. A curious red feather rose from another pin, and a red tassel dangled at the end of the fold. The red color contrasted with his full dark-brown beard. His mustache ends curled up at the sides, and his shoulder-length hair had streaks of gray running through it. Henri's lips had a bluish tinge like he was cold, even though he wore a fur coat draped around his shoulders. The front of the coat was open, exposing a beautiful beaded choker worn around his neck. A leather pouch hung from his belt, and he seemed very protective of it. This made Kallie wonder about the pouch's contents. Whatever it was, it was very powerful medicine. Kallie's eyes fixed on it as Henri, Bear, and some of the others walked down the bank to the traders' canoe. Henri anxiously watched his supplies and directed the younger man to guard the canoe while he pushed curious children away. Kallie decided she did not like the mannerisms of this man.

Vapor clouds steamed from the men's breath when they spoke. The volume of their voices was low, but Kallie could hear that Bear, the translator, had switched to French. "Comment allez-vous?"

Henri replied, "Trés bien, merci." Then Elizabeth came up as close as she dared and translated for the women all she could hear.

Henri spoke. "I am glad we made it to your camp. The weather is turning cold again, and the thickening river ice took us by surprise. We were hit by huge ice floes. Ice was even underneath our canoe. We were wet so many times in the cold water that we ached. Monsieur, may we remain at your camp until travel is safer?"

Bear said, "Yes, Flaming Arrow has offered safe passage, but who is your new partner?"

Henri exhaled an exasperated sigh. He explained to Bear in French, "No, monsieur! No partner. It is only for payment that I bring this young man. This man, Pierre, is to be dropped at a mission far downriver. That will be the last I will see of him. He is a man of God, a missionary. A man of God makes everyone nervous."

Bear and Henri laughed as they conversed.

Kallie and the tribe members stood patiently to see what would happen next and when the trading would begin. The women gossiped about beads and utensils they would acquire, while the men eyed the canoe curiously, attempting a glimpse of what new items Henri had brought this year. It was rumored Henri had brought the firewater which burned the men's insides and made them wild. Kallie heard the men were thirsty for it.

Kallie shivered as she hid in the crowd. She did not want to draw attention to herself. Elizabeth's eyes sparkled with excitement as she said, "Kallie, you see, my prayers have been answered! Frenchmen arriving here, and the serious one looks like a preacher. I wonder if he is married and has left his wife back in some provincial town somewhere. Oh, Kallie, this is so exciting. Now, you promise me, if they visit Lost Buffalo that you'll come get me. Promise me." Kallie could only nod her head at Elizabeth to oblige her. Meadow Grass, Weasel Tail's first wife, tugged at Elizabeth's worn dress and pulled her toward home. Meadow Grass seemed worried that Weasel Tail would notice Elizabeth's infatuation with the white man. Kallie held her protruding belly and fended off a feeling of desperation. She would be traded to Henri if Lost Buffalo and the others had their way.

Disheartened, she made her way home. It was close to her time, and the baby had dropped. Each day, walking had grown more cumbersome, and she could barely bend over to tie her oversized moccasins. Pains shot across her belly sporadically during the day but then would suddenly stop. Kallie took comfort in the hope that the cold weather would draw Yellow Willow back home sooner than expected. She decided to stand behind the tepee away from the others, hoping her absence would make Lost Buffalo forget about his proposition.

People passed by her tepee. When she heard coughing, she became curious and peeked out from behind the tepee. Flaming Arrow, Lost Buffalo, Brave Eagle, and Bear were walking with the white men. As Henri and Pierre passed by, the young preacher looked at Kallie. She was startled to see the clarity of his light-blue eyes when his eyes met hers. He looked shocked, as if he could not comprehend that the tribe held a white woman captive. Kallie thought perhaps he had heard terrible stories of what heathen Indians did to helpless captives.

Kallie was alarmed by Brave Eagle's cold stare because of this unexpected encounter. Henri reacted by grabbing Pierre's arm and pulling him through the crowd, while talking rapidly in French. At the same time, Elizabeth managed to break away and forcefully bump into the white men. Quickly, Elizabeth introduced herself and pleaded for help until Weasel Tail violently pushed her away. The young preacher's mouth opened as if to speak. Kallie heard Henri interrupt. "Keep your eyes to yourself, and go straight ahead. Do not stop."

Lost Buffalo told Henri, "Pay a few boys to guard your belongings in the large canoe."

The trader replied, "I trust no one and with good reason."

Lost Buffalo said, "That is fair. If your merchandise is not guarded, then it will be gone by morning."

Henri replied, "I am very organized. All my supplies are in tied bundles. Everything traded or divided out is written down in my notebook." Henri held out his buckskin-covered book. "I can immediately tell if one item is out of place."

Pierre was quiet while Henri cursed the darkening sky and said, "Now my trip will be postponed for several days until the weather warms up. I had hoped to be the first at the American Fur Company Trading Post in order to obtain the best prices. Now, with this weather, I am stranded."

Kallie could tell Lost Buffalo was amused and strangely content about the situation. She wondered if it had to do with her being traded.

That night, men trickled into Lost Buffalo's tepee. Henri entertained the men with stories of his trades and travels. He spoke by using a combination of Sioux, French, English, and sign language. A sweet aroma filled the tepee as Henri stuffed his pipe bowl with different tobacco blends and then shared. The men smoked as they waited for Kallie to bring tea and food. Henri had insisted on going out and checking his canoe. It became a source of amusement for the other men.

Kallie was in charge because Yellow Willow was still on the hunt. She carefully poured tea and then stayed out of the way. Without Yellow Willow to guide her, she did not know her role with the white men. Pierre seemed ill at ease and kept quiet in the midst of the laughter. He kept staring at her. Henri was an engaging man, but she sensed it was all show. He really didn't want their friendship, only their business. She kept a wary eye on him but eventually became entertained by his stories, even though she didn't understand all his motions and words.

While Henri and Bear conversed, Kallie stood with her head down. Hawk Woman entered and announced, "The guest lodge is almost ready for you two men. Kallie, go with them and help them. You can clean up later." Kallie let out a breath of relief because she was ready for everyone to leave. She missed Yellow Willow.

She followed behind Henri and Pierre as they hastily walked through the dark village. Assuming Kallie did not understand, Pierre spoke in French. "It was unnerving for me to see a beautiful white woman, heavy with child, held hostage. Earlier, the other white captive woman asked me for rescue. Her eyes pleaded with me. May God have mercy on their souls! I will pray for them. This bondage seems most unnatural to me. You, however, do not give it a thought."

"Ah, you take things too seriously for the frontier, my preacher friend. I'm a Frenchman. The pregnant woman is not even French, and the other one is clearly trouble. Why should I worry on such a matter? These things are for the settlers and Indians to work out. I'm a businessman just passing through. I want no trouble, mind you. You must forget them, or your troubles will be just starting. I can assure you of that! Now get ready for some fiddle playing tomorrow night. If the old man trusts us, the rest of the tribe will follow along. We are marooned here until the river clears, so keep away from that Brave Eagle. He doesn't seem to approve of you."

"Why, I've done nothing to dishonor him. I've only met him today."

Henry looked at Pierre with disgust. "I suspect he could see your eyes following up and down that woman. Be careful. I could see anger burning in his eyes. Use caution. We have been invited tomorrow to the old man's tepee to play music. And you must remember—no looking at the girls unless they offer you one. If that happens ... well, that is a different story."

Henri entered the guest tepee. He switched to English and addressed Kallie. "Thank you. This will be comfortable for such a cold night. I am fatigued." He took out a bottle from his jacket pocket and said, "A few precious swigs on this bottle will help things. Tomorrow I have some trading to do." Pierre fell into his bed; he seemed oblivious to Henri's doings.

All the next day Kallie looked forward to the evening. It was then the fiddles were brought out of black leather cases and, after an interlude of tunings, the white men began to play. The fiddle music sounded so sweet and clear. Kallie choked back the tears as her childhood memories returned. She thought of her father's fiddle playing and her mother's sweet singing. The music enticed Kallie to move in closer until she was in the circle. She stood quietly, absorbing each note with joy. It was as if she were home on the farm again.

Soon the lodge was so filled with men that the women and children had to stand by an outside fire. The women listened and danced to the strange songs. As the music flowed, more people crowded outside the tepee to be part of the unexpected festivities. Elizabeth had managed to escape Weasel Tail's attention and push herself close to the entrance. Kallie could tell by the fire in her eyes that Elizabeth would get her way, even with Weasel Tail in the vicinity. An opportunity to speak to the white men would be worth any beating she might receive. It could mean escape. Later, as the crowd thinned, Elizabeth stood by Kallie, knowing there soon would be room inside. After a short while they made their way in, and Kallie reminded Elizabeth she would have to serve and clean if she was to be inside.

From across the fire, Kallie felt Brave Eagle observe her. He seemed angry. Maybe he had never heard such music before, but Kallie stared mesmerized at the two white men. Glowing with excitement, she even clapped at one of the preacher's songs. Lost Buffalo seemed to approve of her manner and laughed softly with her.

Kallie grew uneasy because Lost Buffalo pushed her toward Pierre, who continued to look at her. Kallie glanced at Brave Eagle, who touched the knife dangling from his waist strap. He flexed his shoulders, folded his arms, and stared.

Lost Buffalo let go of Kallie and motioned Brave Eagle to sit by his father, Flaming Arrow. Brave Eagle moved and watched with a bit more constraint.

To change the atmosphere, Pierre played a jig. Henri laughed and grabbed Elizabeth for a dance. Everyone was amazed at first but then encouraged the couple by making more room for their dancing. Henri laughed loudly while stomping his feet in a manner that no one had seen before.

When Pierre finally stopped playing, he sat down close to Bear and whispered something to him. Everyone waited. Bear made a request to Weasel Tail, who then looked over to Flaming Arrow. Flaming Arrow gave his approval. The crowd watched Pierre politely ask Elizabeth to sing a song for them. Beaming with excitement, Elizabeth requested her favorite Bible song. Henri and Pierre instantly recognized the name and softly played it. Elizabeth sang in a forceful and clear voice, for she had loved singing Bible songs at the revival meetings she and Jacob once held. Kallie smiled, thankful it was Elizabeth who had caught their attention. She had no intention of singing in front of everyone. The evening was stressful enough.

After Elizabeth finished her song, Weasel Tail was visibly agitated. He grabbed Elizabeth by the arm and pulled her out of the tepee. Their dramatic exit was followed by an awkward pause. Lost Buffalo took the silence as an opportunity to talk of trade negotiations. After hearing the inquiry from Lost Buffalo about a possible trade, Henri said, "Of course we will trade. You always have unusual items to trade." Henri looked confused. He seemed to sense that something was not quite right.

Pierre looked at Lost Buffalo and boldly pointed to Kallie. Lost Buffalo obliged Pierre's request with an affirmative nod. Pierre immediately moved closer to Kallie, requesting she sing a favorite song. Kallie was trembling as she sang her father's favorite tune. At first, she sang with such a soft timbre that most strained to hear her. While she stood singing the Celtic melody, her voice became stronger with each stanza. She rolled high notes in the Celtic fashion. Her voice was haunting, filled with so much emotion that even Henri sat motionless and listened. Kallie's tears betrayed her at the end of her song.

Embarrassed, Kallie went back to serving. Lost Buffalo came to her and said, "I am sorry I forced you. It was your ancestor's song in a strange tongue and should be kept private. It is not our custom for a woman to sing at gatherings, but you should not be ashamed."

As she served Brave Eagle, he looked directly at her and smiled.

He seemed proud of her, even though Kallie knew she was not supposed to cry. How she wanted to be in his arms. She continued to serve and felt the missionary's eyes following her.

Lost Buffalo abruptly stood up and said, "Brave Eagle, soon the sun will rise. You need to prepare for the morning purification steam bath. After that, it will be time for you to leave on your vision quest."

Brave Eagle replied, "I agree. I am ready." And before he left the tepee, he took one more look at Kallie.

Chapter 26: *Time of Change*

Yuswa: Unravel

Kallie gathered fuel for Brave Eagle's steam bath as Lost Buffalo had directed her. She felt so awkward she could hardly walk. Light contractions had started to come and go. The baby was positioned low in Kallie's belly, and every bending movement was uncomfortable. She was nervous about the baby's pending birth. It would be soon.

Elizabeth approached and could barely contain her excitement. "Kallie, come with me quick. Those white men are in your tepee again. Invite me in, and I'll help you with your chores. Hurry, before Weasel Tail sees me here and beats me, that scoundrel. Oh, Kallie, come along. Hurry and pretend like you don't know a thing."

Elizabeth grabbed Kallie's load and quickly deposited the wood outside the steam bath. Then she dragged Kallie into Lost Buffalo's tepee. The men were negotiating and did not acknowledge the women. Finally, Lost Buffalo impatiently ordered, "Kallie, bring us food and drink." Kallie obediently served the group with her head down. Her demeanor changed when she served Brave Eagle, and they exchanged glances. Elizabeth scurried about, serving Henri and then taking much more time with the minister. She made sure her crucifix dangled between her breasts for him to see. She smiled complacently, but her eyes desperately pleaded with him.

Kallie knew Brave Eagle would soon leave on his quest. By the time he returned, he might be out of her life forever. She sighed with despair at the thought of losing him. Lost Buffalo interrupted her thoughts when he sternly ordered her out of the tepee and instructed

Elizabeth to stay. Confused, Kallie obeyed. Fella whined as they stood outside shivering in the cold. Walks Far, covered in a large buffalo robe, approached Kallie. The woman's eyes glared as she spoke. "Your baby has dropped, and soon it will be time for you to give birth. I will help you since Yellow Willow is still on the hunt." The woman's lips curled back into a smirk, and Kallie glanced around for support. She found none. She looked down and said nothing. She huddled deep within her buffalo robe and waited until the men exited the tepee. Brave Eagle stomped out, and Bear followed closely behind. They both glared at her. Brave Eagle looked furious. Bear said nothing and followed his friend to the steam bath.

The trader, Henri, stopped and examined her like she was a piece of merchandise. Flaming Arrow and Lost Buffalo ignored her as they passed by, leaving Kallie feeling alone and desperate. Lost Buffalo had never neglected her before, and now he avoided her as he hobbled to the steam bath. Kallie stood dumbfounded until all the men were out of sight and then went in to find Elizabeth.

Elizabeth was in the tepee waiting to share the details. "Lost Buffalo negotiated with Henri about trading you, and not for much, I might add. Oh, Kallie, this is perfect. Pressure them to take me also as part of the deal. Our prayers have been answered. I'd best get back before I'm missed and Weasel Tail tries to beat me again. I swear he is starting to enjoy it. Remember—not a word of this to anyone. Try to find out when they plan to leave. I'm counting on you, Kallie." Elizabeth rushed out and then poked her head back in to add, "I almost forgot. Weasel Tail's first wife, Meadow Grass, said I could help you with the birth. Send for me as soon as you need to." Then Elizabeth scurried away.

Kallie gathered more wood. From outside the steam bath she heard the fire crackle and the men talking.

Lost Buffalo said, "Here are magic potions from our special pipe. This tobacco is a special blend of dogwood tree bark and herbs."

The young men must have smoked it, because she heard them coughing and talking about their dreamlike sensations.

Bear said, "I am honored to be your assistant on your vision quest. I have prepared all the things we will need."

Lost Buffalo reminded Bear, "As an assistant, wait below the cliffs with the horses and guard against any possible intruders. It is time now for both of you to paint your faces."

Bear continued to talk. "I am uneasy about the weather. I feel a snowstorm is brewing. It is the pale moon, and that means the weather will grow colder. I think I will take more provisions than I originally planned." They stopped talking. Bear exited and surprised Kallie.

Brave Eagle emerged with his face painted half-black and half-white with four long streaks down his cheek. He was already in a trancelike state and did not seem to see her. He climbed on his horse, Wind Racer, and swiftly rode toward the river cliffs. Bear followed.

Lost Buffalo emerged from the tepee and told Kallie, "Bring that wood for our fire. I am tired and look forward to a nap."

When they arrived home, Lost Buffalo said, "All is as it should be. Brave Eagle's vision quest will decide your fate. I have done all I can to clear his mind and open his heart. Kallie, whatever the final decision, it is now up to the spirits. I will think about it no more." He complained, "My hip is hurting more than usual; the weather will turn for the worse. I hope the hunters arrive soon. I miss Yellow Willow." Lost Buffalo then clutched his robe and fell asleep.

Lost Buffalo's prediction was accurate, and the buffalo hunters returned that evening. They had hurried home because of weather changes. Kallie noticed Yellow Willow was exuberant as she carried calfskins and fresh meat into the tepee. She proudly unpacked raw liver and intestines she had painstakingly saved. She instructed, "Kallie, eat these for the baby's health."

Kallie could barely keep from retching at the sight of it. Not wanting to disappoint Yellow Willow, she sampled a small portion and discovered the liver tasted good. It eased her cravings. Yellow Willow smiled. "It will fill you with good things. My son, Short Bull, provided this for you to give you strength."

Their time was filled with the hard work of caring for the hides and distributing raw meat to the elders of each family. Walks Far had come to help. After the long chore of unpacking, the women were exhausted.

Kallie tried to hide her occasional grimaces. Yellow Willow fell into such a deep sleep that not even Lost Buffalo's coughing fits disturbed her.

Kallie's contractions had grown stronger. She tried to hide the labor pains because Walks Far seemed to be watching her. Walks Far's disposition had lightened considerably, and Kallie wondered why. Walks Far gave her a potion that tasted so bitter she did not trust it. She knew no one would question her death should she fall prey to Walks Far's venom.

Walks Far asserted, "Your pains have arrived. Let us go to the birthing tepee, and I will help ease your discomfort with an herbal drink. The baby will not be born for a while, so let the old couple sleep. You must not burden them. Lost Buffalo is growing weaker from his cough, and Yellow Willow is very tired. I will tell both Running Brook and Yellow Willow to come help when it is time."

Kallie was fearful because escape would be difficult. Her intuition told her not to trust Walks Far's pretense of concern. It was a trap. Walks Far would kill her and steal the baby. As pain skirted Kallie's midsection, she could barely keep from moaning but kept her face expressionless.

When the pain had subsided, she lied, "Of course I will come to you when the time is right, but it is not time yet. I will speak to Elizabeth. Weasel Tail said she could come help." Kallie defiantly stood with her arms crossed and knew she would not comply with Walks Far's wishes.

Walks Far was forced to concede. She smiled curtly and hissed, "You will have your way for now. Here, I have prepared a special blend of red clover and strawberry leaves to help you give birth. You should drink this soon."

As soon as Walks Far stormed out, Kallie flung the drink into the fire. She hurried to Weasel Tail's tepee to ask Elizabeth for help. In a panic, she announced herself and entered. Meadow Grass and Elizabeth were bent over a stretched hide, cutting it. The tepee was much bigger than Yellow Willow's. Elizabeth's belongings were stacked against the wall, and Kallie realized that, for a second wife, Elizabeth had many possessions. She thought to herself that Elizabeth was probably a better trader than the white men.

Elizabeth glanced suspiciously at Kallie and continued cutting. Calmly, she said, "It has gotten so cold the river has frozen solid again. Weasel Tail says a spring blizzard is coming. Have you ever noticed, Kallie, that spring storms are the worst?"

Kallie nodded her head. "Yes, it is getting colder. Yellow Willow said they came back early from the hunt because it might storm."

Meadow Grass went to get more wood from the outside pile. Elizabeth waited until Meadow Grass was gone and whispered, "So do you have everything you need?" Kallie nodded her head yes. Elizabeth continued, "There's no way to talk you out of running away? Giving birth in a cave?" Kallie shook her head no. Elizabeth sighed in defeat. "Well, at least let me brush and braid your hair so it'll be out of the way." Kallie struggled to maintain her composure, as the pains had begun again. They became increasingly stronger while she sat.

Elizabeth wove one long braid down Kallie's back and inquired, "Have you taken a good look at the preacher man? The one they call Pierre? He doesn't wear a wedding ring. I saw you studying his hands. What did they say to you?"

Grimacing through her pain, Kallie foretold, "He's right-handed and has average-sized hands, so he's a practical, logical sort of man. His palms are a square shape. This means he's a hard worker and likes to play by the rules. But he could be stubborn, you know … thinks only his point of view is right. His fingers are long with knobby knuckles, so he's a planner and likes a challenge. Once he's decided on something, he's not easily discouraged. He probably has just a few friends, and he doesn't like to take many chances. Elizabeth, you'll have to inspire him so he'll take up your cause. And if you are successful in that, he'll fight for you until the end." Sharp pains disrupted Kallie's smile, and she bent down as she held her midsection.

Elizabeth looked pleased. "Well, I'll have to be persistent. Kallie, if you come out of this alive, at least your hair will look good. If you have a son, a dark son, you might get the man you want so badly. Although the latest news is, Kallie, that Henri is thinking about Lost Buffalo's proposition. You know, the deal about trading you. He'll take you in trade but not the child. He doesn't want to travel with a baby."

The contractions grew stronger in closer intervals. After talking with Elizabeth, Kallie decided to leave for her cave immediately before the storm hit. With Yellow Willow and Lost Buffalo sleeping through the evening, this might be her only opportunity to leave undetected. If she left now, she could pretend to be going out for wood and water. No one would suspect her true motives.

Kallie squeezed Elizabeth's hand good-bye and, with great effort, pretended everything was fine. Kallie slipped outside and closed her robe around her. The wind was beginning to howl. She stopped at the tepee for her collecting basket and water container. Then she and Fella walked out of the village. Snow flurries swirled around, covering her tracks. Even though moving was painful, she did not pause until she reached the entrance of her cave.

Kallie could no longer eat but drank a long swig of water. Her labor increased, and she was overwhelmed with fear. She wished Brave Eagle was protecting her and that she would be allowed to keep the baby. Tears ran down her face, and Kallie screamed. Despite her experience delivering babies, she was terrified.

She grasped her belly and bent over in pain. Fella whined and moved to a corner to lick his paws. Kallie was trembling but managed to make a small fire and prepare the items she needed. The pain spread throughout her lower body with an intensity she had not anticipated. She rocked back and forth. No position was comfortable. Her long braid had begun to unravel. Desperate for relief, she found the herbal potion Yellow Willow had made for her. Kallie gulped it down praying the concoction would help her.

Her pain intensified throughout the night. She was uncomfortable but was warm and protected. The snow began to pile up in front of the cave entrance. Kallie did the best she could to remain calm during the sharp contractions and took more of Yellow Willow's medicine. The root tea tasted so bitter she could barely tolerate it. Kallie thought it strange because Yellow Willow's potions were usually sweeter. She paced, soaked in sweat and trying to endure each contraction. Finally, it happened. Bending over in pain, she had the urge to push. She pushed with each contraction until her body took over. The contractions came again and again until Kallie thought she could tolerate no more. Screaming, she finally pushed her baby through.

Her little, dark son was born in the early morning. He let out a strong wail as he entered the world. Kallie smiled as she held him close and smelled him. When he looked up, searching for her breast, she noticed he had his father's dark, intense eyes. She began to nurse him. After a time, she tied off his umbilical cord and moved the soiled grass away. She snuggled with him under the robe and listened to the howling wind. The little boy's skin was like silk. For the time being, all was calm inside the cave. She fell asleep.

When Kallie awoke, she was disoriented. Her baby boy seemed healthy and strong, but she grew concerned. The storm had intensified, and she felt herself growing weaker. With her last bit of strength, she sipped water and nursed the baby. She gathered a new moss diaper. Kallie lay down and stared at the smoldering fire. She saw herself put more wood on it, but when she awoke, the fire was cold. Snow completely blocked the cave entrance. In the darkness, she called Brave Eagle's name and then almost lost consciousness. She heard Fella whine as he nudged her face with his nose and smelled the baby. She tried to call out. Fella paced back and forth at the cave entrance and poked his nose out like he was searching for any smell that would calm him.

Chapter 27: *Vision Quest*

Hanble: To Fast and Attain Visions

Brave Eagle reached the cliffs and tethered his medicine shield and weapons to Wind Racer. His horse would be under Bear's protection. Brave Eagle, already in a deep trance, carried his medicine bundle, sage, fire starter, and wood. He moved along the icy trail. When he slipped, the ice cut his hands, but he could not feel them. Climbing closer to the spirits, he hiked up the highest cliff and entered a cave. Brave Eagle started a fire, huddled close, and stared into its dancing flames. He smudged by burning dried sage leaves. He cupped the sweet-smelling smoke in his hands and spread it over his body, creating a sacred space. He sang songs to help ease his confusion.

The memory of his departed wife haunted him. He still missed her. That was why he felt an intense loyalty toward her family. Dawn Star's face appeared before him, and her beauty mesmerized him.

During the night, the storm intensified. Brave Eagle listened to the wind blasting through the valley and thought back to the first time he had seen Kallie. He had first spotted her from a distance. He had signaled the others to hide in the vegetation while she unknowingly walked toward them, calling for her horse. His eyes had not left her as she had approached. Kallie had been so close he had seen her exotic green eyes.

Bear had called out to her with a horse call, and Brave Eagle had been impressed that she had known instantly it was not her horse that had answered. She had stood still. Suddenly, she had turned and run. The way she moved, with her long skirt flowing, had intrigued him. Kallie had stopped once and glanced back before she had headed into the trees. Brave Eagle and his fellow warriors had stayed close to her camp that day. Camouflaged by the bush, they had watched the white peoples' curious activities while the warriors had planned their raid.

Brave Eagle began to dream he was a wind spirit soaring high above his village. He saw Kallie in labor. His insides filled with anger when he remembered the white men watching her with their hungry eyes. His memories blended together: Lost Buffalo's proposal to the trader, losing his wife, and Dawn Star's enticing smile. In his vision, Lost Buffalo came as a shadow and reminded him to use animal guides.

Brave Eagle called out to the spirits: the elk spirit for love, the spirit of the bear for courage, and the wolf for cleverness. He was in a deep trance and could no longer determine if the wolf howls were from this world or another. He took in a deep breath and exhaled his repressed anger. With each breath, he became more accepting of himself. Brave Eagle relaxed, confident that Bear would look after things in this world as he let himself slip deeper into his spirit journey.

Throughout the night, Brave Eagle hallucinated. Even though he had always respected elders, provided for his family, and followed the ways of spirit, everything had been taken from him. He let go of his bitterness and purged anger until he was left shivering and exhausted. When he woke from his trance, his mind was clear. After the death of his first wife, his heart had become stone until the moment he had seen Kallie. Only she broke the dark spell. Brave Eagle knew his answer. Now courage and integrity would be needed to deal with his family's expectations.

His mistake had been one of pride. He had never fully trusted anyone. He had been too proud to enlist the help of the grandmothers, whose role it was to keep tribal relationships in harmony. They would have helped the two families come to an agreement that balanced everyone's needs.

Snow clouds filled the sky as Brave Eagle fell into intervals of sleep and hallucination. He dreamed the hunt had been successful and the hunters had safely returned to the village. Brave Eagle woke and shivered from the cold. The fire had turned to ash, except for a few buried coals that glimmered when the wind stirred. He used the last of his dry prairie grass kindling and ignited the fire again. Hunger gnawed at him. Still hallucinating, he saw a wolf spirit run past the cave entrance. Brave Eagle knew the wolf represented danger. Firelight danced upon the rock wall, and shadows shaped into the face of his enemy, Hawk Claw. A strange fungus smell, not unlike the smell of death, permeated Brave Eagle's nostrils. This unusual sign greatly unsettled him.

He tried to stand but could not. A mountain lion, which was Kallie's animal spirit, pranced on the rocks. It leaped from ledge to ledge, guarding Kallie and her baby. Brave Eagle wondered if it was possible the baby had been born. This pleasant thought was disturbed by his spirit eagle's harsh scream. It was trapped; its talons were being grabbed, and its neck was being throttled. Brave Eagle awoke from his stupor and experienced a fear he had never felt before. The cave was completely black, and he had no sense of time. Although confused, he was consumed with concern for the safety of his village, his family, Kallie, the baby, and himself. Something was terribly wrong.

Snow accompanied ferocious winds. Brave Eagle was panicked and could hardly breathe. He slid down the trail not caring about scrapes or cuts. He sensed there was a dangerous threat, and he had to warn the other warriors about the threatening omen he had experienced.

He called out to Bear with a wolf howl. Bear answered with a yelp call guiding Brave Eagle through the darkness. He found Bear sheltered from the wind and covered in his robes, sitting near a fire. Bear looked confused at Brave Eagle's abrupt appearance, and he said, "Sit. You are cold. Your lips are blue. You are shaking, delirious. Put this robe around you. I will not listen until you sit by the fire."

Brave Eagle said, "We must go back immediately," but he could not find the words to explain more.

Bear shook his head. "No, drink tea and calm down. You are not making sense. It is perilous to journey during any storm, especially a pale moon blizzard." Brave Eagle tried to stand, but Bear firmly told him, "Sit. We travel at first light. Here is tea Lost Buffalo prepared for you." Brave Eagle drank it and fell asleep immediately.

At dawn, Brave Eagle and Bear left the shelter of the cave. The wind was fierce, and the blistering snow obscured their vision. Brave Eagle was not to be thwarted. He and Bear rode steadily into the storm, unaware of the danger lurking just beyond their valley.

Chapter 28: *The Storm*

Iyapa: To Run Against

Brave Eagle and Bear slowly made their way into the village. The two men's faces were frozen with ice, and Brave Eagle could no longer feel his feet. His fingers grasped Wind Racer's reins, but he could feel nothing. He looked around and saw only white. Every tepee entrance was buried in a snowdrift. Even the sentry dogs were hiding in dugout snow shelters.

Quickly, the men tethered their horses and entered Short Bull's tepee to escape the unrelenting storm. Once they were inside, Bear scooped twisted dried grass for the tired horses. Brave Eagle's mother, Pretty Shield, hurried in with warm compresses, extra blankets, and a nourishing hot meal. Bear shivered as he ate several helpings of stew. Brave Eagle collapsed on the floor. He called for Lost Buffalo, but no one seemed to hear him. He had heard Short Bull say he was going to sleep at his parents' home, where it would be quieter.

In the morning, Brave Eagle awoke. His thoughts were beginning to clear. He ate cold stew but still was deeply troubled by his vision quest. Something was wrong. When Brave Eagle's belly was full, he stretched his legs, gathered a robe, and walked to Lost Buffalo's tepee.

When he arrived, Short Bull muttered for him to enter. Brave Eagle sat silently at the cold fire pit while his eyes searched for Kallie. It appeared she slept under her robe.

Yellow Willow started a small fire and heated water for redroot tea. Lost Buffalo struggled from his bed, sat in his willow chair, and said, "I can see by the expression on your face you would like to discuss your vision quest now. Do you mind if the others are here?"

Brave Eagle shook his head no, and the old man encouraged him to describe his experience. Brave Eagle did not hold back. He unraveled his visions of Hawk Claw, and the fear of being trapped and then strangled. He spoke of his decision about Kallie and the need for the tribal grandmothers to help him. He expressed his fear of impending danger.

The shaman seemed lost in Brave Eagle's insights. Lost Buffalo had put on his magical elk skin, which was as creased as his own face. The long tears in it had been tenderly repaired. Brave Eagle knew Lost Buffalo derived great power from it. He wrapped the skin around his shoulders, positioning it so that Brave Eagle would not disturb him.

Brave Eagle sat in silence while Lost Buffalo contemplated the vision. He finally said, "Brave Eagle, I had hoped your vision quest would solve my own dark premonition, but it has not. More patience will be needed to sort out the meanings of your vision quest. I need more time to see in the darkness, so you are welcome to leave or sit and drink tea."

After Brave Eagle was served, Yellow Willow said, "Short Bull, get up."

Short Bull slid deeper into his robe and said, "Wind is blasting snow throughout the village. I was planning to sleep."

Yellow Willow said, "Then at least nudge Kallie. I need her help."

Short Bull opened his eyes in surprise. "She is not here. She has not been here all night."

Confused, Yellow Willow said, "She must be in the birthing tepee. Quick, Short Bull. Get up. Go inquire."

Disgruntled, Short Bull pulled on his winter shirt and ventured out in the storm. When Short Bull returned, he shook off the snow that filled his clothing and gave the details. "She is not there. Walks Far said she did not come to her. No one knows where she is. She left before dark with her basket and water containers. Nothing unusual."

Yellow Willow shot a concerned look at Lost Buffalo, who said, "Don't worry. She is probably with Hawk Woman. There has to be some explanation. Not even Kallie would be foolish enough to wander off during a pale moon storm."

Brave Eagle said, "I am not so sure."

Yellow Willow agreed. "We must search for her." Determined, Brave Eagle, Short Bull, and Yellow Willow left the tepee. Yellow Willow bent her head down to avoid the brutal, stinging wind. Her hands tightly clutched Brave Eagle and Short Bull. The landscape was a blinding whiteness. Having found no clues from Hawk Woman, Yellow Willow told the men, "Elizabeth must know something about Kallie's disappearance. Kallie would not take such a risk without confiding in someone."

They struggled to make headway and trudged toward Meadow Grass's lodge. Brave Eagle asked Yellow Willow, "How will you get information from Elizabeth?"

Yellow Willow replied, "It will be easy."

Once they arrived, Short Bull, Yellow Willow, and Brave Eagle were quickly ushered in and served hot tea as the family huddled by the fire. Meadow Grass whispered to them, "She knows."

Brave Eagle observed Yellow Willow work her way to Elizabeth, who seemed preoccupied in the corner. While inquiring about the disappearance of Kallie, Yellow Willow looked directly into Elizabeth's eyes. She extended her hand to Elizabeth's and rubbed it while asking Meadow Grass, "The white men will come to talk to Lost Buffalo today. Could Elizabeth come help me?" Meadow Grass looked up to Weasel Tail, who had no opinion, and she nodded her head yes. Elizabeth eagerly grabbed her worn buffalo coat and scurried out the door with them before Weasel Tail changed his mind.

When they had settled in at Yellow Willow's tepee, Brave Eagle let her handle the situation. She resorted to promising Elizabeth she would be permitted to entertain Pierre when he came to visit. This could be arranged if she would tell them where Kallie had gone.

Elizabeth blurted out, "She must be at a cave just past the last water trail. She told me about it and said she was going to give birth there. I told her it was a foolish idea, but Kallie never listens. She is fearful that Walks Far will take her baby. She must have left in the storm."

Short Bull said, "I know where her hiding place is. Bear told me about Kallie's wolf encounter by the river and how he had noticed her tracks going up in the hills. I used to explore those caves when I was a boy."

When Short Bull saw his mother's pleading face, he said, "I will go search for her. Brave Eagle, you are tired. You stay here."

Brave Eagle said, "I am going."

Short Bull replied, "Brave Eagle, you are weakened from your vision quest. Can you even separate the dream world from reality?" When Short Bull heard no answer, he shrugged. "Do what you want, but I am taking the lead."

Yellow Willow said, "Thank you both. Here are food pouches to put inside your robes. Take two of our best horses."

By the time Brave Eagle and Short Bull entered their tepee, snow had already crusted upon their faces. The warmth from the tepee fire began to melt it, making their chins drip. Brave Eagle's mother was cleaning up. Short Bull told her, "We are going to search for Kallie. She is missing."

Upon hearing news of the captive's disappearance, Pretty Shield said, "Oh, that poor girl. She will surely die out in this storm. Brave Eagle, you must stay here and rest. Let Short Bull do this for Yellow Willow."

Brave Eagle continued gathering his warmest clothes, so she held out a nutritious broth with thinly cut meat and insisted, "If you must go, at least eat so you will have strength."

Pretty Shield pleaded with Short Bull, "It is crazy to search for her in this storm. The she-wolf will come back when she is ready. Why would you risk your life for her?"

Short Bull agreed with Pretty Shield but added, "I am doing this for my mother. It will help to have Brave Eagle along."

Bear, who had been sleeping in the corner, woke up. He appeared confused at all the activity but followed the other men's example and began dressing in his warmest clothes. Bear said, "Wait. I am almost ready to go. Where are we going?"

Pretty Shield answered, "On a hopeless mission for a stupid captive. Bear, talk sense into them."

Brave Eagle hugged his mother and followed Short Bull and Bear into the storm. Soon, the whirling wet snow obliterated any trail left by the men. It pelted their eyes and clung to their heavy robes.

Short Bull led the way to the approximate location of the large caves above the river bend. Brave Eagle cupped his hands around his mouth and asked Short Bull, "Why did you not say anything before this?"

Short Bull shouted against the wind, "I did not care about Kallie's hiding place. It was not my business until today. Now I am risking my life for hers." He smiled. "I guess I should have said something sooner." His horse stopped abruptly on the icy path. Short Bull prodded his reluctant horse to go slowly forward.

The river path was treacherous. A horse could slip, throwing its rider into an icy death. Sleet pounded them, and they were covered with ice. Eventually they reached the place where the hills met at the river bend. The men huddled in their robes and scanned the area for the cave where Short Bull suspected Kallie was hiding. As Short Bull peered through sleet, trying to pinpoint its location, Brave Eagle thought he heard a yip. He strained his ears and heard the muffled sound again. Short Bull headed in the direction of the sound. Directed by Fella's frantic barking, the men located the cave's entrance and dug. Fella wagged his tail and jumped with excitement as the men crawled through the opening.

The interior of the cave was dark and cold. The fire had died out long ago. Short Bull rapidly twisted his fire starter, blowing the sparks onto the tinder. Brave Eagle repeatedly called Kallie's name, but only after Short Bull started the fire could he see the body outline of her robe against the cave wall. He knelt over her and whispered her name, hoping her eyes would open. When they didn't, he felt under her nose for a wisp of warm air. He spoke with relief as he called out to Short Bull, "She is still alive." Short Bull smiled as he fed the fire and waited for Brave Eagle to direct him.

Kallie opened her eyes, looked at Brave Eagle, and asked, "Am I dead?"

Brave Eagle smiled. "No, Kallie. You are alive. Short Bull, Bear, and I are here." He turned to Short bull and whispered, "Her breath is weak, and her forehead is hot. These are bad signs." He lifted her head and offered her water. When the cool water reached her parched lips, she took in a little. Kallie was conscious but no longer seemed to know where she was.

Brave Eagle said, "Kallie, try to stay in this world. Please, do not go away. Stay with us."

Kallie was delirious. She mumbled something about the trader and Walks Far taking the baby. She became more agitated.

Brave Eagle pleaded, "Kallie, calm down. Stay with us."

She asked him, "Have you seen the baby?"

He shook his head no. Anxiously, he pulled open the robe and saw the infant nestled by her side. Brave Eagle looked down in awe. The newborn's dark eyes stared up at him. Brave Eagle felt as if he was looking into his own eyes. The baby was a healthy and strong son. Sheepishly, Brave Eagle lifted the little one and held him close to his chest; then he raised him up to profusely thank the Creator.

Short Bull pulled two small pouches from his shirt and presented them to the proud father. One pouch was shaped as a turtle, and the other was shaped like a lizard. These shapes were selected because turtles and lizards lived long lives. Yellow Willow had made the pouches to protect the little one. Later in the child's life, the turtle would serve as a reminder of how precious life is.

Brave Eagle knew part of the umbilical cord was to go in the turtle pouch. This was vitally important for the baby's spiritual survival. He did not know how to speak of this with Kallie. He decided to ask later and put the pouch necklace on the baby's neck. Yellow Willow would know what to do in order to protect his son. The baby nudged Brave Eagle's chest, and the men laughed, knowing it was time for him to nurse. Brave Eagle helped Kallie, for she could no longer sit up without support. Her eyes had a vacant look, and it was apparent to him she had lost much blood.

Brave Eagle, Bear, and Short Bull discussed their limited options. They had to get Kallie into Yellow Willow's care. The only way to save her was to leave immediately, although traveling during a storm might prove deadly. Brave Eagle would not sit and wait for her death. This he would not do. Short Bull and Bear decided they would do whatever Brave Eagle requested of them.

Brave Eagle decided Short Bull would carry the baby, and he tied his tiny son to Short Bull's chest. There, under Short Bull's massive robe, the baby would be protected against the cruel winds. Bear helped Brave Eagle carry Kallie. Wrapped in a buffalo blanket, Kallie moaned as Bear lifted her upon Wind Racer. Brave Eagle held her tightly.

Short Bull threw Bear a pouch to sling around his horse's neck. In a quick motion Bear scooped up Fella and placed him safely in the pouch. They traveled as fast as possible, battling the raging storm. Snow drifted across the trail, making travel treacherous. Eventually, they reached the shelter of the trees along the river.

Brave Eagle felt Kallie stir, so he knew she was alive. He felt her body lean against his chest, and he embraced her. In the blinding storm the riders could not see the trail. But even under the desperate circumstances, Wind Racer knew the way to his herd, food, and shelter. The horses stopped only once. Brave Eagle noticed the nervous horses were acting like they had encountered the smells of a strange herd, but he paid no mind.

The storm spirits hovered above them. Blasts of snow swirled, and cold penetrated them, but they were determined men. They reached the village with Kallie and the baby still alive. Yellow Willow pointed toward the warm birthing tepee. In the blinding snow, Brave Eagle gently lifted Kallie off Wind Racer and into the arms of Bear, who carried her into the tepee. Lost Buffalo and Yellow Willow followed them, apprehensive but grateful. Lost Buffalo said, "The spirits have watched over my adopted daughter."

Brave Eagle acknowledged Lost Buffalo's statement but could not shake his anxious feelings. His vision quest still haunted him. Even though he had found Kallie and the baby in time, something was not right.

Chapter 29: *Uneasy Feelings*

Hahake: Anxious

In the birthing tepee, Brave Eagle, shivering from the cold, knelt close and called out Kallie's name repeatedly until he realized she could not respond. Kallie slept and did not stir even when the baby squirmed at her breast. Running Brook gave the baby a concerned look as she tenderly sprinkled mushroom powder on his umbilical cord.

Yellow Willow gently massaged Kallie's belly and said, "I've administered yellow poppy tincture, which should reduce swelling, but her breath is shallow. Death is stalking her." Yellow Willow sadly shook her head. "I fear I have done all I can, and now it is up to the Great Spirit."

After his son had nursed, Brave Eagle stood to leave but then boldly asked Yellow Willow, "May I take my son with me?"

Yellow Willow weakly nodded and said, "I cannot refuse the father of the child."

Lost Buffalo, wearing an owl headdress, waved a painted plum stick with a pouch of sweetgrass incense hanging from it. He spoke to Yellow Willow but was loud enough for Brave Eagle to hear. "Kallie ran away to protect her baby, and now her actions have set off a chain of events beyond her control. Brave Eagle carries the baby toward Pretty Shield's tepee. Now the baby will be separated from her. Kallie's premonition has come true." Lost Buffalo chanted over his adopted daughter's still body. Yellow Willow sang a healing prayer, and Running Brook kept the fire going.

Brave Eagle hurried to his mother's tepee and entered with a wide grin. Pretty Shield joyously hugged him. Brave Eagle beamed with happiness as he pulled the baby from beneath his thick robe. As he presented his son to his father, Flaming Arrow looked upon his first grandchild with pride. He said, "My grandson resembles our family. I feel a strong bond with the little one." Flaming Arrow said to Pretty Shield, "Take this young warrior from your son's shaking arms." Then Flaming Arrow said, "Son, you are swaying. The vision quest and rescue have drained you of your strength. Rest. We will take care of this fine grandson." Brave Eagle sat covered in buffalo blankets and listened to the excited women.

Pretty Shield cuddled the infant and then handed the baby to Dawn Star, who had come for a visit. She said, "Word is traveling throughout the village. Kallie is not well."

His mother smiled. "It will make our lives simpler."

Dawn Star gazed upon the baby and agreed. The women gathered around and cooed at the little one. Walks Far said, "What a handsome baby. He looks so much like his father."

The women discussed the preparations they needed to take care of the baby. Dawn Star spoke about finding a wet nurse for the child since Kallie was so ill and not expected to recover. Pretty Shield proudly presented a beautifully beaded cradle board she had used for her own children. The cradle was elegant, with a simple design of delicate beaded flowers circling the rim. Its interior was lined with soft rabbit skins. Blue-beaded pouches holding charms were attached to the sides of the cradle board. It was a wonderful gift that Pretty Shield gave to the small child. This powerful gesture meant Pretty Shield had accepted the little one into her family. The baby now was the youngest member in her large clan of strong warriors. Brave Eagle felt proud.

Family friends came to celebrate the birth of his son. The women became busy with preparations. Despite the raging storm, the women scurried outside to collect supplies and returned with their arms full.

Flaming Arrow told Brave Eagle, "I am joyful about my new grandson, but I need to talk to Lost Buffalo."

Brave Eagle replied, "I would like to go also."

Flaming Arrow said, "Let's go then."

Lost Buffalo welcomed Brave Eagle and Flaming Arrow as they entered the tepee. He invited them to smoke his special tobacco to celebrate the birth. After they had smoked a bit, there was a long silence. Flaming Arrow shared, "Lost Buffalo, I've come for advice. I am haunted by a strange dream I had last night. Its visions were most unsettling. If it is possible, I would like an interpretation." But then suddenly he changed the subject and asked, "May I visit Kallie?"

Surprised, Lost Buffalo replied, "Yes, of course," and followed Brave Eagle and Flaming Arrow out.

When the men entered the birthing tepee, Brave Eagle noticed Kallie was still pale and close to death. His father told her, "You have brought a fine son into the world and a fine grandson. I thank you, Kallie."

Yellow Willow administered a powerful concoction of black currant root to her patient. She told the men, "Soon we will know whether Kallie will come back or journey to the spirit world. I will sit with her. Go back to the tepee and relax. There is nothing you can do here. Leave me."

The men complied and went to the tepee. As the men smoked, Brave Eagle grew light-headed. After Lost Buffalo contemplated the unfolding events, he said, "This is a perplexing puzzle. The pieces include Brave Eagle's vision quest, my own premonitions, and, now, Flaming Arrow's ominous dream. I shudder at the depths my thoughts have taken me. Perhaps the stones will provide more details."

Lost Buffalo unfolded his sacred bundle and removed his stones. He asked his troubling questions out loud and rolled the stones. Lost Buffalo lapsed into a trancelike state and said, "In the village a screeching eagle hovers over a tepee, and a mountain lion crawls from a cave. The river flows blood red. Crows circle above, and I see Flaming Arrow's war headdress. It is carelessly thrown on the ground. A fierce warrior I do not recognize stares up at me. There is no life left in his eyes. The warrior is an enemy and painted for battle. The dead man grips an eagle feather, cut diagonally, signifying he has cut his enemy's throat."

"What is the purpose of this?" Brave Eagle asked.

Lost Buffalo answered, "Stones tell me the river flows with life or death. We must protect and defend ourselves from an enemy. If we run from him, he will claim us. He will kill us all."

The shaman continued, "I see a hand grasping an eagle's talons as it lands on a trap pit. Whose hand, I cannot determine. I see a strong arm swiftly pull the eagle into the pit while twisting its neck. I see Brave Eagle running toward me for a fleeting second, and then my dream fades." Lost Buffalo looked off again. "No, wait. The stones have more to tell me. They show me a vision of an infant being cuddled with love but in grave danger. An enemy creeps toward him. This enemy warrior shoots an arrow, but where it lands I cannot say. I hear screams of a woman. In my vision, the storm has subsided and the river ice floats with the current. All is quiet now except for the wailing of people. I see Kallie standing by Yellow Willow as they mourn over someone. The body is facedown in the snow. I am told no more."

Brave Eagle put down the pipe and shot a look of concern at Flaming Arrow. As Lost Buffalo regained his senses, he said, "I am relieved this vision is only a dream journey. I am glad to be back in my warm and quiet tepee." Putting his stones back in their container, Lost Buffalo said, "There is danger coming. We must heed this warning from the spirit world before it is too late."

Flaming Arrow agreed. "We will alert Black Hand to post sentries at the village's edge as soon as the storm dies down. No one will attack in this storm. It would be a bad omen. Lost Buffalo's vision showed calm weather."

Lost Buffalo nodded his head in agreement and said, "Go speak with Black Hand. Tell him danger is coming. Brave Eagle, let us check on Kallie. I also want to see Yellow Willow and make sure she is all right."

At the birthing tepee, Yellow Willow gave an update. "Kallie still clings to life. I am concerned her condition has not improved, but I will continue to administer medicine." Then, looking at Brave Eagle, she said, "I have asked Running Brook to retrieve the baby."

Lost Buffalo gently kissed and held Yellow Willow. He said, "Brave Eagle, my wife is a good healer. She will take care of Kallie."

Upon returning with the baby, Running Brook said, "Pretty Shield resisted giving the child to me. I had to politely insist, and in the end, I won. Next time will be harder. Brave Eagle, I will need your help to go against your mother's wishes."

Brave Eagle agreed. He left and slogged in the snow until he arrived at the herd of horses. There, he gathered two of his finest horses and roped them behind Wind Racer. Brave Eagle squinted against the gusts of wind that blasted snow in his face until he arrived at the tepee of Lost Buffalo. He tied the horses to a post outside the tepee and then rode back to Kallie.

Brave Eagle slipped in without announcing himself and was infuriated to find Elizabeth and Pierre hovering over Kallie. Elizabeth's huge silver cross dangled in Kallie's face. Elizabeth cried as she held Kallie's hand, while Pierre boldly said his prayers. He waved his hands as if he were performing a death chant. Brave Eagle looked angrily at Running Brook, who held his son. Running Brook reacted by forcing her way in between the two white people. She sternly explained that Kallie needed privacy to nurse her son. There was an awkward moment of silence, but Running Brook insisted. She brusquely pulled Elizabeth out the door, and Pierre followed. Brave Eagle stared with hostility as the three of them exited.

Brave Eagle knelt beside Kallie and listened to her shallow breathing. Just then, she opened her eyes, slowly at first, and looked at Brave Eagle. Her voice weak, she asked if Elizabeth and Pierre were gone. A look of relief washed over her when Brave Eagle nodded yes. They enjoyed a quiet moment until it became obvious the baby needed changing. Kallie pointed, saying, "There are moss and cattail pads in the corner. Would you get one?" Brave Eagle gathered a moss diaper and heard Kallie struggling to get up.

He objected. "No, do not get up. Running Brook left with Elizabeth and Pierre, but I will do this." Soon he was on his knees, laughing, rubbing his son's head, doing his best to clean him.

A flustered Brave Eagle, kneeling on a robe, comically attempting to change his son, was interrupted when relatives stopped by. The men stood silently while Yellow Willow and Running Brook chuckled.

Yellow Willow said, "Shoo, Brave Eagle. We will take care of this. Running Brook, give Kallie the last of her medicine. It will make her sleep in order to heal. Brave Eagle, do not sleep here tonight. She needs quiet."

Brave Eagle patiently waited for the old couple to retreat so he could observe their reaction to the horses tied outside their tepee. When Yellow Willow and Lost Buffalo noticed the two beautiful horses tied to their post, they looked at Flaming Arrow. Such a generous gesture could be interpreted only as Brave Eagle asking permission to marry Kallie.

There was an uncomfortable silence until Lost Buffalo shook his head and said, "We cannot accept this gift with Kallie being so close to death. This might be a bad omen."

Yellow Willow looked gravely at Lost Buffalo and said loudly, "We accept this gift!" She boldly moved to touch the horses in acceptance.

Brave Eagle felt relieved but noticed his father bite his lower lip. He mentioned nothing about the horses as they walked against the headwinds. Brave Eagle stopped to say good-night to his mother before retiring for the evening.

His mother, Pretty Shield, told him, "I will fetch the baby early in the morning. Kallie is too ill to care for him." Brave Eagle nodded in agreement and left. He found Short Bull and Bear sitting by the fire smoking pipes. Their firewood supply was dwindling, so they retired early to stay warm. As they crawled under their buffalo robes, Short Bull muttered, "What kind of enemy would strike at us during a storm such as this? A storm is a bad omen. To go against nature makes no sense. Such an attack would bring bad luck upon the perpetrator."

Brave Eagle yawned. "An enemy with a twisted heart, so twisted he does not think like a normal man." But he did not speak the name Hawk Claw out loud.

Bear whispered to Short Bull, "I saw two of Brave Eagle's finest horses tethered behind your mother's tepee. So now the real battle begins."

Short Bull laughed as he rolled over and said, "Bear and Brave Eagle, I think we should gather all our weapons and sleep with them at our side." They agreed. Soon, with their battle gear beside them, the warriors slept.

During this night, the winds died down, the snow stopped falling, and the storm quieted. It was peaceful. All the people in the village slept deeply, except for two. Brave Eagle tossed and turned. He could not sleep. Dark dreams had invaded his thoughts again. He anxiously ventured outside, where he unexpectedly met his father. Flaming Arrow marveled, "It is quiet. Not a dog bark or howl can be heard. Every living thing must be resting after the storm except you and me."

The men entered the birthing tepee and encountered a sleepy Running Brook, who was rocking the baby. She said, "The baby has eaten and should be fine. Flaming Arrow, take him to Pretty Shield, because I could use sleep." Running Brook quickly exited, leaving Brave Eagle and his father to tend to the baby. Flaming Arrow held the little one. Before they left, Brave Eagle checked on Kallie. She looked very pale and did not stir, but she was not dead.

Chapter 30: *Hawk Claw's Revenge*

Watoga: Revenge

Hidden in a cave, Hawk Claw's large war party huddled around a fire. Hawk Claw laughed to himself as he stared at the glowing embers. His warriors had come to raid horses and take buffalo meat back to their hungry village, but Hawk Claw had come for blood revenge against his enemy. He imagined the salty taste of Brave Eagle's blood as Hawk Claw slid his knife blade across his tongue.

An excellent war leader, Hawk Claw had led many successful raids, and he assumed this encounter would be no different. He was seething with anger and hatred. Hawk Claw envisioned winning in hand-to-hand combat against his enemy. He planned to strangle Brave Eagle and leave his mutilated body for his relatives to discover. Strangulation would ensure that Brave Eagle would never reach the spirit land and join his spirit family. Instead, Brave Eagle would be trapped inside his rotting carcass, feeling the slow decomposition of his body until his bleached bones held him captive forever on the earth. Flaming Arrow, Brave Eagle's father, would bear the weight of his son's terrible fate.

Hawk Claw reflected back to the time of the harvest moon, when his younger brother, Raven, had just earned his first warrior feather. He had been so proud. Soon after, Brave Eagle's band had raided their village. It had been a surprise attack, and Hawk Claw had not posted enough guards around camp that night. During the scuffle, Brave Eagle had fought with Raven. Brave Eagle had swung his war club at Raven's head and had left him for dead. At first it had seemed his brother would recover, but then, after several days of unconsciousness, he died. Hawk Claw had vowed to avenge his brother's death.

The surprise raid had caused some of the tribe to question Hawk Claw's leadership abilities. As he had grouped the younger men to retaliate against Brave Eagle, the older chiefs had intervened and stopped him. Now, on this stormy night, the timing was right for an attack, but his men seemed hesitant under his leadership. Hawk Claw suspected a few men were waiting for him to make another mistake so they could prove his medicine bundle had lost its war magic. One thing hadn't changed. His men still feared him and knew he would fight to the death in this retaliation.

Hawk Claw's face held a cold, dark expression. He listened to the bitter wind intensify. The storm had swiftly closed in on them. While most war chiefs would interpret a spring storm of this magnitude as a bad omen, Hawk Claw had rejoiced. He knew it was the Great Spirit helping him make his attack more lethal. Brave Eagle's tribe would never suspect a raid during such weather. He was relieved his scouts had discovered caves hidden in the bluffs. These provided protection for them. The bluffs sheltered even their horses during the storm. The men would have to wait and ration their meager food supplies. Hot tea would keep them warm until the weather changed; then his raiding party would attack like a cougar leaping upon a thirsty pronghorn at a watering hole.

His men gambled and laughed loudly, knowing their presence would not be detected on such a treacherous night. They spoke of the many fine horses and women captives they would take. No sentries would be posted around Brave Eagle's village, for every person would have sought shelter. Soon Hawk Claw's men would be eating the enemies' spring food supply and hanging scalps from their belts. They boasted about past raids as the howling wind echoed throughout the cave.

Hawk Claw was impatient. Thoughts of revenge for his brother's death had consumed him. He would not wait any longer, despite the weather. Hawk Claw painted his powerful body with red spots. He dipped two fingers into red paint and covered his forehead; then he finished with a white stripe cutting across his face. He would wear his buffalo headdress and rawhide wristbands and hang a war club from his belt. The club held powerful war medicine, and its blunt end could kill a man with one mighty blow. The long silver blade of his knife shone by the fire. After everyone was painted, it was finally time to depart. His raiding party was prepared to attack.

He and his war party traveled steadily. The snow was deep, and the night wind was bitter cold. The dark and icy conditions slowed their horses, but they pressed on. While his unsuspecting victims slept in their warm tepees, Hawk Claw's scouts had traveled toward the village.

Hawk Claw knew the timing of the raid would be crucial. They had to attack the large camp before sunrise. His warriors would obtain scalps, steal precious meat supplies, and drive off the horses before most of the tribe was awake. He would set an ambush on the north end. After the raid, his warriors would quickly ride back to where the trails converged. Any enemy foolish enough to follow them would ride into an ambush.

The war party arrived at the perimeter of the village. Hawk Claw was eager to finally avenge his younger brother's death. After scouts surrounded the main herd, Hawk Claw used the caw of a crow to signal it was time to attack. Some of the men siphoned off the herds and started driving the captured horses away. Hawk Claw motioned other men to steal the supplies of meat. His warriors infiltrated the sleeping village. This was easily done because even the sentry dogs slept in dugout snow caves. Painted warriors scattered to collect coup and scalps.

Hawk Claw moved with another warrior whose face was painted completely black. The man's muscular body was painted in yellow stripes, and he wore tufts of feathers on each side of his head. Hawk Claw and his partner chose a tepee located closest to the river on the village outskirts. It was in the most defenseless place.

As the intruders crept forward, a dog whined. He came out of the main entrance growling and with the fur rising on the back of his neck. The dog's nose was sniffing the air. Hawk Claw pointed his arrow at an old man standing in the tepee entrance. Just as the old man looked up at him, Hawk Claw's arrow tore through his heart. The old man clenched his power drum with his feeble hands and remained standing for a few seconds. He turned and fell facedown halfway through the tepee entrance. His blood splattered his drum and power satchel. Hawk Claw shot again, and his arrow pierced the dog's neck. The dog quietly crawled away from the entrance

Hawk Claw watched as his fierce companion tore an opening in the tepee's wall. His companion crept through the hole but quickly backed out before Hawk Claw could enter. The other warrior lowered his voice and said, "A trail of blood oozes from a woman's bed. It is cold and dark. She has been laid out for burial. This is a death tepee and a terrible omen. Hawk Claw, you have killed a powerful medicine man. His power items are strewn out on the ground. I recognize him. This medicine man's spirit can attack me. My battle here is done."

Shaken and not wanting to jeopardize his own power medicine any further, he motioned Hawk Claw to slip back into the safety of the vegetation. Wanting to maintain his power, Hawk Claw told him, "You will fight. Come, let's gather the others to attack the other side."

As he slipped into the main encampment, Hawk Claw recognized Brave Eagle's mother, Pretty Shield. She was outside gathering kindling in the early morning haze and noticed one of his warriors' fleeting movements. She screamed, probably alerting whoever was inside the tepee. Hawk Claw knew he was close to flushing out Brave Eagle, when Flaming Arrow raced outside. As one of his men and Flaming Arrow locked in combat, another warrior struck Pretty Shield in the head. She dropped, and no more screams would be heard from her.

A beautiful woman stood at the entrance of the tepee and peeked out. He raced toward her with his weapon drawn. She screamed in horror and pulled the skin door down to block him, but Hawk Claw barged in. He stared at the young woman, and she stared defiantly back at him. Showing no fear, she stepped back. Hawk Claw thought he might take her captive, but just then, something moved under her robe. Hawk Claw pulled his bowstring and pointed his arrow at the moving robe. As he released the arrow, the woman dove to protect the bundle. The arrow lodged deep into her side. She looked up at him in disbelief. Hawk Claw spit on the ground and left her bleeding.

Vowing revenge upon his brother's killer, Hawk Claw finally spotted Brave Eagle's horse tied to a tepee post. This was where he probably slept. Hawk Claw crept silently on the snowy ground toward the back of the tepee. Whoever slept inside seemed unaware of the impending danger. Hawk Claw laughed to himself, pleased his revenge had come so easily. He drew his double-bladed knife and contemplated whether to take sleeping Brave Eagle's scalp before killing him.

As Hawk Claw approached the tepee, two men came out and looked surprised at the chaos. Then Brave Eagle emerged and did not see him coming from behind. Hawk Claw decided to first touch Brave Eagle with his coup stick. This would give him very powerful war medicine for future battles. As Hawk Claw bent to touch his enemy, he heard someone running toward him. A man was charging straight at him.

Voicing a war cry, Hawk Claw held his tomahawk's blade in the air. The two men collided in combat. Blade hit blade. The downward stabbing motion of Hawk Claw's knife plunged deep. As Hawk Claw pulled away, Flaming Arrow slumped to the ground. Brave Eagle screamed out when he realized his father had been stabbed.

Hawk Claw waved his bloody knife in front of Brave Eagle and taunted, "I will take his scalp after I collect yours." He sprang forward and swiped Brave Eagle's chest with his knife. Brave Eagle seemed wild with grief and acted like he did not feel the slice. Brave Eagle kicked the knife out of Hawk Claw's grip, and it slid across the ground.

The two men fought each other in hand-to-hand combat. Brave Eagle was no match against Hawk Claw's brutal strength, but somehow Brave Eagle knocked him to the ground. Brave Eagle tried to grab the fallen knife, but Hawk Claw was able to break his hold and pin his enemy down. Hawk Claw once again had control. He tightened his hands around Brave Eagle's throat and began to choke him. Hawk Claw laughed, knowing he had finally killed Brave Eagle in the most humiliating way. But then he recoiled from a sharp pain. Brave Eagle had thrust a blade deep into Hawk Claw's lower back. Stunned, Hawk Claw released his grip and fell back. Hawk Claw could not feel his breath flow into his body. His throat burned, and no sound came out as he attempted a war cry. The last thing he felt was Brave Eagle's war club smash into his head.

Chapter 31: *River Flow*

Agli: To Arrive Home

Brave Eagle walked among the dead and wounded. Women shot arrows into enemy bodies so their spirits would be burdened by the additional injuries. This action ensured enemies' ghosts would be bound to the earth forever and never be capable of harming the tribe's loved ones again. Once this task was completed, mourning for the dead ones could begin.

Pretty Shield covered Flaming Arrow's body with hers, wailing sad mourning songs. Her crying was interrupted when Brave Eagle called out to her. She acknowledged him in a weak voice. "Brave Eagle, you are alive." He knelt beside her in the snow, and they embraced. As mother and son clung tightly to each other, they prayed Flaming Arrow would journey quickly to the spirit land. There, ancestors would honor his brave act.

Brave Eagle said, "Mother, I cannot believe Father is dead. Where is my brother, Speckled Eagle? I lost sight of him during the raid and cannot find him. Where are my relatives? Why are they not here helping you? I must find Kallie and my son."

Pretty Shield's swollen eyes spilled more tears as she desperately looked at her grief-stricken son. Shaking him, she said, "You must find your brother first. Ask the spirits to assist you. The baby was with Dawn Star in my tepee."

Upon hearing this, Brave Eagle loosened his mother's grasp and immediately left. Blood dripped into his eyes, and he limped past survivors shrieking and crying as they discovered their dead loved ones.

Brave Eagle could not contain his despair. He could not think clearly. His stab wounds were bleeding through his makeshift bandage.

When Brave Eagle entered his mother's tepee, he discovered the cradle board was empty. Speckled Eagle was kneeling beside Dawn Star. He covered his eyes with both hands and sobbed.

Dawn Star's beautiful eyes were open, but Brave Eagle knew she was dead. An arrow had fatally pierced her side. As Brave Eagle knelt by Speckled Eagle, he heard the muffled cries of a baby. He lifted the robe and discovered Dawn Star had protected his son by hiding him.

Speckled Eagle caressed Dawn Star's soft skin with the back of his hand. He touched her shiny, smooth black hair, and spoke. "I do not fear her spirit ghost, for Dawn Star was the most beautiful woman in the tribe. Perhaps she was the most beautiful woman in the world of grasses, and now she is dead. I have always loved her. I have kept my feelings hidden for so long and was the one who deserved her. I had already spoken to the older women of the tribe about it. Now I have nothing. I am numb. My body and mind feel as if I am floating away."

Deeply shaken, Brave Eagle could not answer. Speckled Eagle softly spoke to Dawn Star. "I remember the first day of the full moon when the black cherries were ripe. Our tribe had moved to the gathering grounds for the Sun Festival. I had intended to hunt but found myself at a small lake close to the camp. It was early morning, and the bluebirds were singing. Bog mud squished between my toes. The wind rattled the grasses. I patiently listened for your approaching footsteps because I knew you would be gathering water for your family. When you finally arrived, the cottonwood trees hid me, and I stretched to get a better view of you. Somehow, I decided, doing this would be okay, since I loved you so much.

"On this beautiful morning, I crawled through the tall green grasses to look at you. I shamefully admit that I watched you shake out your blanket and throw your buckskin dress and beaded belts upon a tree stump. You stood, so beautiful. Your long brown legs looked so strong. I followed the curves up your back meeting your single black braid flowing down to your waist. You lifted your little niece Morning Star and placed her upon your hip. The muscles in your arms curved as you held her tightly against your body. Little Morning Star shook her head with laughter, making her ivory earrings dance. I stood mesmerized as you, with your niece, stepped into the shallow waters to bathe.

"The wind carried the smell of yellow lotus. In my mind, I created the best song ever played, each note sweeter than the last. Embarrassed that I had watched you more than I should have, I stood up and turned to leave. But first I took one more glance your way. Our eyes met for a brief moment. You tried to hide your head behind Morning Star. I smiled inside all day. I will always remember your laughter and your womanly body standing in the clear water.

"You were the melody to my flower songs, my loved one. I will always treasure you, even if only in spirit. I pray your journey is swift and peaceful, for my heart goes along with you."

Speckled Eagle wiped tears from his face and bent down to kiss her lips. Holding her cold hands, he chanted over her for a moment longer. Brave Eagle gently put his hand on Speckled Eagle's shoulder. He and his brother backed out of the entrance and met the bright sun. The death of so many seemed impossible.

Brave Eagle held his baby son close and kept moving. He had to find Kallie. His wound was bleeding, and dripping blood splattered on the ground as Walks Far came running toward him. They embraced tightly, but the bile taste in his mouth did not leave.

Walks Far said, "Speckled Eagle and Brave Eagle, you are alive. I have been looking all over for you. You must search for others. Many of our horses were stolen," she said, with a desperate, worried look. "Wind Racer is also gone." Walks Far noticed blood on her hand. "Brave Eagle, you are bleeding. Let me take the baby. Come, I will stitch you up."

Brave Eagle felt the clamminess of her hand and told her, "Speckled Eagle and you must help my mother. The baby stays with me. My wound is nothing. I must go to Kallie."

Walks Far grumbled, "The skirmish happened on this side of camp. Kallie will be fine if she has survived her sickness."

Brave Eagle was not so sure and limped among the frantic villagers. He came upon Bear, who stared at him with stunned, reddened eyes.

Bear held his broken war shield. He was silent. It was obvious Bear could not help him.

Brave Eagle continued on without him and saw Henri, Pierre, and Weasel Tail standing in the middle of the chaos. Henri said, "Pierre and I heard nothing. We are astounded a raid has taken place. I am trying to help." Henri explained, "We came upon this grisly scene. Elizabeth lies among the dead and still grips a hatchet in her hand. Her bloody victim is next to her."

Pierre knelt close to motionless Elizabeth and held her wrist. He said, "I found throbbing, but it is so weak. I am surprised she is alive." Pierre tilted his head close to her mouth and heard a slight rattle. He shouted to Henri and Brave Eagle, "She is still breathing."

Upon seeing Pierre's reaction, Weasel Tail proclaimed, "Elizabeth saved my first wife, Meadow Grass. From this day on, if Elizabeth lives, Pierre will take care of her." Weasel Tail's bloody weapons hung from his side as he looked at Brave Eagle and said, "You'd better get that wound looked at." Brave Eagle shook his head no and cradled his son.

Henri explained, "It seems Elizabeth is the talk of the village. Enemy braves invaded Weasel Tail's tepee, and Elizabeth protected Meadow Grass by charging the intruders with a hatchet in each hand. The enemy warriors were so surprised by her screams and wild looks it gave Elizabeth a slight advantage. Her worn black dress flapped as she chased the warriors outside and mortally wounded one of the intruders. Then Elizabeth swung hatchets in the air, even though no one was close by. It was the act of a crazy woman. None of the enemy would physically touch her. Finally, an arrow brought her down, but in Elizabeth's honor, no scalp was taken. She was left intact to travel to the spirit world as she was: strong and swift, if not crazy."

Pierre nodded while Henri recounted the story. Pierre said, "Elizabeth is such a strong woman. I am proud of her bravery. She will make a good missionary wife. It is hard to find a woman who can endure the hardships of frontier life." Henri did not reply, but his face reddened.

Brave Eagle noticed Bear limping toward them. He looked like he was coming out of his stupor. He told Brave Eagle he was going to search for Running Brook.

When Brave Eagle and Bear arrived at the birthing tepee, Brave Eagle tightened his hold on his son. Yellow Willow bent over a body in the entrance. It was facedown, but Brave Eagle and Bear knew it was Lost Buffalo by his moccasins. This medicine man, who had been like a father to them, had been killed. Brave Eagle and Bear looked at each other with profound sadness. They would gravely miss their mentor who had been so wise in the ways of spirit.

Yellow Willow had cut her long gray braids and placed them upon her husband's body. She said, "Brave Eagle, Kallie is alive. Running Brook is with her and will tend to your wound." Brave Eagle acknowledged Yellow Willow with a single affirmative nod and drew silent strength from her. Even in sorrow, her eyes projected grace and dignity.

Bear motioned to Brave Eagle and said, "Come through the tear. This way Lost Buffalo's body will be undisturbed."

Walking past Yellow Willow and entering through the tear, Brave Eagle stepped over Fella. The dog was lying in a pool of its own blood. Brave Eagle looked at the bed and saw Kallie. She was still breathing. He put the little one at her breast, gently kissed her on the forehead, and rubbed her cheek. Running Brook told him, "I've got to check the strength of Kallie's heart."

As Running Brook gripped Kallie's wrist, she shifted her eyes so Bear would notice Fella. The dog had left a trail of blood across the tepee floor. Bear gently lifted Fella and removed him from beside the bed. He placed the dog's body close to Lost Buffalo's corpse, so Fella could accompany Lost Buffalo to the spirit land. Lost Buffalo would welcome this loyal companion.

Running Brook said, "Bear, come get the baby. Brave Eagle, you are bleeding through that bandage. Pull off your shirt so I can stitch you up."

Bear lifted the baby and said, "This little one is a fine son."

Running Brook cleaned Brave Eagle's cuts, stitched his knife wounds, and managed to stop the bleeding. Brave Eagle was oblivious to the needle pokes. After she was done, Bear bent down and kissed Running Brook on the top of her head. She stood and gave him a full embrace, held him tightly, and cried into his shoulder. Bear kept saying how thankful he was that Running Brook was alive.

Sorrow filled Brave Eagle as he thought about the distraught villagers facing the news of the deaths of both Lost Buffalo and Flaming Arrow. He resolved to stay strong. His thoughts were disturbed when Short Bull arrived.

Short Bull's face held an expression of disbelief. He embraced his mother, Yellow Willow, and motioned for Bear and Brave Eagle to help move Lost Buffalo's body to the shaman's own tepee. This way, Yellow Willow could clean and dress him properly in private. After this dreary duty was done, the men walked back to the birthing tepee.

Brave Eagle, Bear, and Running Brook huddled close to Kallie and the baby. Short Bull also sought comfort from his friends. They sat together in quiet despair, and no one had the heart to say anything. Brave Eagle was thankful they had survived, and together they would help the village in this time of sorrow.

Brave Eagle heard a familiar neigh. He and Bear peeked outside and saw Wind Racer running away from the prairie hills and toward their camp. The brown-and-white-painted horse still had Brave Eagle's long feathers hanging from his mane. "Ah, he has broken free," Bear said, and then he added, "This is the first good sign I have seen on this dark day."

Brave Eagle glanced at Short Bull's worried face. It was smeared with blood, but Short Bull seemed not to care. Brave Eagle knew it would soon be time to meet with the other men. The council members would take official account of the village's losses and decide whether to make a retaliatory raid. Bear sighed and said, "Even though our losses are great, I hope that we will not chase the enemy. Surely, Hawk Claw's men would have planned an ambush. I have no heart for battle until the dead are given a proper funeral. This will allow our loved ones to make their journey to the spirit land. Besides, the twisted one, Hawk Claw, is mutilated and dead. He can hurt no one. That is enough revenge for now."

Brave Eagle did not answer. He was dreading going to the council meeting without its most important members. It sickened him with utter despair. No matter what the decision, he would follow the elders' dictates and do whatever was deemed necessary.

A single drum sounded. Bear said, "Come, brothers. It is time to go."

The council tepee's fire burned brightly. Many men were inside, smoking and discussing retaliation; but Bear, Short Bull, and Brave Eagle sat quietly and smoked, still too saddened to offer much counsel. The empty seats next to the fire made them feel lonely. Their political allies were gone. Only a sacred buffalo skull occupied the medicine man's customary spot. A simple feathered arrow lay in Flaming Arrow's place. These symbols demonstrated the men's great respect and love for their dead leaders.

In the innermost circle, the men wore only breechcloths. The ceremonial pipe was passed around, and as each man exhaled, it was his turn to speak. The debate went on for a long time. Ultimately, the men awaited the reply of Short Bull and Brave Eagle. Because they were the sons of Lost Buffalo and Flaming Arrow, the group wanted their opinion.

Short Bull's voice was barely audible as he said, "We need to take care of the dead first before retaliating. I know my stepfather would have wanted that."

Brave Eagle nodded in agreement. Black Hand, the war chief, took a long time to draw from the pipe and blow smoke out of his nostrils. He said, "I agree with Short Bull and Brave Eagle. We as warriors should wait for a clear vision before taking revenge. I would like to remind all the young men that it is spring. Soon it will be time to migrate for the buffalo hunt. We now need to replenish our stolen food supplies in order to survive the Moon of Crying Babies."

Short Bull and Brave Eagle nodded their heads in agreement. The older men voiced they too were willing to wait. The only objections came from younger, inexperienced warriors who wished to retaliate immediately. Eventually everyone voted, and it was agreed to wait until after funerals and hunting before discussing retribution.

Chapter 32: *A Visitor Comes Calling*

Icimanipi: Traveling to Visit

In the birthing tepee, Kallie slept. Death hung in the air, even as the wind chimes swayed and sounded with the spring breeze. Kallie stirred. Her body ached, and she was still feverish. Kallie could not determine whether she was in this life or another. Slowly, with effort, she forced herself to sit up, crawl, and then with resolve, finally stand up.

She heard Lost Buffalo call out, "Kallie, comfort Yellow Willow. Tell her to put on a robe because the winds still blow cold." Kallie's legs trembled as she walked outside. The sun stung her eyes, and she extended her arms to shield them. She walked a few steps at a time. Pausing to rest, she saw her adopted father, Lost Buffalo. She gave him a warm hug. She felt much love from his embrace, yet she could not feel his body.

Kallie inquired, "Oh, Lost Buffalo, did you see my baby son? He is beautiful and strong like Brave Eagle. He will make you proud."

Lost Buffalo smiled at her and acknowledged, "Yes, a strong grandson is a very good omen. You are feeling better, Kallie?"

She nodded her head while explaining, "I feel weak and light-headed, but look at you! Why are you so pale? Come, Lost Buffalo, and sit upon this old tree stump. Rest your weary body, and let me bring you something to drink." She made her way slowly to Yellow Willow's tepee and fetched a horn of cool, refreshing water. Kallie watched him bring the rim of the horn cup up to his parched lips. She saw that Lost Buffalo pretended to drink, not out of thirst, but to show his appreciation to her. He held her hand, but Kallie wondered why she could not feel his touch.

Her concentration was broken by Lost Buffalo's gentle voice. "Kallie, look over there. The first flower of spring pokes through the snow. It reminds me of when I was a young man and would spy the first spring plant. With its hairy stems and bushy white head, it looked like an old man. I would pull out my tobacco and offer it in the directions. Then I would sit, smoke, and reflect upon the last twelve moons. When I was finished, I would come home and sing the flower's song to Yellow Willow."

He smiled at Kallie as he reflected, but then he turned serious. "You must take good care of my grandson. Have patience with Brave Eagle, for he will be a good provider, and most importantly, he knows the ways of our people. You must be vigilant. Be a good wife to him. Remember to touch him often, for when you touch his skin, you touch his soul. He will not beat you, and in return, you must show him respect. Do not be stubborn. Sometimes, like a blind horse, you walk fearlessly when you should fear. Be truthful and generous. Always listen to Yellow Willow. She will guide you and help you find your way. As her adopted daughter, promise me you will provide for her. She has been a good wife to me. For her, I have great respect; we had a productive life together. Now go! Bring her a buffalo robe and tell her to wear it before she becomes ill. I will see you again, Kallie, but now my spirit calls me. I must begin my journey on the ghost trail, and you, Kallie, must journey back toward life."

Kallie protested, but it did no good. He turned his back to her. He and Fella simply faded away. When Kallie woke, she was sitting up in bed. Her shaking hand touched only the still air. Bewildered, she could not tell what was real. Suddenly a gust of wind drew her out of the strange trance. Although walking was difficult, she gathered a buffalo robe and headed for Yellow Willow's tepee.

Kallie found Running Brook, the baby, and Yellow Willow in the tepee. Yellow Willow was rocking back and forth, crying over Lost Buffalo's body. Kallie draped the robe over her and stood next to her for a brief moment. Kallie was deeply confused at the scene before her but said, "Know that Brave Eagle and I will take care of you."

Yellow Willow did not look up, just simply pleaded, "Go back to your bed." Then she continued wailing and swaying. Short Bull put his arm around Kallie and guided her back to the birthing tepee.

Chapter 33: *Funeral Preparations*

Itokaga: Going South to Spirit Land in the Milky Way

Brave Eagle and Speckled Eagle had left the council meeting to help prepare their father's body. Their mother, Pretty Shield, was careful not to speak her husband's name out loud now that he was dead. Holding her tears inside, she took a knife and slashed her wrists and calves to release the pain. Blood flowed from her self-inflicted wounds. It pooled onto her soft brown dress and then spilled upon the ground. Brave Eagle could not bear to see his mother in pain, although he knew her physical cuts were nothing compared to her sorrow. Pretty Shield lifted the knife, dripping with blood, and cut off her long braids. Tenderly, she laid them in her husband's palms and closed his stiff fingers around them.

Brave Eagle and Speckled Eagle wrapped their father's body in his favorite buffalo robe. Pretty Shield had carefully packed his medicine bundle, coup stick, and battle shield for his long journey. Speckled Eagle had gathered Flaming Arrow's favorite weapon, pipes, and food pouches, ensuring his needs would be met. The rest of his belongings would be given away when it was time.

Later in the day, Brave Eagle gathered with other tribal members, for in life or death they were bound as one. On this day the spirit world hung close. The dead would be properly prepared and dressed in their finest robes for the funeral ceremony. Their most precious possessions would be placed with them on scaffolds far above the ground. This way, their spirits would be free to rise toward the sky and begin the ghost trail journey to the center of creation. There, the ancestors anxiously waited for them. All village life had slowed so that only the funeral necessities were done. The day lasted forever, and the shock of loss reigned. When the sun finally set, the village remained quiet. The night air was sharp.

The next morning, Brave Eagle woke beside Kallie and his son. He left and walked along the path. The spring snow was melting, and the river current dislodged sheets of ice near shore. Small, brown patches of mud appeared on the village paths. The raging blizzard was a faded memory against the warmth of the day. Food was being prepared for those who had lost family members. Brave Eagle was relieved no one was expected to mourn alone. As was the custom, the young and old who had the strength to carry on hung prayer feathers. The sight of the feathers fluttering in the wind offered hope, as Brave Eagle whistled to Bear to come with him.

Brave Eagle noticed Pierre had moved Elizabeth to his small encampment at the far edge of the village. No one had objected, and only Brave Eagle seemed to notice. He observed Pierre's blue eyes twinkled as he doctored Elizabeth back to life. She begged for water, a good sign. Elizabeth stared at Pierre with the prettiest face she could muster. She weakly held out her hand and asked Pierre to read Bible verses to her for comfort.

Brave Eagle and Bear watched Henri pack and rearrange the merchandise to go in his cargo canoe. They overheard Henri tell Pierre, "I am so relieved my belongings are still here. That raid was nasty business. I am anxious to leave this place. I'm thinking we should go before the funerals. No one will miss us."

Pierre protested, "We cannot leave just yet. Elizabeth needs a little bit more time to heal before traveling."

Henri replied, "It is past time to leave. I have to reach Steamboat Landing to get my furs on the steamer heading for Independence. You are too attached to that woman. She's trouble. I'll have none of that."

Pierre said, "You will need to drop me and my soon-to-be wife at the church site to receive your payment. The missionaries stationed there are expecting me and will welcome Elizabeth. You will not receive any money until we are delivered there safely."

Henri began to pace and grumble while rearranging his things once again. Bear said to Brave Eagle, "Elizabeth did help out in the battle. It was a good thing Weasel Tail did, to release her."

Later that day, while the mourning songs were heard, Brave Eagle visited Kallie. His reddened eyes revealed the pain caused by his father's death. Brave Eagle was haunted that he had not aided his father in time to save his life. To ease his suffering, he asked for his son. Holding the baby to his chest, he smelled the newborn's freshness. He rocked the child, and it soothed them both.

Running Brook had prepared mashed winter turnips and told him, "It is good. Kallie had an appetite and devoured her meal." Running Brook pried the baby from him and explained, "Kallie needs to feed him." She put his son to Kallie's breast. As Kallie fed him, his little fist grabbed her finger and held tightly. Their son nursed loudly as Kallie deeply inhaled and then let out a long, relaxing breath.

Brave Eagle rested his hand on Kallie's shoulder. He informed her, "Wind Racer came home running strong and was wearing his war paint and feathers. I have few horses left after the raid. The two horses I gave Yellow Willow have been stolen."

Kallie interrupted, "I did not know you gave Yellow Willow two horses." She paused. "Only two?"

Brave Eagle smiled and admitted, "Of course, there were more horses to be given after my intention was formally accepted. Yellow Willow is now a widow. She must stay with us."

Kallie was confused. "Is Lost Buffalo gone?"

Brave Eagle nodded his head. "Yes, and I am deeply sorry." He avoided the topic of Fella by saying, "Kallie, I must go now and help my family with funeral preparations." He kissed her on the cheek and left.

Brave Eagle smelled sage grass used to smudge tepees. The burning sage cleansed the space from lurking evil spirits left behind after the destruction. Hawk Woman, who carried Lost Buffalo's ceremonial tools, paused when she saw him. Hawk Woman recounted to him how painful it had been to collect them. Although Yellow Willow had agreed, she cried as Hawk Woman rummaged through Lost Buffalo's things. Short

Bull held his mother tightly. Brave Eagle hugged Hawk Woman but did not know what to say.

Brave Eagle found his brother. Together they finished dressing Flaming Arrow in his favorite war shirt. Pretty Shield had added beads she had bartered from Henri. Speckled Eagle gently tied eagle feathers to his father's hair and sadly painted his father's strong facial features with black stripes. Brave Eagle held his father's headdress. The beaded strip along the front was in blues and whites, contrasting with the colored beads wrapped around the buffalo horns. The headdress held many eagle feathers, each one ending with a tuft. The sons straightened Flaming Arrow's bone necklace and gently touched his war shield, decorated with his personal medicines. The brothers smiled through their tears as they remembered their father's singing and dancing. Flaming Arrow still looked important and handsome in his ceremonial clothes.

The two brothers remembered earlier days, when their father would raise them up to his massive shoulders, their mother following behind laughing. Flaming Arrow would swing the boys around in the prairie grasses and play animal songs on his flute. Brave Eagle and Speckled Eagle had respected their father. They were proud of the way their painted tepee had reflected his brave deeds for all to see.

Brave Eagle had felt secure when his father sat close to him on lazy winter afternoons. Flaming Arrow had taught the boys to sharpen arrows and knives. His father had provided great quantities of meat for the family and had given generous cuts to the elders. He had taken good care of his tribe.

Sadness swept over Brave Eagle. He felt the shadow of his father's spirit journeying onward. Brave Eagle was relieved Hawk Claw's body had been pierced with many arrows. This enemy could not harm his father again. Brave Eagle was consoled knowing his father was free, not bound to the earth by strangulation or scalping.

The brothers knew their tribe would soon travel on, following the great buffalo herds to replenish their stolen supply of meat. This hunt would distract them from their grief. During the summer, they would meet with many cousins and extended family. Their presence would fill the hollow spots in their hearts. The tribes would gather at the Sun Festival, where their members would officially choose new leaders.

Brave Eagle looked around the tepee. A dark emptiness enveloped him. For the first time in his life, his father was not there to help him. When he and Speckled Eagle finished preparing Flaming Arrow's body, they would try to comfort Pretty Shield. She cried so inconsolably that Brave Eagle worried he might lose her also. It was time for him to be as strong as his father would have been.

The brilliance of the sun shining upon the valley contrasted with the solemn occasion. Men circled the encampment beating drums. This was a signal the funeral procession was to begin. The people came together under the huge sky and walked as one to the ancestral grounds. This sacred land of the dead held special meaning. All their lives intersected. The earth bound the living to those who had traveled through life before them. This sacred ground was created from their ancestors' bones. As the dust blew, their dead ones were free to go with the wind.

The dead, dressed in their finest clothes, had their weapons and possessions circled around their bodies. Each body was covered with buffalo robes and then elevated on strong wooden scaffolds. Each platform stood high. Feathers and hooves dangled from the platforms. They clanged and swayed with each gust of wind. Brave Eagle wove through the procession to get Kallie.

Chapter 34: *Ice on the River*

Cahnajuju: Ice When the River Breaks Up in Spring

On this saddest of days, Kallie noticed the first spring flowers of the prairies had come alive. Dots of white poked out of the melting snow and swayed gracefully in the wind. Kallie treasured the beauty of the flowers and smelled their fragrance. Even in the midst of the sadness and despair, Kallie thought of Lost Buffalo picking the first flower, singing its song, and bringing the treasure home to Yellow Willow.

Brave Eagle stood between Kallie and his family. Her body leaned against Brave Eagle's side. She carried the baby's cradle board on her back but chose to hold the baby in her arms. Her hair flowed freely in the wind as she slowly turned to Brave Eagle and buried her head into his warm chest. He drew her even closer to him.

Pretty Shield turned her head away and asked, "Yellow Willow, why is the baby not in the cradle board where he belongs?"

Yellow Willow stood close to Kallie and said nothing. Kallie appreciated Yellow Willow, who would be a powerful ally and help guide her in tribal life.

Kallie noticed Henri and Pierre stood with heads down and held their red knitted hats at their sides. Next to them, Elizabeth rested on a stretcher with Meadow Grass standing beside her. Elizabeth did not take her eyes off Pierre while she called to Meadow Grass, "You must gather my things, for I will be leaving on a long journey. And here—give my crucifix to Weasel Tail. He should have it."

Meadow Grass said, "It will be done."

Elizabeth smiled at Pierre and suggested, "We should baptize the baby before we leave. Why, he can be the first convert of our church." Henri nervously shuffled his feet in the mud and looked flustered. Kallie thought a baptism might be good, as long as Pretty Shield did not find out.

The elders spoke at the gathering, each taking a turn to eulogize Flaming Arrow, Lost Buffalo, and the others. Their words brought both pain and comfort, while the people tried to gain strength from them. There was much crying. When Black Hand spoke, sharpness ran through Kallie's heart. She longed for Lost Buffalo's soothing manner and Flaming Arrow's protection. Just when the emptiness grew so large she could not endure it, the baby squirmed and distracted her. To appease him, Kallie offered her small finger for him to suck upon. She smiled down at him and thought Michael or Caleb would be a good name. She would name him after one of her brothers.

Brave Eagle gazed down at them, and his grieved expression lightened. He told Kallie, "Soon we will name our son. Earlier, when I went to the river to speak to my father's spirit, I noticed a lone white wolf on the other side. Right then I knew our son's name will be White Wolf." As he looked down at their son, Kallie knew Brave Eagle was thinking about Flaming Arrow's death. Running Brook had told her about how Flaming Arrow's fight with Hawk Claw had saved Brave Eagle.

Brave Eagle said, "I will not hesitate to die for my son. In his blood flows my father's and all those that came before him. Flaming Arrow's strength and guidance will always be with me."

Kallie observed the swollen river. A chunk of ice broke off from shore and floated downstream with the current. It glistened like a crystal as it slowly spun in the murky waters.

As she watched the ice chunk melt, Brave Eagle whispered to her in a low voice, "This is our life now. We must live on and do our best with what the Great Spirit gives to us." Kallie looked at Brave Eagle, who stared into her eyes. He told her, "You are getting stronger. We will live a good life together and have many babies."

She nodded knowingly and then watched the last of the ice break away from the shore. It bobbed up and down until it was caught in a great sweeper and slowly swirled in a whirlpool.

When she could see the ice no more, she picked up a raven feather that fluttered past her. Brushing it against her cheek, Kallie said quietly, "I was always searching for my destiny, but instead, my destiny caught me. Like crossing at Sweet Grass, fate took me into its flow, just like ice on the river."

As part of the tribe, Kallie watched the sunset behind the burial scaffolds. The platforms became dark shadows against the starry night. The spirit world hovered upon them in the sorrowful darkness. Children stayed inside, and every dog lay quietly, even though the wolves teased and enticed them with distant howls. On this night, the wolf pack received no reply, for the village was in absolute silence.

About the Author

Laurie G. Robertson has ventured into the American West seeking voices from the past to influence her writing. The poet and author lives with her family in Fairbanks, Alaska where she teaches high school science, enjoys downhill skiing, snowshoeing, the study of herbal medicines and gardening. *Crossing at Sweet Grass* is her debut historical novel.

Come visit her website laurierobertson.com or contact her at laurie.robertson@rocketmail.com

Printed in the United States
By Bookmasters